SEARCHING FOR AN ENEMY

SEARCHING FOR AN ENEMY

KRISH BHARADWAJ

PARTRIDGE
A Penguin Random House Company

ISBN:	Hardcover	978-1-4828-4354-5
	Softcover	978-1-4828-4353-8
	eBook	978-1-4828-4352-1

To order additional copies of this book, contact
Partridge India
000 800 10062 62
orders.india@partridgepublishing.com

www.partridgepublishing.com/india

A FICTION, WITH IMAGINERY CHARACTERS, DIALOGUES, WITH NO INTENTION TO HURT ANYONE, NOR REFERRING ANY SPECIFIC SECTION, ORGANISATIONS, INDIVIDUALS OR MOVEMENTS.

CHAPTER I - DEC 2014

"OUR MISSION IS TO SILENCE THE VOICES. YOU TALK OF FREEDOM OF EXPRESSION? SHOULD WE TOLERATE?"

Disturbing the silence of the air conditioned room, the rhythm of the computers keys are humming with a low beat. Like fire alarms the telephones and mobiles are chiming with different tunes. 'TIMELINE' the national headquarters is buzzing with callers, reporters and telephone operators. This daily magazine is a most debated paper among all political groups. If a minister does not see his name in this newspaper, even for a greeting for his birth day celebration, he will be happy. Problem is, if his birthday bash is exposed and expenditure is questioned, Income Tax will put him under the net. If the greetings are really a benign from well-wisher, party headquarters will call the minister and question him of his love affair with TIME LINE. The Private line of Chief Editor suddenly came to life.

"*Telephones are tapped, come to DoCoMo mobile*", with a curt warning, the line was disconnected.

"*From, Parliament lounge, Sir, voting on the presidential form of government may be defeated in 2/3 voting. Rishi Bharat literally tore the amendment and even senior leaders of NPP are feeling that it will undermine the democratic process. Total pandemonium and violence marred the whole day. Fear is that friendly parties of NPP may refuse to co-operate."*

"Totally exiting sir, I sat through the entire session to witness our Rishi Bharat's mesmerizing speech. Next to me NEWS TO-DAY, the official news reporter of NPP, Devraj was sitting. He commented that Rishi is using crow bar to break the dreamy castle of their Prime Minister and he is removing that brick by brick"

"He turned and jovially told 'Your man is the first brought bull dozer in the road and here is a member, using crow bar inside the parliament, as bull dozers cannot enter here. Achar, don't think our fellows will swallow bitter venoms. Tell my ex-boss, Sameer to be silent or be careful for some time? Some of our fellows are man eaters, now with no cage."

With a deep breath the voice continued. *"But the cabinet is firm, if they cannot purchase, that too including the opposition leader,they may blackmail. Most of the M.Ps are shocked and silenced by the ruthlessness. Sir, including the dissent voices at ruling front, especially old guards are bitter. Yet afraid to offend their winning horse."*

After a deep silence, *"Mini emergency, Sir, you are not safe"*.

"Yes man, I know, Achar, did you meet Madame" without naming the Barathiya Congress President.

"No sir, I tried, she is almost under house arrest with her own Z security. They refused entry into the gate".

"Achar, *then meet Shankar or Mallik, they were her most trusted vice-presidents*"

"No Sir, they have no access to her, only her daughter is with her. She has switched off her mobile line."

"With this voting, will the government fall?"

"No sir, two third M.Ps. have to vote for the amendment. May be the amendment gets defeated. Law ministry seems to be planning to ask the speaker to consider some technical changes to introduce 99th and 100th amendments without sufficient and separate notice as though it is necessitated by the emergency condition prevailing because of the terrors faced by people. Government need not resign, even if the bill fail to get 2/3 majority. PM`s men are confident."

"Left, New Age Party will take advantage. But meek noise. Home Minister Pramod says that Left will blast a bomb every time, but government will release only smoke."

"Indian Central Investigation Agency has withdrawn action against Madan Vyas. Four charges of fake encounters. Who is another person J.B.Shetty", asked Mr.SameerBasu, the editor, Time Line.

"Sir, ICIA has one major role, now-a-days "After pause he spoke, *"Destruction of records and evidences and redraft the files, according to the directions of home ministry. The government is trying to delete all the historical evidences and one lakh files are listed to be destroyed. Madan Vyas has got seven criminal case out of which four are murders. J.P. Shetty is*

a known illegal iron ore emperor. He controlled entire iron ore export in south. More than one lakh crores had been exported without any payment of royalty and tax. He is capable of redrawing the state border maps".

"Difference is in the position of friendly parties. They are dead against the Presidential form which will ultimately switch off their power centers. Secondly, large corporate dictations are known to everyone. Madan Vyas, NPP secretary called them and told that `their pre-election payments includes the post-election loyalty.' P.M, every ten minutes appear in T.V. and say, the Political stability is very much important with Presidential form, for further flow of foreign capital and investment climate. He is bringing 3 trillion dollars as investment according to latest promise. He says stable Presidential government alone will create confidence of those huge foreign capital. Confidentially, the biggest losers will be state parties. This may put an end to the third front bubble, every time being organized by the Left but buried by the minor partners in that process. Sir, a breaking news".

Achar cannot leave his TV anchor language, Sameer mused and asked, "*What?*"

"Even before the amendment is placed for division, Home ministry has changed the top bureaucrats and trusted are placed to meet an unexpected political chaos. ICIA chief, national defense headquarters, Presidential office, top home ministry position, Propaganda ministry-all are revamped. Sir, another 32 strategic places are identified."

"Did you check up, why?"

"The whole system shall be customized to function under one Processor -PMO"

"ACHAR, I have heard human brain has got unique mapping, now computer, but I have never heard a nation required a unique mapped brain, O.K, continue"

"Sir, your favorite WISE MEN OF ZEONS, top genes, have not left the party headquarters for the past six days. Even Rashtirya Rakshna Samiti, the religious front of the party, seems to be kept one step far off. Amending the constitution for PRESIDENTIAL FORM of government at the same time, centralizing all the powers in the hands of president are being discussed. Draft programme is ready and the PMO chief advisor Mr. RAMSEY is the total in charge".

"In a week a huge three days RRS convention is arranged and PM is bending upon launching the nationwide programme for a presidential form of government. Now their leaders are making extensive arrangements for a three days national convention."

"Sir, if you are going to write editorial, now itself do it for to-morrow`s edition. I am reaching our office in 10 minutes. Already you have printed the amendments, which is inflaming the whole parliament."

SameerBasu, the editor of the TIME LINE disconnected his line. Slowly he walked to the Library. TimeLine, India`s leading news magazine, known for its fearless, forthright expression and sharp editorials, with its circulation of twelve lakhs in seven states, is known for its frontal attack on the policies of any government. When V.P.Singh was the PM, then, his advisors, being perturbed, told him to stop SameerBasu from criticizing his government. Singh said, *"Why cannot we shut him by committing zero error in our administration?"* V.P. Singh privately admitted that he himself is a fan of Sameer and what information he is not able to get from his department skull heads, are somehow reaching Time line magazine.

Basu opened a file on various constitutional amendments. Report on 42nd Amendment in 1976 and an application from government for the reopening of Kesavananda Barathi vs state of Kerala 1973 on fundamental rights came before Justice A.N.Rayand others.At the argument stage to a specific observation, can parliament conceive a law for the return of monarchy, Hon`ble Judge of Supreme Court reacted that such things are merely fanciful flight of imagination and no sane government will do. Mr.N.A.Palkiwala, eminent constitutional lawyer immediately replied, *"My Lord, the test of constitutionality is not what a sane parliament may probably do, but what an insane parliament can possibly do."*

Sameer murmured, *"So return of insanity, end of democracy!"*

Mentally, he was much disturbed. He moved to the shelf, opened the Book `DERFUEHRER-HITLER`S RISE TO POWER by KonradHeiden. He read back the lines once marked by him for an article.

"This is the demon who speaks out of the book. `We shall talk with people on the street and squares' says the demon, and teach them the view of political questions which at the moment we require".

"We -the demon always says 'we'-shall create unrest, struggle, and hate in the whole of Europe and thence in other continents. We shall at all times be in a position to call forth new disturbances at will, or to restore old order."

"Unremittingly, we shall poison the relations between the peoples and state of all countries. By envy and hatred, by struggle and warfare, even by spreading hunger, destitution and plagues, we shall bring all peoples to such a pass that their only escape will lie in total submission to our domination".

"We shall stultify, seduce, and ruin the youth. We shall not stick at bribery, treachery, treason, as long as they serve the realization of our plans. Our watchword is force and hypocrisy! In our arsenal we carry a boundless ambition, burning avidity, a ruthless thirst for revenge, relentless hatred. From us emanates the specter of fear, all embracing terror". Engrossed in that book Mr. Sameer Basu looked up. The whole concept said to have been conceived centuries back, tested eighty years before in Germany, Italy and many more nations. To-day the devil started speaking, here!

It was 01.00. P.M. Sameer ordered for a tea and continued his reading, *"Outwardly, however, in our official utterances, we shall adopt an opposite procedure and always do our best to appear honorable and co-operative. A statesman's words do not have to agree with his acts."* Suddenly, he was disturbed. *"Are we heading to build an evil empire?* "Sameer could not concentrate, again disturbance, this time louder.

Sameer heard the ringing sound and the door opened, his P.A. Shia was standing with a trace of hyper tension and perturbance, which Sameer had not seen her like that. Very bold lady, who can handle the entire company affairs independently.

"Sir, I am receiving number of calls, highly threatening and disturbing to hear. Any time our office may be attacked ransacked by the thugs. Our securities have witnessed the movement of several TATA Sumos and Scorpios vehicles with rowdy elements".

Sameer raised his head and simply told, *"Do take suitable action with the consultation of admn.Head: Go ahead. You are capable of handling in hard times".*

Pages of the book was turned again, *"twenty years had passed before this knowledge found the right man. And thus the book `The Protocols of the wise men of Zion` since become so famous, fell into the hands of Alfred Roshenberg, a Baltic German a close cabinet of Adolf Hitler, who built Nazi theory on Aryan supremacy incorporating the ideas of Wise men of Zion".* Sameer groaned and slowly got up. Wanted to discuss what shall be done on security issue.

`He is near, he is hardly by the door` was ringing in his brain. It is often quoted over the turning of devils.

His mobile rang. *'Just hear me, Home ministry is trying to frame you. Anytime you will be behind the bars, Department may have to sign the papers. Why not you go underground for some times`.*

The Home secretary was nervous at the other end. Coolly answered Sameer, `*Let me face the ordeal, I will have at least thousand friends here to discuss in jail. If I fly, who will be with me in London, Moscow or Washington? All those Governments will extradite me at any time, saying it as bi-lateral or I have to seek political asylum, which will be a disgrace and temporary solution."*

"O.K. I will call you"

The door opened and Achar rushed inside. *"I am sorry, to enter without permission"*, hesitantly he advanced.

"O.K, O.K, tell me what is happening."

"Sir, Cabinet is unanimous and the hard liners are now planning to take the propaganda to high pitch with riot and anarchy activities and trying to advance need for a national emergency. Alternatively, there is a plan to arrest a few to silence the voice of opposition. A virulent and provocative discussion is taking place in parliament, even before the actual bill is placed on the table. Your friend Rishi Bharat is to lead the opposition with all documents he collected from our board. PM wants all arguments gets exhausted and oppositions are thrown out or expelled. Home ministry is preparing the list of anti-socials, anti-nationals and publics are going to be mesmerized with tales of horror and conspiracy. The Brain group is preparing the whole conspirators theory and training is given by a big advertisement firms to propagate, to write and to mislead. Sir, your name is listed. They are linking you with Bihar criminal gang, on whom we wrote two articles last month."

Basu was observing Achar`s shocked reaction to the Home ministries' plan. But how he gathered- not an issue! Role play of Ranadir Sena President in massacring the Dalits was discussed in TIME LINE and the matter was taken to parliament. Home Minister`s constituency which secretly provided asylum for the leader of the Ranadir Sena became the bleeding needle for the H.M.. The press reporter reached the farm house of the minister, under the pretext of selling country made pistol. He prowled a little more unsuspectingly to photograph the hiding Sena leader in that farm house. When photos were released in press, minister coolly told that the sena leader had come to surrender. But parliament did not show any mercy nor swallowed the tales. How the man who came to surrender again allowed go free and under which provision of law? Minister was virtually massacred by the opposition. Old tale, but vengeance unabated,

Basu turned to Acharand told him about the warning now received from Secretary Home Ministry. Government is still hesitant. He can still have fresh breath at his office, than at Tihar Jail.

Suddenly, commotions was noted, pushing and jostling someone was making his way towards the glass partition of the Library. Sameer Basu`s secretary tried to stop huge powerful man and told him that his boss is not willing to meet anyone. He did not mind but surged forward and two RAF men were following him. Achar was wild and in a fit of anger menacingly, he stepped forward. Doors opened.

He was shocked to find that the insurgent was smilingly raising his hands and asking him to be calm. He neared

Sameer and apologetically bowed, *"Hi, I am sorry Sameer, to terrify your secretary"* and turned to the doors, where the lady was standing, blushing with anger and red face. Sameer broke into a loud laugh and shouted, *"What the hell, you are doing to add to the chaos here. Home ministry has broken their nerve two minutes before".* Colonel Fernando took out his mobile and dialed.

"Colonel Fernando speaking sir, he is safe sir"

Yes sir, I am with him, giving to SameerBasu-my old boss".

Achar was puzzled, what is going on between these two men. Boss is relaxed and calm. He is able to realize that the invader seems to have come from a close quarters. Yet it is a head splitting suspense "*What happened to me, I know him*". Suddenly he recollected, Col.Fernando, chief of RAF, the whole country is talking about him now, and he is in our office: That too friend of our Boss? In the tension, one minute he is not able to recollect. Sameer Basu took the mobile and addressed more politely to the man on the other side.

"Sameer, you are leaving to Kolkata by road immediately. I have made all arrangement for travel and even your uncle is informed about your arrival. Colonel had already packed your things and your wife is also waiting in the car standing few building away from your office."

Minister for police and internal administration, West Bengal was on line. Sameer turned to Colonel and shouted, *"Why, the hell all are kidnapping me, what is the problem?"*

Colonel responded, *"when my ex-boss says, I will do man, do what he says"*. Minister was an ex-brigadier and came out of Army at the age of 55 and after few years, he entered politics, got elected and was elevated to Minister for Home Affairs. His daughter Neena Ghoswal fell in love with Sameer, while she was doing her journalism and they got married after two years, once she completed her post-graduation. When she was being honored on her article on the Drug Mafia of Delhi city, they asked her how she was able to gather so much information about dangerous Mafia. She immediately commented that she is born to dangerous sword and married a wildest pen.

From the other side the rough old voice continued, *"Aay! Why do you shout at him? I have got two vital informations. One they have a plan to put you inside, for harboring and giving refuge to two terrorists whom they have kept inside Special Central Reserve Police office right now. If you do not escape, they are going to link you to Bihar Criminal gang. The drama of capturing or shooting some members of this gang at your yard will be done to night or to-morrow. I am anticipating more danger to your life and to your workmen. CRAB chief came to know and stopped this cynical dramas. Now get out. Tell your boys, not even the security to stay at your premises. I fear local mob is going to attack the office. 18 TATA, sumo, turbo vans are going round with rowdy elements. RAF men are there, so they are afraid to come nearer. Local police is not going to help you. Rapid Action Force cannot be deployed as it will be against state regulation. Col.Fernando will tell what is to be done"*.

Sameer face has gone red and his B.P. started rising. Col. Fernando caught his hand and softly told him to calm down and seated him in the chair. He asked for permission to give instruction to his staff. Sameer depressingly nodded. In a flash of moment, he and Achar and came out and called the sub editors and other working staff to follow his the instructions. *"All of you please switch off your mobile and hand over to Mr.Achar, You can collect after an hour"*

He gave instruction to Achar to disconnect outgoing lines. Sheepishly he asked Mr. Fernando *"So you do not believe even employees?"*

Col.Fernando smiled, *"I am known as meticulous schemer, that is why I am Rapid Action Force Chief, got it?"*

Tersely he advised them to follow whatever he says. *"No fan or light shall be put off. Too two cameramen shall wait for my instructions. Now you go round and take a video of all the machines, materials and building and come back. Don't cause any suspicion. .Await for my next instruction. Press vans are coming to the godown area and 20 persons shall go inside and then place paper bundles. Achar you supervise that and give instruction. My men will come with you."*

Ten vans were kept in the line. Sameer was waiting there with the two RAF men in civil dress and he was literally bundled into the backside of the seventh van. Some more were inside by that time. The van moved out and after five hundred meters a black BMW moved from the side path and followed the van. Next Street, twenty men from the van got down and it further proceeded.

After crossing ten kilo meter the van turned from the main road entered a cross road and stopped. The RAF man jumped out and walked few steps and looked around. Assured of no suspicious movement, they signaled and Mr. Sameer slowly stepped out. The van moved and in two minutes from the other side of the road the black Ford reached the spot. Sameer saw his wife with a shocked look. She seems to have been briefed and she hugged him once he got inside, he warmly held and kissed her. *"God, you are safe"*.

She poured black coffee from the flask and gave it to him. She served some biscuits and coffee to the RAF men and thanked them. The mounting tension slightly relaxed in a minute and in the darkness they were able to hear the lady slightly chuckle. Sameer turned to her, *"why"*.

"Sameer, last week you told that you have no time to visit Kolkata to see my dad. Sorry, from to-morrow you are going to be his prisoner instead of government guest here".

Sameer look above, *"I would rather prefer the honour of being government guest"*

"No problem, Sameer I will tell my dad". She lifted her mobile. Sameer hugged her and caught her mobile.

Tearing the High ways, the ford flew at the speed of 110k.m. towards east, crossed the border of Delhi and entered Utter Pradesh. BMW returned with security men after crossing the borders.

While Sameer`s memory was travelling back in the time zone, his vehicle was heading towards Lucknow at a speed of 80 to 100 k.m. and he is soon entering Kolkata after a gap of two years.

In the falling darkness in Delhi, a few vans carrying hirelings and ruffians were moving forward from various direction towards LIFE LINE building.

CHAPTER II - JAN 2014

THE LONGEST HISTORY OF AN EMPIRE AT LAST ENDED IN A SHEPHERD`S TALE

January, 2014, the chill winter is haunting entire Delhi. Delhi as a capital is very rich with largest junk of poor in old Delhi area. It has several strange specialties, not available to any other city in India. It will preserve all the old Mogul look of 600 years old on one side and build one special enclave on the other side with hundred crores apartments. Every third person will tell you that he will talk to Prime Minister and solve your two and half acres land taken over by government in Pune-Bangalore High ways for expansion. He will be solving your 7 years Supreme Court appeal as Chief Justice has invited him for a supper, to discuss about Haryana state 1000 acre land allotment case. A visitor to Delhi will be amazed to hear, these lies, trained cheaters bold promises, half-truth and a few mediators' business profiles. A largest fake liaison offices are available, with photos of ministers and board chairmen along with the managing director of the offices. Files will move inside every ministry, but will not see the exit route. These liaison lobby do keep the same file in their office to get seal and signature for your file instead of the tedious process of moving the same from one seat to another in a single window clearance process. But orders and notifications will be fake. When you come back, you can see new occupants and new liaison board. In the country as a whole politics will be discussed as a form of social changes, but it will be discussed in terms of bullion bars and government printed notes here at Delhi.

In this city no event is important or awesome matter for a common Delhites. To them, even M.P.s or Ministers are one rank below. All decisions of the bureaucrats will be decided only at the three or five star hotels in the late nights and will be released in the department next day. Rules and notifications language will be debated and discussed over a Chicken 65 and bottle of beer in Coles Park or Karol Baugh area.

January chillness did not affect the heat of the election announcement of May 2014. An important meet was organized that day by the Indian National Chamber of Commerce inviting Prime Minister for a vital agenda has gone unnoticed even by the Press. INDIANNATIONAL CHAMBER OF COMMERCErepresents 90% of Indian industrial and business houses but serves the interest of 10% of the emperors of powerful industrial houses. Top 30 High Net WorthIndian corporate giants were the invitees to the meeting.

Prime minister was requested to preside. He is a man of few words, even that he did not speak in this meet. A bitter contempt and anger is able to be traced on his stony face. The focus of the discussion was not in the language relishable by Barathiya Congress government.

President of the Chamber of Commerce was in his own remorseful world. If he succeed in his attempt, another three years he will be renominated. The very intention for a closed door meet is to extract some last minute assurances and commitment from the government. Once next government is installed, these promises can be superimposed. If public criticism arise, bygone rulers will be blamed. This is corporate political dice: Played cleverly in the current stream of political transition. Even though, last nine years, the Indian corporates had extracted highest state favors, out of the reforms, they were skeptical about the government ability to build a robust market to compete internationally. Their central committee member even cynically asked them once, *"It is a shame that we call ourselves market leaders and international players, but behind the screen fall on the feet of government to ask them to build a robust international competitive environment with all protectionism! Reason is we are still feudal corporates."*

Government did not allow the foreign market players to capture the retail market and agriculture by investing foreign funds, which will cause public protest and even unrest. But the big houses wants to bring in foreign funds as collaborators of capital. At the same time, the mantles of powers of each corporate, these corporate leaders wanted to retain or pass on only to their sons and son-in-laws, who had international doctorates and master degrees specially purchased in U.S. or some European remote universities or B-Schools, along with their whole sale purchase of their 6 seater planes, joints at Swiss or holiday homes at Italy or Spain or Rolls Royce. Prime Minister was totally cramped because he could not bring a total market strategies with these Feudal corporates, who were controlling 70% of the national economics under monopoly.

Finance Minister was the government spokesman. He quietly asked the president to initiate the subject of the day.

President of the Chamber got up *"Honorable Ministers, we are happy that you have come to our special session to discuss an important agenda. We find it is the right moment for the government to release a clear policy statement on privatization of all public sectors, opening FDI 100% in all sectors including agriculture. 10, 15, 20%tax slabs to corporates as per their earlier memorandum submitted one year back. But your government failed to respond and this year our foreign account inflow and our GDP are all sliding down. We feel that your hesitation is causing a reversal in our overall business and production. Our Chamber has placed this demand in clear terms and I appeal to you to table it in the present session of the parliament and take a bold decision to adopt it. We are also assured that the opposition party NPP will not create any hurdle in passing and we have their assurances. Minimum wage act and contract labour act, trade union act, Factory Act and industrial dispute acts need to be repealed. You assured to look into it and your labour minister on the other day rejected our meeting. He commented that wages in other countries are 27% of the corporate cash flow and in India, it is 7 to 9% even though we have sufficient labour force employed in all sector with lesser support of technology. Labour minister sarcastically commented in our Chamber meets that I.T.Act or Factory act are more to control labour struggles and once these acts are repealed labour force will be wild cats. He warned us that a nationwide labour struggle will not be able to be controlled by using violence and oppressive police. Sir, he smacked us and told not to throw burning carbon stones on the sky, it will fall on your head. Is it a way a minister of your government speak? That too in a forum organized by us?"* Finance minister bent close to P.M. and told that Labour Minister had given the more beating with red rods and these guys deserves. They did not remember that man is form Kerala and blood is red first and dress is white.

*"We are afraid that such attitude of your ministers will force us to close the industries than diverting our profit towards expansions. With this short appeal, place the memorandum before you on behalf of this chamber. Thank you sir."*Mild but conspicuous language of blackmail from these large corporate feudalists was sensed. Threating and blackmailing a government?

Finance Minister took the mike, "*Gentlemen, You please exercise a few minutes of patient hearing. For various political reason I cannot make public confession. I repose confidence in you and speak frankly. Secondly, transparent exposure is not going to harm, as major damages have already been done in the quid-pro-quo deals. I do not understand how a government, without time to implement can issue a policy statement or notification-now? Secondly, what we did not agree for the past ten years due to our political compulsions, cannot be altered in a private gatherings. But let me place spread sheet for your consumption or perception.*

Nearly 7, 10,000 crores of tax concession were extended in last five years. First five years, we had to rely upon trusted allies like left parties. They never allowed to favor the corporates and diverted government spending only on socio economic improvement schemes. They were unfavorable to you, but we *gained another five years term with a higher mandate. Despites opposition, through state governments, one lakh forty thousand acres of land was granted at notional value for industrial use. It was almost a free gift by the government to the industrial and business houses. Tax write offs and waivers, export subsidies, waiver of tax for 10 years to new investments, exemption to capital in agriculture-my list will elongate if time permits. Countries oil cost was going up and $120 per barrel is the import cost. All subsidies, the general public were getting, corporates too. Oil exploration and crude sale are now $ 8 per barrel. You are the beneficiary. What benefits we failed to provide?"*

The hosts were getting restless as they are painfully pinned by the Finance Minister sermon. Someone whispered *"He is singing eulogy for his government".*

F.M.noticed the uneasiness yet determined to needle them for their closed door meet with NPP leaders two days back and comes with a draft to get thump impression of Prime Minister. It is the one time opportunity for him to shut their mouth as he had determined to vacate his seat forever.

Finance minister continued sharply, *"Sir, sorry to be so blunt, the government has never audited the accounts of total export and payment received back from abroad, since the day of scrape of State trading corporation." "When we made a sample tests, one MNC of Indian origin is holding Rs. 1,00,000 crores in foreign banks. It is not reflecting in their GAAP Balance sheet. If we point out their fine in dollars will cross 3 million in US alone. If the files are opened and balance sheets were questioned by Ministry of Corporate affairs and I.T. departments, 17* *companies will be black listed and we will face an irreparable damage in the international trade. Government observed all silence. Eight days back someone filed a Public Interested Litigation challenging the government, either to pass an act decitizening the people, who failed to bring back their foreign reserve or under criminal provision or conspiracy against the state by economic terrorism. Can you imagine he had made an assessment of 462 billion dollars? In all fairness he had put listed corporates as major defaulters with 310 billion dollars and others are bureaucrats, politicians and religious heads of all five major religions in India. Our Ministry officials confided that this group was gathering more than 89 files under RTI. Case is admitted by Supreme Court, making Government of India and 13 international financial institutions as parties. Brilliant international financial experts, former Reserve bank deputy governors and two corporate undersecretaries have worked before filing the 1200 pages petition.Had you all repatriated what you traded in the foreign land, my government would have had 17 lakhs crores in our international balance of payment, we could have saved the food security of a nation. I know that you are commenting that this will be last speech as finance minister. Never mind, You were patient enough to hear twenty seven lectures in the past and this is the 28th with a full stop."*

After a breath, he started again, *"Government was asked to keep away from production and distribution. Government industries accounted intentional loss and factories closed. Government products actual selling price was 40 to 55% of the Maximum Retail Price of private production. Closed factories were auctioned at scrap value and many of you directly bought the same. We artificially reduced your production cost by 24% including labour cost. Where is that surplus? You are supposed to show 8% growth, failed. Let me not mince truth gentleman, you called us to discuss about your future. But, it is not linked with our governance and parties future, you assure someone one trillion dollars"-is it not correct?*

A burly, gasping, business leader was red faced and gesturing his disagreement, *"No we did not discuss anything politics with any party. Invitation for a chamber meeting to Premath Mawa is a courtsy."* he dragged.

F.M. looked sharply at him. The statement that One trillion dollars brought a sense of shock in the minds of the chamber members. That man sat down as though he was trapped rat. He found that some of the corporate M.Ds were nodding their head accepting the lyrics of the F.M.PM passed on some note to FM. FM nodded and continued.

Sir, most of the states are giving BPL ration subsidies. You were critical and one of your President of chamber of commerce called it a wasteful subsidy turning the nation a beggar's colony. I tell you the truth, If food subsidies to 17 crores people are withdrawn, you have to pay a minimum wage of Rs.15000-00 per month to meet there family per capita income. You have to create 20 crores of employment. Your expenditure to labour alone shall be 29% of your income as per the economist. Government will have to go back on the beaten track of reopening their Public Sector and to support this unemployed army or we will collapse. European unions are bearing that much load of labour expenses and pension in their balance sheet, you know that. Now as per the statistics most of the companies are spending maximum of 11% as wages to labour. Who is subsidized gentleman? Industrial houses or Below Poverty Line work forces? Subsidies are unethical and most unscientific economic evolutions. But we did it as we wanted to protect the corporates.

"Sir, banking sector itself has written off three to four lakhs crores. You know for the past 7 years industrial houses and business barons have not repaid Rs.4,95,00,00 crores. Banks were transferring their income earnings to bad loans and one time settlement of bad loans. Silently, we postponed our 'Each Indian One Account' scheme as we have to open 5, 60,000 Branches in villages. Banks were refusing to oblige as the bad debts you created are haunting them. One lakh crores have been gobbled by 13 companies. Had we spread it over to rural debts, urban small trade and industries, this money, confidentially I tell you, would have lifted high my vote shares solidly by 6%. We committed a grave error and we are afraid we will face the curse. Even after defaults, 1780 companies including four in this meet have taken another Rs.1, 410,000 million even though norms are strangely violated.64 international instruments were created for external borrowing and investments, circumventing or slightly subjugating all the Foreign Exchange Regulations. Tell me, what this government did not do? More than 20 lakhs million tax income, in 7 years you failed to remit, we accounted under unpaid tax account. Strangely, I face wrath from press run by your corporates. GDP has grown and it had multiplied effect on personal wealth of the corporate directors and less in the balance sheet figures of the corporates."

Analyzing the political changes, *"Sir, with the help of corporates, the left parties and trade unions were unarmed in every state. No doubt, you paid a huge money to TU leaders belonging to our party and NPP. Sir, all the labour reforms were orchestrated and unions- free environment was created. We elevated a few anti-labour judges and even at Supreme Court, labour, human rights judgments were deleted. As per statistics the production cost in India does not exceed 11% for manual payment. Work turnover had gone by 11 to 12 hours a day on an average not eight hours. After doing this you were asking us to remove all labour laws. What is your logics? Mr.President please understand, you can suppress them and disorganize them to certain extend, if they unite and rise up, even armed force in this country cannot control them. Premnath promised you privately three days back, when some of you met him."* President of the Chamber was really turned pale.

"*Remember, work forces are not ill-equipped nor run by old illiterate masses. They can disturb your board meeting, your corporate finance and make you sleepless. Better, visit some European state and learn to induct 50% of their labour administration. You will have excellent production result. Premnath told that I will not be there in government. No issues, use your brain to run your industries and not his politics.*" President realized that they had one or two black sheep in the team that met Premnath.

FM was rubbing the salt on wounds. He covertly explained how at the cost of his party, chamber of commerce played a major role in funding and implanting the alternative party in West Bengal, how much CIA funds were injected only for finishing the 35 years of communist regime. "*Your corporates decide, what food the Indian middle and upper class shall eat; how at the cost of small traders huge Malls be built. Corporates decided what dress Indians shall wear at the cost of handloom downfall and what income each sector shall pay, at what wage structure. Only in India, these debates are open as corporate-government nexus is an approved culture of corruption.*

"All we did for you. How many delegations you all made. Even our budget underwent changes before prints and after prints. I stop now. Tell us how you are going to back our party in this election?" On a point blank manner, the Harvard trained F.M turned the table.

The last sentence broke the silence. Anger was mounting among the audience. Someone whispered *"finance minister`s great oration on his political funeral".*

CEO of RENAICENCE got up as soon as Finance Minister stopped his unfrequented open speech. The huge figure with all pain of lifting the whole body got up. Everyone is aware that he is capable of shutting the mouth of the FM. Mr. MUSAANI, the leader of largest empire in India with the personal wealth of 1.8 billion dollars and internationally tenth MNC, with two billion person assets turned to the Prime Minister, *"F.M. speech is fine. But not a word, on the subject of this meet. Internationally our reputation and image had gone very low. If the economy has grown and our market competition should have gone high; how come the dollar against Indian currency that was Rs.8-00 in 1981 now costs Rs. 72.00? Is there any major flaw in government policy? All are telling that this Government is now in a state of bankruptcy due to huge scandals, bad governance and accusations of worst corruptions. International investment is seriously affected and inflow of capital to an extent of one billion is withheld for my own corporations. The Indian investment summit organized by a section of foreign based Gujratis in November 2013 gave a clear direction to Indian business houses, not to back present ruler. What we were telling is only to declare a policy statement so that we can attract foreign investors. Whatever our President told was with an eye on revival of industries…"* He continued. Someone in third row commented to his neighbor that Mr.Musaani score in the total scandal exceeds one billion dollars, in telecommunication, oil and coal! How can he put the PM in the stinking basket and claim himself clean?

Majestically, another corporate leader, Mr.Sathish Dawan, known for his corporate integrity rose up. Indian corporates consider him as roll model for new innovative market magics. Government used to call him as expert member for all corporate law reforms. The whole house was suddenly had a jerk. He never cares for the big bosses. Nervously, the chamber observed him, *"Sir, I come directly to subject raised by my friend. I use some harsh words, I believe it is rather foolish to sanctify ourselves. The whole ICIA enquiry has indicted and jailed the ministers who had allotted all the transponders and communication rights or coal mines or iron ore mines and so on. Beneficiary corporates are not holy cows. Coal scam and corporates involvements, can anybody disown? Or without corporates how this deals or scam could have taken birth? Ministers are corrupt, I do not want to dispute, who paid them bribe? The list of payments are already in the internet and in the court. Now stop, the blame games. Not with any big good intention, but we shall not take the charcoal power and do cosmetic beautifications. Secondly, why the dollar rates are hiking? F.M. answered first we raised the question later. He told billions of exports earning income. But profit is retained in some other country and in some other account. While digging pit to others we shall also understand we are inside the pit to dig deep with shawl. An unbiased judiciary if exist, noose will be on our neck with the famous brand phrase "crony capitalism."* He turned to the PM and said, *"Sir, we apologize if any remark hurts you".*

He again turned to the president of Chamber of Commerce, *"If you have any table papers to be placed appealing the government to consider, Place it. As for the Gujarat Summit resolution is depreciable and all such fanaticism are to be banned. First of all tell us who are they? You have some parallel president? We are indulging in party politics or responding to someone`s instigation. Their Language is too much: End it or it will end the chamber`s co-existence."*

Now the black mail is in clear language. Even if Bharathiya Congress government signorders in dotted paper, the ruling party is going to be coffined by this Financial Empire. Of course, people will not vote if the business leaders-`say`, but people will vote, if the same barons-`Pay'- through their political agents.

P.M. left the venue with a sense of betrayal and humiliation as old wounded tiger. Had he diverted the billions of the treasury income to all alternative development schemes, to million micro enterprises, they would have changed the face of whole state economy with wide spread growth. Office of PM would not have been humiliated and treated like enslaved labour by these monopolies. Now, he is a thrash, sorted for shredder. Normally, ordinary workers used to shout that corporates do use them and spit out. Now, the highest office of the country is facing the spit out. Alternative political leader is now tracked by this fortune billionaires. Now their treasury will divert flood of currencies in different directions.

"Sameer, I am Satish Dawan, to-day what happened, you know, is an inexcusable insult to a national head. You have enough documentary and video proof and my letter."

"Hi Dawan why of all the press, you want to hang LIFE LINE editor?"

"Because, you look so smart and strong, my wife told me- bloody, I am jealous!"

CHAPTER III - JAN-14

THE PLAY IS DONE
THESE KINGS ARE TO MORROWS
PEDESTRIANS
WITH THEIR ROYAL EXECUTIVES
THEY SHALL FIND PLACES
ONCE DISPENSED WITH

"So,Dawan, is it wise to take the risk of publishing the whole debate? Parliament session is going on" Sameer was talking to Sathish Dawan, managing director of AFTA CORPORATION LIMITED

"I do not care if my name is out at any time. As a matter of fact I have already purchased two acres in California in my son`s name and I am settling in three months after the election and I am stepping down from my company board. In ten minutes, I am sending a pen drive video. I do not know, how my assistant got it so clearly in the closed door summit. Three or four members' dissent notes are recorded in writing to chamber of commerce that copy is also sent to you in printed form. I know, you are the one who do not jerk at the bottom, when you sit on hot iron bar."

"Sir, are you praising or putting me in the acid jar?"

"My dear Sameer, both"

O.K., I will release it. You are planning to run away in two months. Sir, but why you are so perturbed?"

"Sameer, never in the history, these rogues had treated a PM with contempt and humiliation. 28 times, I am telling you 28 times, I had gone to this PM and FM on deputation for various industrial concessions and we got it. In fact, they tried to coerce him to sign blank documents. 14 corporates committed foreign exchange violations and were caught. Finance minister helped them to come out. It was I who mediated. Tell me, which corporate has not grown? I myself have grown from $.100 million to $.3, 700 million in 8 years. Had, he not opened the market and given us opening to international market, we would have remained in our own drying lakes or pissing in our pants with no investment, no expansion in trade." Sameer Asked *"Did he sign? I mean any policy statement issued?"*

Managing Director of AFTA corporation replied, *"No, and Sameer, all these guys had their first round talk with* **PremnathMawa**, *the NPP nominee for Prime Minister. Under his advice only these business houses came with their package."*

Sameer repeated, *"Did he sign?"*

"No, a blunt No!"

TIMELINE flashed a most sensational article next day. Openly editorial in the front pages. The high light was that the corporates have insulted the national head under the guidance of Mr. Prenath Mawa, Prime Minister Candidate of NPP.

Parliament was becoming more and more a meat market as it was nearing the date of election. NPP was firing salvo against the Prime Ministers and other ministers every day and come to the lawn, where the news channels are waiting with their channel brand, color mikes. They will drums about the chaotic tale as hot news with samosa and tea. Sometime Samosa and tea will be much hotter than news. Too many news channels, with too little interesting news try to release all those parliamentary lawn news channel tit bits. Sometimes member who was in fish market at the precious hour of parliament will also give thriller tales on issues which he never participated nor his presence was there at the time of debate. News channels will treat those thrillers as time fillers.

Morning 10.30 parliament commenced its business.

While entering Sameer accidently met a minister. *"Ayer, yesterday TIME NEWS debate was very excellent. A good election campaign"*

"Hutt, what is the use. When our man with zipped mouth and stony face spoils all our chances? Did madam tell him not to smile, not to open his mouth? All bakwas, the opposition will speak and tell prime minister alone shall make statement! He will make a miniscule reply. My god he is going to delete 20% of our urban votes. See to-day, more thing are going to rot. You also added acid"

Again that minister shouted, "*O, oh, bloody shit, I mistakenly opened my loud mouth to you. That too to-day! Hi! Don't quote me in your column!*" Both laughed.

What is your problem, Ayer? Sameer Jovially asked.

"*Nothing, nothing man, I wrongly pissed in my pant while talking to you*" Ayer's satires are famous in the parliament. He rushed inside.

NPP members were on feet and shouted at the PM, "*How can you talk about our leader in Chamber of commerce meet? Is it not a shameful act on the part of Prime Minister to accept demands of Chamber of commerce which are policy decisions?*"

PM got up and was about to make a statement.

R.M. Gupta, Vijay Andhra party got up and asked the leader of NPP to clarify, "*Honourable speaker, I have to raise a point of order. Sorry to intervene P.M. Whether NPP is against these corporate demands? Secondly will it take a firm stand rejecting these demands of the Chamber of commerce if we pass a resolution against the PM approval? Please clarify your position.*" P.M. sat back and Finance Minister sitting nearer asked him to wait.

"*That is not an issue here. We want the PM to make statement*"

Again the same member got up "*NPP to make their stand clear before they are asking PM to make his position clear. Or otherwise I place a motion, condemning all these corporate demands, will the ruling party vote, will NPP support?*"

Barathiya Congress members got up. "*Yes we are prepared to vote.*"

Entire ruling party and other opposition got up from the seat and asked NPP to answer this issue. There was a blazing attack on NPP that they were collaborating with industrial houses. Shouting continued. Communist members got up and shouted, *"Corporate agents, One trillion rupees How many suit case?"*NPP walked out amidst the chaos.

PM curtly said, *"Government has no intention to consider any major change in the economic policies. As for dragging the names of NPP in that chamber meet, I request the honourable member to investigate, who are those who glorified Premnathji and who denounced his role in inducting polarisationin the chamber. Premnathji had agreed to support these demands. I am not willing to indulge in divisive politics"*

Left group got up asked whether it is true that Corporates invited him for a meet, demanded to make policy changes and also insulted him for his refusal. PM looked embarrassed.

"Is it a fact that Gujrat International Investors Summit had advised the business houses not to back the ruling party?"

"Did corporate asked you to sign a policy statement on FDI in agriculture, sale of Public sector industries including SAIL, Oil and others?"

The NPP allies who were still in the house were anxious to get the reply. They know well that NPP is involved in chamber of commerce politics. They were shocked when the angry PM shot back,

"No such recognized body named Gujrat International summit do exist and even if some unrecognized group makes any senseless resolution, House will not waste its valuable hours in answering these cheap publicity stunts. Who are they to call International? May be some unpatriotic foreign nationals-do you want to respond these unpatriotic groups? Point two, yes, these issues were the Private corporates consistent demand. Not a sudden origin. The chamber members told that Premnathji is also supporting. Our reply is also consistent `NO`" Entire Gujarat bench turned pale with shame.

Sameer who was witnessing the live discussion, *"See, See, if he had done this in all past discussions, government would have retained its bold image."*

FM called him, *"Sameer come to my chamber, Ayer told me that the man who poured boiling water in the parliament is sitting at gallery counting the red spots."*

FM said, *"Your story, Conspiracy of the Corporates! Is Premnath behind?"*

.

"But sir that is not my head line? In fact, your role and PM were much exposed, Sir. As a friend I also feel".

FM replied, *"Yes, you have exposed the role of crony capitalists. More than anything, you washed all our five years sins. We were the bearer of cross, you shifted them back to the shoulders of the guilty. But it is too late and nobody is going to recognize that. Thank you."*

"Secondly, your climax exposed the cunning game of their future Prime Minister. I reveal one fact, if the corporate felt the heat of the investigations on scams directly, Indian industrial sector could have come to a standstill. Fearing the collapse, we protected them and made ministers and officials alone scapegoats. No body is a holy cow to-day and in future even if they come to power they will be worst collaborators. Yesterday you tracked the whole discussion with video! Come on, who is your insider?"

Sameer,*"Sir, can I quote you?"*

An uncontrolled laughter made the ministry office to astonish, how come FM is able to burst after facing the onslaught and wrath for the whole day.

Next day, *"Sameer Basu"*.

A hoarse voice called, *"Mr. Sameer, I am Madan Vyas. Do you remember me boy? Your head lines charges NPP is in nexus with corporates. You wrote against our party and Premnathji. They are utterly obnoxious and defaming. He is disturbed."*

"Mr. Madanji type your objection and say what is correct, we will release."

"Not necessary Shameer, TIMELINES life line ends after this election. How long we can tolerate? Tell me!" Line disconnected.

The main opposition NATIONAL PEOPLE`S PARTY head quarter suddenly started buzzing with feverish activity and their CHINTAN BAITAK, the brain ware of the party was called to meet in 2 hours at their Head Quarters.

Time Lines wrote

"Corporates have chosen NPP leader as their Shehansha"

CHAPTER IV - MAR 2014

ANY HISTORY THAT IS DISTORTED TO DIVIDE PEOPLE SHALL BE DESTROYED AS NATIONAL CURSE

National Central Committee of Rashtrya Rakshna Samithi had an urgent meeting as the elections for 16thLok Sabha was announced as May 2014. President of the Samithi as usual was sitting in one corner of the hall and silently observing the happening. Normally, as soon as the meeting officially starts, he will move to the stage. Until then he will sit on a window seat and silently view the surrounding nature. He will speak less with cadres in the meeting hall. The most revered leader, Rashtirya Rakshana Samithi, Poojya BAJI RAO, joined the RRS at the age of seventeen. He pursued his studies in the Banaras Hindu University. His political education also commenced along with his study on Hinduism. Later in British rule in India, he served as the Diwan of Maharaja of Marwad, who was again in the roll call of British. To interact with British and to negotiate BajiRao, the elite B.A. (Hon) service was often required. Baji Rao slowly recollected his own biography forgetting the crowd around him. *'He hated the British, but the impotency of his king finally converted him as a talented negotiator. He witnessed the rise of freedom movement against British. Like forest fire people revolted against the White rules.*

Congress was demanding participation in British governance. Muslim League took birth with similar demand but for separate representation of their leaders. Communists were there with their Soviet flavor. Many of them were in underground, many in jail. Most of them in other parties as communist Party was a banned organization all through those decades. Congress and Muslim league line of collusion with British caused revolt inside the party. ' Poorna Swaraj' slogan took birth and Balagagdhara Tilak and other extremist lead internal revolt. Later QUIT INDIA cry rented the air. BajiRao was passionately reading about the BalagangadarTilak, Lajpath rai, Bipin Chandra Pal, the extremist, as the British called. Rise of Gandhian Movement on one side. Subash Chandra Bose militant movements, ChandrajitYadav, Bhagat Singh, Arabind Ghosh the name of the martyrs slowly waving in his brain. BajiRao tried to bring back the names of those freedom fighters one by one. Remained, as bachelor all through his life and dedicated to the creation of a Maha Hindurashtra. His mind rolled back the names of Hegdewarkar and Golwankar, Deendayal Upadyaya, What was their role against British? Nothing! Veer Savarkar, why he fought against British, arrested and sent to Jail in Andaman Island?

Some name vaguely came to his memory-Namboodripad? Where he met that Brahmin! He was not able to recollect how this name came to him? Finally, he recollected. Namboodripad, once happened to meet him at Thiruvananthapuram hotel, where both were provided rooms by their respective local leaders. EMS! He was in congress or communist movement, he could not recollect. "Mr.BajiRao, tell me why your Maha Hindurashtra is not fighting against the British, the `REAL ENEMY'. India *is enslaved by them. Our economy and culture are invaded by them. Our wealth are looted.*" Both of them engrossed in discussion for more than two hours, forgetting that they represent two different ideology. Finally departing BajiRao told, "*Yes EMS, do you say that Muslim League is participating in all this independent struggle.*"

EMS responded, "*You are correct, Muslim League and Liaquat Ali Khan, Jinnah and others rather want to have a participation in British rule, rather than national independence. We shall be happy that, at least, they are not pro-British. But basically earlier Muslims rulers' war and struggle against British is historic. Like that several Hindu kings and queens in India. It has two faces in our perception. One, heroic wars against British is against foreign aggression is not ideological, but purely defending their feudal ownership. There is no strong motivation to drive the British out of this nation. Because there is no single nation in the political map to call Bharat or India!*"

"*EMSji, you are all different breeds and you will think beyond, with certain parameters which will crack our basic concept, but nothing harmful or incorrect in your perception and realities. I am not willing to accept that shape nation which you display. I can see the shape- torn cloth of the map. But you also wish and know that we shall stitch them together as one spread. Time will erase the borders and we will display a different map. Both of us will live to see that.*"

EMS addressed "Guruji, in 1857 India had 20 crores of population more than 560Princely states or Indian kingdoms were there. Two lakhs Indian soldiers in British army and a major section were revolting. British were only 40000, still the

Indians could not drive the ruthless British out. Your concept of Akanda Bharatha did not exist any time in the minds of Indians, even though that word originated in the Vedic period and live among the orthodox but learned. I am also longing for the birth of one independent nation. But any such conceptions, if it does not percolate in to the grass root, what you say will remain in holy script and we will remain under British slavery."

Baji Rao smiled and told, "EMSji, you called me Guruji, whereas, I am receiving upadesha, a different perception of nationalism from you to day". "In Rig Veda there is a saying `Let the noble thoughts come from every direction`. Your point is correct, I will present your idea in our MHR meet."

Next day, when the news spread about the closed door meeting. Neither communist nor Maha Hindurashtra spoke about it.

Some pressman met and asked Namboodripad "*What is the significance yesterday's meet, can you give us in detail? Both are enemies, have you planned any joint action in your freedom struggle?"*

EMS smiled, *"We two Indian nationals met: We are not enemies: Our real enemy is Imperialism. In the national freedom, every Indian can join, even if they represent different ideology. If they come to anti-British movement, it will be strengthened. Since he is an intellectual and respectable leader of the movement, we exchanged our ideas on various issues."*

Baji Rao read this prodigal statement of EMS and smiled. When some pressman approached him. He gave him the paper cutting and told that nothing more to add. British Viceroy sent a warning to all the Hindu kingdoms to restrain Maha Hindurashtra from discussing this subject. MahaHindurashra did not take up this struggle to drive the British out nor indulged in any debate with the spirit of nationalism. Baji Rao looked around, the RRS meet is yet to start. They are waiting for some NPP leader to make an important announcement.

Baji Rao again trounced back as there was no initiative or interest from any member to discuss any subject in relation to Rashtirya Rakshna Samithi.

Akanda Bharat now divided in to several countries like Afghanistan, Burma desh, Sri Lanka, Tibet, Nepal, Pakistan, East Pakistan i.e. Bangla desh. Hindurashra dreams were deeply buried in sand. When Pakistan division took place, their core issue was decimated. Instead of crying for the breach of their holy land to pieces, the RRS cadres took part in the unprecedented human carnage, migrations and drove out millions-like beasts driving the enemies from their jungle territory. In fact, driving Muslims were done by land aggression gangs in many states. This brutal game from both sides resulted in transit of 4.5 million Hindus and Sikhs from Pak and 5 million Muslims from India. One Million people died in this exodus. MHR cadres were rejoiced over the most horrible and inhuman partition. Death, burning, rape, murder, loot and massacre of lakhs of people in the name of religion broke the heart of patriotic people of the nation. History of these two to three years were written in blood, flesh and burnt homes and broken tales of families and heart. Now AKAND BHARATH was eternally a ruined dream. Yet some of them still holding in their blog, their posters, web sites, that Pakistan and Bangladesh are non-liberated part of India and it will be part of Akanda Bharath in the future times. Baji Rao was often asking them, should we compulsorily keep these dead concepts alive? Did we not drive millions out and told that is your land? What way it will serve a nation and people? Most of RRS men do not find proper answer. Without receiving an answer to that question, Baji Rao had spent his life for this nation. Some praised his vision and some treated this as an illusion. He is afraid to drop these visions as dead, because it is this mirage that is keeping him alive and running the whole movement for half more than half century.

British divided the nation, gave freedom and made the nations to bleed. Mr.BajiRao looked around. RRS is yet to commence any discussion. What we have done as the political and social organization? One crore members, what is their real contribution except in the time of calamities or some mass struggle against government atrocities or national emergencies? For whom the leaders are waiting for? He turned his attention to the hall. 75% are senior leaders, who are living for this movement. Are they also living with the same luminous illusions? Hundred times they met in a year and talk about Nationalism, patriotism and try to bring more youths to shakas. Hundred boys enter as cadre 150 are absenting to the shaka. RRS has become a permanent appendage to NPP. NPP is nothing but another degenerated political party now according to Baji Rao. Proudly, RRS leaders used to boast that NPP takes decisions only after consulting RRS. Fact is, decisions are announced in the name of RRS in order to avert inner debates within the party. Guruji went back to his political meditation once again.

Madan Vyas was in his BMW moving across the streams of Delhi traffic. He is late to the RRS meet. All units will wait for him.

His secretary Vishal placed the budget. *"Sir, how you are going to transfer the funds to U.P."*

"Who said we are transferring? As on to-day, all are oral promissory notes. Eighteen corporate companies are going to give Rs. 60000 millions No 2 a/c fund. They will move their funds in account or in cash or withdraw through their sellers as advances, payment of purchases and so on. In six days, these donations are going to be parked in 117 district headquarters. Seven thousand millions are going to be for three constituencies - Rai Bareli, Amethi and Varanasi. RRS we pay Rs.1, 00, 000 million?"

"So much sir! How we are distributing sir?"

"They have their own couriers all over India. But headquarters is not willing to involve. Money is released on the state headquarters according to the list given by their vice-president. I tell you, this organization is only one wing which will spend with 80% honestly and our 30% of votes will be mobilized by this wing only. There is an in house counter force to meet the muscle power of other political parties."

"Sir, Mr.BajiRao seems to be unhappy about this corporate funding and campaign money."

"There are only two ways of dealing with evil persons or thorns. Crush them under your boot or stay far away from them"- said Chanakyya. We stay away: Vishal, I am not a RRS man with bundle of ideology. NPP has given me only one area of operation. Distribute and monitor the corporate currency now flooding. I am a trader, I know where to put money at what season it will give a good return. First I offer peace through currency payment, create enmity with the same instrument where peace offers are not accepted and use the same to buy stick for a different brutal operation, as per our sastra. In NPP also I am a CEO without any share holdings. But controls everything and the power is derived from the major shareholder to day Mr. Premnath. If I contest for a M.P. post on my own I will lose deposit and at the same time if Premnath goes without me, he will lose the party.

"I tell you that we had a thorough study of Presidential campaigns as we are changing the strategy of projecting not the party but one man above the party. Obama campaign reached a stage of One Billion dollars. NPP is going to spend 1.5 times more. See five billionaires alone have agreed to take care of the entire campaign. There personal net worth is 5,240,000 million rupees. I have not gone to any corporate company worth less than Rs.10,000 millions. More things I confide to you because 30 to 40% of the monitoring is going to be under your supervision. We have purchased 197 opposition MLAs and old 30 MPs, who will remain in their own camp and sabotage their party candidates."

Vishal looked at his Election guru and wondered about the brilliance of this campaigner. He is confident that NPP is going to route other parties. Slight shiver came in him. If, by error, if he fails in the test of loyalty to this gentle monster, he may vanish. Smilingly he touched the leg of Madan Vyas and did namaskar. Jovially he told *"Guruji by your teachings, I have obtained Political wisdom. Sorry I cannot name it as wisdom. I have passed 10th std public exam."* Madan Vyas laughed and got down from the car before the RRS headquarters.

Mr.BajiRao's dreams were shared by every hard core of Rashtriya Rakshna Samithi. But hard core with personal integrity and political commitment are shrinking in digits. Leaders like BajiRao were aged wounded tigers. Never he aspired nor contested for any electoral position. Never preferred posh life style that are enjoyed by other political leaders. His colleagues revered him for his Spartan religious life and religious dharma practices as poojiyashree, a venerable nobleman. Eighty eight or ninety years, yet physically active due to his daily yoga for two hours. As an excellent organizer, funds raiser had gained the reputation of soft dictator. He was not in any government, still his directives will come out as ministerial notification in governmental orders. His wing Rashtriya Rakshna Samithi which is having more than 50000 shakas or branches and more than 1, 00, 00,000 membership, claims as a most potential political force with complete administrative and organized structure. Top leaders of Rashtriya Rakshana Samithi, wise men of the Hindu Zionism, do share his thesis.

Meeting has not commenced and the organizers at the stage were restless. Time schedule is one of the discipline of RRS. Bajirao may walk out anytime, if he is presiding. But he is clear that he will not preside any meeting arranged for NPP representatives to participate and address. Even chief ministers many time found him walking out for their unscheduled programmes.

BajiRao, travelled back with time, mapping the past history. The MHR shortly known, the pre-independent movement had an idea to keep as many as seven to eight Hindu Kingdoms with in Indian Territory as independent state without annexing or merging with Indian Union. This preposterous proposal received a firing opposition and condemnation. Government of India feared that this will invite great peril, as kings who have signed the agreement of Accession may go back. There was already a civil war in Hydrabad-Bidar region between the communist and Nizam`s Army. Communist who were trained in armed struggle had valiant fight earlier in Chittagong and many parts of the British India. In fact, In India, British were afraid more about the communists uprise and their political allies who are extremist in the liberation movements. Even after national independence 1949, 1950 communist party was a banned organization. National Congress, Mahatma Gandhi and Jawaharlal Nehru on many occasion were forced to take strong political line against British. That pressure was built by the left forces called congress socialists inside congress. Congress also knows that once if they take compromise line as they were doing in 1885 to 1918, Indian people will reject them totally. British knows that liberation of India is an inevitable retrograde move and in this retreat if the communist succeeds and takes *over the government in India, they will tilt the international polarization against West. Already One third of the world was dominantly supporting USSR. 516 colonies of the Western countries one after another were removing their shackles and chains. When the contemporary conditions were adversely ruining, the last effort of the British is to keep their economic hold and industrial wealth under their regimes. British also felt that they shall go with Congress in transferring the power. Baji Rao was in a remorse mood. Why we MHR remained as audience to such an historic transition? Did we lost not all the boats till 1947 and failed to capture till 1977 or lead till 1996!*

RRS were finally able to restrain congress in annexing Kashmir and Nepal, Bhutan as Hindu Kingdoms. They were backing the feudal ideals of retaining the kings as head of the states. Some Portuguese colonies were left untouched then. But, the error of Pakistan arming border Razakkars attack on Baramulla and occupation of Musheerabad by Pak backed army, forced Maharaja Hari Singh of Kashmir to annex the kingdom with India in October, 1947. Then why this special status in 1954 included in the constitution of India for Jammu and Kashmir? Baji Rao is not able to collect in his memory. Why it was drafted by Gopalasamy Iyangar, former minister of Hari Singh and government of India was forced to accept: another blunder?

Battle against privilege to Muslims getting an adverse popular opinion now a days. RRS is not able to impose its ideals. Secular thoughts are deeply implanted in the minds of majority Indians. The left intellectuals are an incorrigible force to deal with and to be finished politically and ideologically other wise they never allow the party to establish a `Baratha continent'. In the present *environment, is it a correct line? Baji Rao was totally confused as no political line is giving a revival to his movement. Even the success of NPP in election is not a solution to RRS.*

"*Guruji,*"some one gave a cup of milk. Mechanically collecting that Baji Rao went back to his world of thoughts.

Isolating Muslims even though was not much successful, RRS cadre built bases everywhere. A promise to build Ram temple resulted in creating a good mass. A chosen line for consolidation of a political wing on ideological path! But, what is RRS mission, independent of NPP? Again it is an answerless question! Are we heading for Himalayan blunder?

A Promise to give a good governance against the corrupt existing ruling party will give 15 to 20% votes. After centuries, the SC and ST are being wooed by the cash rich NPP. Thus after 60 years the NPP party is once again gaining maximum seats in the parliament as per the poll predictions. Perhaps, it may independently form its own government. But 25 or 30% vote share! To reach this, it took 90 long years and hundreds of defeats and failed coups. Baji Rao felt that He, above, is writing whatever destined to be followed.

On the other day, Purandhar Vittala contradicted him. Vittala always speaks with his detachments to Samithi path. What you did as RRS, you built a consolidated vote bank to NPP. But what you did to a nation with that? But the nation has suffered an invisible partition all over the nation; fundamental suspicion among communities, divided business, forcing ghettoes for some communities, markets isolations, political untouchability, linguistic divisions, separated caste-communal educational Institutions, localities, business links with communal identifications, rigorous grip of religious fundamentalists over their community people, fury and violence over the inter-religious marriages,oppressions against women in the name of religious laws, hate campaigns, bloody riots, burnings and rhetoric speeches of fanaticisms of religion- all have virtually demolished the vision of a monolithic nation. With all these disease, whether RRS has achieved its noble aim? Why Purandar is missing? He cannot tolerate these corporate carbon monoxidepollution-this is the word he used on the other day? Purandar may part with movement once I am no more"

Baji Rao again looked around. He found that, the cadres are not happy to be kept in waiting for half an hour. Their culture is now corroding under the influence of NPP. For him time has no relevance.

'Now the confidence is that once the state power becomes absolute, thing will change. Good days will come. What way NPP is going to bring change? Is it wise to effect it? We have to make a search for an answer. In the whole world, in many countries, ruling majority had implanted their religious ideas on their own people and people have silently acknowledged the dominance. Why not in India? It is Israel, it is Pakistan, it is in Myanmar, in Sri Lanka and many Arab nations, dictated democracy are running for decades. R.R.Samithi, the heart and soul of the party and its philosophy carved out of Natchez and other fascist ideologies, suffered all set back in establishing a nation dreamt for a century. But the very character of a state and culture changes, how these restoration of old order is going to bring a golden era? Who will reply me with a rational

thought? His mind was crisscrossing endlessly. Others were thinking that he is planning deeply how to organize the election strategy for the success of their new Messiah Mr.premnath Mawa.

'Samithi`s historical wounds are still on the loss of Afghan kingdom ruled by Kusha, son of Lord Rama. Burma with 2000 temples were removed from Indian map, Thailand, Sumitra, Indonesia, Borneo, Kamboja, Ghandara, Takshasila, Purushapura(Peshawar), the legendary holy lands of Hindus are no more in map. "Political borders are manmade and he can alter too" -Mein Kampf sentences reverberated in him. What is this alteration means? Bloodshed and loss of thousands of human life and brutal massacres and destructions with modern weaponry. Is it worth or an act of insane brutes?' Om Namashivaya, his mind slowly caved in and he stated meditating which he will do unmindful of rumbling and noise around.

Poojya BAJI RAO, came back after a few minutes of silence. Some sevak leaders raised from the seat to mark their respect to some visitor. This disturbed the silence of the hall. RRS top leaders started discussion on the political strategy of the parliamentary election.

Secretary called upon the presidium to allow Madan Vyas to address. Baji Rao, President was not even asked to occupy the front seat. A hoarse voice of the NNP`s secretary, Madan Vyas is heard. No courtesy, no formalities normally observed by seeking permission of the President to speak out. He is a special nominee for dealing with Third Alternative front and UP. His role is more or less a Political power broker. He is a known excellent horse trader in politics. Opposition called him a predator vulture, a patient bird, knows the contemporary strategies, conspiracy and political chess movement. Making PremnathMawaas P.M. candidate was decided by them, two years back. A whole team of ten to twelve brain wares, score of intellects sat for 3 months and presented a blue print of 290 pages, with eighty sketch of Indian states. While Kerala state were found in one sketch U.P. state, the largest province, was divided into seven for analysis. Their research was not only on the opposition, but also about NPP leadership. Campaign tone was changed from ideology to party and party to individual image.

Guruji knows that none of the RRS ideas and views are going to be followed. These exercises are not for any consultation with grass root but fixing a price tag for one crore cadres for campaign. Block vote purchase scheme best suitable alternative chosen by NPP basing on local conditions. Politics is now the first resort. He raised his head. Madan Vyas is still addressing the gathering.

Madan Vyas did not go much on the subject as there election strategies are yet to be shaped according to him. He was terse and talking with a monotone. That showed his aversion in reporting the whole political strategy even though it was drawn and blue printed in this NPP headquarters. One fact is clear, that party has to report its activities to all RRS top level. This was a political decision 25 years back. One crore cadres are to be activated. But this time Shakas are not waiting for the command from Head Quarters. Secondly, Madan Vyas is not going withhold any of his programme, whether they accept his actions or not.

"Sir, I make a brief report. There are more than 28 parties, allies of NPP. They are contesting in the seats where NPP had less than 15%vote's percentage. Strategically each state we have framed different policy and posture, so that we score 300 seats and our allies 100 seats. We have entered into a crucial deal with the CM of Tamilnadu in a different terms. We have formed third alliance with smaller entities there with total different formula. Her party and NPP will publically demonstrate a hostile posture. Main oppositions, left and Congress will lose their vote shares partly to us and to her in this conflicting posture. All hostile votes she will capture along with her vote share in the state. Small allies will capture their vote shares and our vote pockets. We will capture our vote shares and allies share, and votes hostile to the madam`s party partly. Candidates nominated by us will win a good number of seats. In TN, Gurunath and Ramji were nominated to mediate, moderate and madam is properly guided. If NPP is elected, she will be relieved of her a major judicial dagger hanging on her head. If, NPP is short of majority, her party will join the ministry. NPP and its paid allies in Tamilnadu will form alternative front. Three, she will betray the left parties in the last lap so that opposition group may not able to release seats to them in the last moment. There will be another division in the opposition vote share. We have to pay Rs.860 crores to our allies in cash."

BajiRao was shocked when Mr. Madan Vyas reported that NNP alliance have been pumped with Rs.860crores for seat sharing in Tamilandu. There was silent pain. Political virtues and public morale are having no place in NPP. Someone wanted to know how many seats the party is expected to win with so much financial input. A terse reply was that three to four maximum. Madan with contempt opened a sheet and showed the amount of unaccounted cash provided from Singapore sources to Ramkanth, an influential politician, who is holding more than 12% of Votes in Tamilnadu. Even if the lady gets 35 to 36%, all oppositions will divide the remaining vote shares with four in equal parts. None will reach 20% vote full. She herself is diverting her vote share in to NPP in three to four constituencies as per the arrangement.

"Sir, Andhra, the seat share is not settling as the demand from Nayaka is Rs.1800 crores. Nayaka is afraid of Jayanath Rao, who is loaded with Rs.3700 crores for this election." Bajirao, the world of idealism has collapsed and he found that his Hindurashtra is going to be built on, corruption, malice, fraud, and bloody money of corporates, checkenry, betrayals and blackmails. Baji Rao mind started exploring, *"Is there anything called Vanaprasta in politics, abandoning all human links in life and leave alone to jungle to spend remaining part of life doing penance? Yes, olden days Maharajas went to jungle after 60 years. Time is ripe now. No I am too late here."*

Tulisram, Maharashtra leader asked who is funding all these huge financial warehouse. Madan Vyas curtly responded to discuss it with Boss. RRS chief was pulled from the peak and thrown into a dustbin. Someone is their boss. First time, in his life the top man of RRS think tank has received such an impolite reply. To everyone`s shock, he got up and without a word, left the room. In the last 65 years, never anyone try to talk a word to humiliate him. To-day surreptitiously someone told him that he is dispensable. Once reached the outer room, he held the wall as he felt some giddiness. He sat on the stool used by the security guards.

Inside, the narration was continuing. *"Sir, UP is our prime target. Here too, four party contest is going on, we plan to buy surplus from each party in each constituency. It is not Gujrath Module but Gujrat Money that is going to secure votes. 3600 Leaders of NPP are nominated officially to conduct the campaign. 1100 other party leaders are unofficially identified and they will work from their own party base but canvass for our candidates. They will capture block votes and shift it to us in the final hour. Even before six months we had stored Rs.11, 000-00 crores, other than the normal methods. Our calculation is that we will capture 28% votes and 70 seats minimum.*

"Are they going to engage RRS shakas in this process?" "Mockingly Vyas responded "*No sir, we have entered contract with Village Punchayat presidents or vice-presidents to transfer 60% of the vote of the village and each president were paid 20 lakhs to 50 lakhs. Each one assured in front of 10 to 12 village members. NPP village council is established with an agreement that Rs.30 to 35 lacs will be paid to villagers and Rs.15 lacs will retained by village NPP council for party affairs. They are our future ranks. We thus establish permanent professional relations in every village instead of lunging for party, ideology or loyalty. An out and out, President Bill Clinton and Obama Campaign we have drafted and being implemented."*

Madan Vyas got up from his seat and told *"my respected leaders, I am leaving to Lucknow. We know how RRS will work for our party."* He shook his head and told, *"We have reserved Rs.10,000-00 crores for RRS Shakas and their election Expenses. State wise requirement will be discussed in two days and money will be shifted. Is it o.k.?"*

Old guards are furious and got up. He had conveyed the message to those who waited for that word. He left the hall. Senior leaders rushed out.

President BajiRao found missing.

CHAPTER V - MAR 2014

WHEN ONE WITH HONEYED WORDS BUT EVIL MIND PERSUADES THE MOB, GREAT WOES BEFALL THE STATE—EURIPIDES –ORESTES

20 days before election, Sameer Basu was with `Guardian` reporter Frank More. Frank always like to spend more time with Sameer as his intellectual discussions are much fascinating with national objectives. Frank had more Indian friends, who are in social and governmental line. Frank wrote an article on the total transfer of wealth estimated by an Indian economist from India to U.K., the British Parliament rose against Guardian Magazine. House of common member, John Maxwell said, *"You cannot deny, that is why you do not want someone tell that to the world. Drop this debate. Nobody asked you to repay. Don't blow it much. Another 267 colonies will sit with their excel sheets. "Again on International black money matters, Frank exposed the role of two MNC banks of U.K. origin and those two CEOs warned Guardian that they will sue the magazine. Next week a large leak of names of Indian Businessmen and their account operations in these banks came out. Bank`s turned deaf and dumb.*

Frank More was really fascinated about the world gigantic event, the elections in India. It is more than a mere democratic exercise. The massive campaigns, multi- parties involvement, money involved, caste, creeds and communal over tones. Public meetings participated by lakhs of people in burning sun, hearing nothing and knowing nothing- what leader is speaking. In the burning sun standing and eating the pockets of food served in most unhygienic conditions, drinking waters from open drums filled by Lorries-were amazing scenes to the reporter. Indian Immune system is so powerful that virus and germs in food and water do die once it enters the human stomach. Guardian reporter asked how come so many lakhs do participate, in public meeting addressed by the leaders.

"Yes, they are vagrant millions with political nomadism. Disillusioned masses move in million one to another oasis, which is also a mirage. Leaders spends 20 to 30 million to mobilize their crowd. One day wage, they earn by participating in mass programme. But more than that, they believe god, they believe their leaders images. They refuse to acknowledge that the corrupt behavior of their heroes are harmful to a nation." Guardian reporter and Sameer sat for the dinner in the roof of Obroi tower. Reporter sought to record. Sameer nodded.

"Indian electoral politics has got certain historical blunder. The electoral system had reached people at grass root, but the roots were not able to reap benefits of the democratic process. Seven national parties did register so far with a minimum of 6% vote shares, that too in more than one state. 36 regional parties holding a combined majority vote share together, but

seat holdings of their own in Lok Sabha are less. 316 parties registered with no electoral participation. But they procure, sell votes in wholesale to one or other major parties. Political parties have become go down of unaccounted cash which we term black money. Gravity of fraud is in allowing political parties to receive donations unaccounted, retain apart and spend apart unaccounted is the most rotten part of democratic process: Corruption sanctified by law."

"With all holy gospels the election commission drama opens with the declaration of election. Candidates will sign under oath on constitution and canvass under the robe of castism. Ministry of corporates' affairs, Income tax department, land registrars, bankers turns mute spectators. When a billionaire declare that he owns money only for his square meals, holds no land bigger that his grave pit, zero tax dues or no loan defaults, all state machineries turns deaf, dumb and blind. His declaration can be sent to various departments to certify the facts. After all 11,000 candidates are in the field. Any defect will result in deleting the candidates from contestant lists."

"Not one criminal`s nomination gets rejected. No funding sources identified, nor expenditure monitored. Sometimes some candidates will have no space to declare list of names their wives"

Sameer raised his face and looked at the face of Frank More, the Guardian reporter, who is closely observing and responding with lot of enthusiasm.

Frank opened his mouth, *"Basu, is there no ceiling on expenditure on candidate or party. Is there no government funding? Some European states fund the candidate for contesting because that will encourage good citizens to come inside the parliament? Since they do not suffer for running their campaign nor do suffer for money to contest the election. But every dollar they have to draw in account and spend through accounts. If they are found to have spent beyond or for some other personal purpose, they will be barred to contest and their name will be removed"*

Basu smiled, "Yes, there is a regulation that candidate can spend only Rs.7 millions, whereas their party can spend even ten thousand millions. Top most leaders of the NPP had already spent more than Rs. 3000 millions in helicopter alone. More than Rs.500 to Rs.1000 millions spent to pull the crowd and paid audience. Funds are moved in physical form, across the country escorted by ministers, police and candidates. Electronic and paper Media contract is in the latest scheme entered by NPP and cost is near about Rs.200,000 million. The whole skies are covered with their master, with the new avatar images. Star campaigners expenses are unlimited and someone as candidate will have a limit of Rs.50 or 70 lacs and the same candidate in the name of star campaigner can spend 1000 crores. Don`t you find this as quixotic?"

10 to 12 parties will have above 5% vote shares. The elected one for governing, the ruling party, mostly used to get the majority with 26 to 35% vote share polled. Votes polled are always 55% to 60 % of the total registered voters. Total registered voters are again 50 to 55% of the population. Nationally 15 general elections have taken place and in six or seven general elections both ruling party plus the main opposition have together got less than 47% of vote share and more than 60% of the seat *shares. Other parties which had more votes polled were of regional in nature and they were cornered in the name of coalition to meet the short fall by the party which had secured maximum number of seats in the final tally. However, never these regional parties took wise decision, by forming alliance, to defeat Barathiya Congress and National People`s Party, in the election to parliament. Most of these parties do not come out of their territory. Can You Imagine, More, Some national party with 6% vote will get 21 seats and a state level party with 3.8% will get 38 seats-democratic anomalies"*

'Now a general election is announced. Media is releasing Mega movie, making Mr.Premnath Mawa as their new clean imaged crusader. Left called both Barathiya Congress and NPP, twin slaves of Indian corporates called other parties to put common candidates. Every political pandit was able to predict that the two national parties will have the worst defeat, if all other forces come together. The two largest parties also did not know how to break the game of the left parties with a few arrows. However, MNCs, Media, NPP and Barathiya Congress all came together and framed their Chakra Viuha. Third front fell flat after it was fully shaped".

"What is Chakra Viyha Sameer?"

"Ho, that requires an extensive analysis. In the famous Indian Epics Mahabharata this is defined. In ancient wars, the army will have several formations in the war field. One such formation is drawing seven circles of soldiers around the king. Enemy shall break and enter every layer and sometimes when he breaks the third layer, the first layer will close behind him and he will be trapped inside."

"My god, with all these ancient skill of war science and wisdom how British ruled the Indians?"

"Formula one is simple-divide and rule. Formula two is the caste system accepted one more upper layer above the Brahmins. The caste is called foreign white lords -in power for two hundred years "replied Sameer.

Sameer continued, "See to-day, before election, empty promises already crossed trillion dollars budgets. Ganga water, which shrunk from 15 lakhs cusses to 5 lakhs cusses over years because of nuding the Himalayan fauna and flora, was promised with a diversion to dried Cauvery basin peasants. You know how many kilo meter far off? 2500 k.m across the country, a new canal is to be built. Is it a possible scheme? No body questioned-People believe that! 10 million jobs were promised in IT and industries, where human inputs were reduced by several millions by introduction of technology. I.T. industry has caused hara-kiri because of overexploitation of its work force and loss of new venues, ventures or market. Imaginary promises are rather marketed. Leaders display the doors of heaven in their mouth. People believe that. Those who made more promises were treated sons of god.

People has a bitter sentiment and disbelief over the democratic process of election. They have nothing to lose other than their votes, even if these promises are hoax. Many do have not even that lose because they sell one vote to three candidates at market rate. But political objective to build a good governance is defeated."

Time line editor showed a statistic of 15 election results with expert's analysis. "See, *Whatever the percentage of lose by Barathiya Congress is shifting to National People`s party. That is enough for its victory. But, the regional parties too will lose sizable votes in the last round campaign called "Vote for Note." This time, NPP has determined to pay double than what regional parties are planning to pay. Money bags have already deposited with the Panchayat Presidents, to town secretaries and city level party offices. What is the tacit understanding among them nobody knows? But black money distribution is day light crime of all the major parties.*

Guardian released an excellent article on Indian Election *"Indian Elections - neither fair nor democratic. Black money elects its representatives more."* Election campaigns ended, booths were opened, votes were electronically polled, debates commenced with lot of predictions and votes were counted.

NPP had a roaring victory in lok Sabha election and the local parties were waiting for signal failed to get as NPP had absolute majority. Frank More called Sameer and asked what is the total vote share of both Barathiya Congress and National People`s party. Sameer told 51%. With 290 seats, PremnathjiMawa was chosen as their Prime Minister. Share market shot up but not industrial productions. Promise to bring back trillion dollars black money silently vanished in darkness. .

Two months later, from GUARDIAN, Frank More called him. *"Sameer, why don`t you come to U.K. I am told that you are being targeted."*

"You know myself and Colonel Fernando were class mates in Manchester University for three years. We were discussing two days before. When I told him about your association, he told me this. Don't bother man, I got Colonel Permission to talk to you about this matter. You can sign official contract with GUARDIAN and stay at U.K. for some months or years as you please."

After election blood will spill and at least 100 to two hundred will be hacked and shot. This is normal political culture of settling the score between parties. But Madan Vyas found that time has come to eliminate as bleeding thorns that are striking them every day. Time Line will end and that will send a right message to other press groups.

Date of destiny is fixed for TIME LINE.

CHAPTER VI – AUG-2014

"PSYCHOLOGICAL WARFARE IS NOT PROBAGANDA. IT IS POLITICS"

- Behemoth-Franz Neumann

"THEY EXPORTED TERRORISM TO SELECTED COUNTRIES AND INDIA WAS ONE AMONG THEM. WE CONDEMNED THEM AND TRIED TO CRUSH, BUT NEVER TRIED TO GET AN ANSWER, WHY WE WERE ONE AMONG THE CHOSEN TARGET OF THOSE DEMONS?"

DELHI INTERNATIONAL AIRPORT was swarming with thousands of passengers. Morning was as usual with the beauty parade of the air hostess, trim and stylish pilots and thousands high flying business communities, popular heroes all in one basket with different languages, color, creed, dresses and other terminologies of global characters. They are landing or boarding on various terminals, in some corner some thousands or millions are waiting to see these faces, in airports they are in a hurry to avoid their recognition.

Thousands of taxi drivers are swarming the parking lots, waiting for their turn to come. Private cars of high flying business and executive groups are waiting for the bosses to land.

Suddenly the blaring siren of Olive vehicles attracted the attention. May be a Prime minister or President of India- everyone was disinteresting minding their business. The Security guard turned his eyes to the front parking lot. God it must be for President or Prime Minister of some other nation, whose death warrant is signed by his own terror forces. Why so many Rapid Action Forces are cordoning the whole airport? Not less than 300 troops, armed to teeth, dog squads: His sixth sense started sending red alert. It is not mere security exercise nor an arrangement for any VVIPs. Terrorist bomb blast or encounter or gang war! He is not willing to put a toss. Cross fire bullets or bomb pellets may finish him, if he spin the coin and wait read its fortune. His wife children are waiting in his hamlet. All the way he had come from Gaya for livelihood. The security waited one second and checked the movement of the Rapid Action Force to choose opposite direction. He started rapidly moving on high way to Delhi. From 200 meters away he turned to look back choosing a small rock for better sight. First squad ran towards airport entrance with stun guns and drove the car drivers to take a `U` turn and go back. One drunkard driver ran into a RAF man and a hard slap threw him down. Others were stunned and unnerved. Another RAF man enter into the car and drove it hundred yards and push it on the side field and returned back. Suddenly not able to respond to the furious drive of RAF men many taxi drivers displayed their

Delhi lordship. A few RAF men simply got in the taxi and drove it by joining the wires below the dash board. Wherever drivers were inside, the gun was shown to threaten them to move. A few seconds were remaining. RAF men are aware that in the capital except president of India or ministers, all are having a lobby even in taxi stands and no law is above them. Many vehicles are belonging to Member of Parliament, police, government officials and the drivers are more arrogant than the M.Ps. A few slaps and hit by butt showed them, the R.A.F. is meant for real business. The whole car parking was stormed by another troop. The cars drivers who were having their group meeting and tea were shocked by the site of the menacing men and in five minutes the whole parking area was booming with sound of hundred cars. An arrogant BMW owner was dragged out and his car was driven 100 metres and pushed on the slope of the road. Another M.P. came out of car ferociously. Major. Rampal who was in charge of the operation took his pistol and lowered the gun against the face of the M.P. This is the toughest message. Delhi Airport is totally getting deserted and more than 7000 travelers and others who regularly throng are driven one kilo meter far off. Standing on the six lane road the whole crowd was gasping and looking at the Airport as though a volcano is going to burst at any second. Three or four squadron of Rapid Action Force men stormed the whole lounge. No body was allowed to get down from the jets on the ground and Air controller diverted the other flights.

"Move, fast, Clear the lounge, out, out". They did not wait for the passengers to push their luggage. Frantically, a mad rush blocked the entrance. Never had they bothered to

check, who is who, ruthlessly dragged the people out of the premises. Operation lasted 10 minutes. Securities were told to vacate and bomb squad with mask entered started moving around. *"Colonel, all clear, moving to the arrival lounge". Move to terminal No.4, passengers from Saudi landed 20 minutes before".*

"Sir, Saudi Airways departed and the whole arrival security zone is emptied" Answered someone. *"Alright, Comb the hall for unclaimed luggages, be careful"*

Thirty armed men crashed in with stun gun. Colonel Fernando saw the coffee vendor machine and as a cheetah jumped over its top. Whole hall was empty. No trace of any animate thing. Still his instinct did not accept the truth. Something wrong, innate pulse started beating fast. His men were moving forward slowly. Suddenly he froze: all around him suddenly turning fog a wave of chillness rushed through his nervous system. From the last row, below the T.V. something moved slowly, dragging a bag. Yet not fully visible. Having seen no one nearer, the animate bundle got up. Four and half feet, bulky figure took one step. He was in a traditional Arab attire with a new grey coat. He was literally dragging the luggage. He saw more than 20 to 25 guns are pointing out directly. Unfastened by the steel tools, coolly the stranger stepped up against the riflemen as though nothing is seen by him. Shocked at the bold move despite seeing twenty gun muscles against him, Colonel sensed the danger and shouted *"don't shoot, run out".*

Short human, as a robot was moving towards them straightly. His right hand slowly moved towards his chest. Flash of second, horror struck the alert minded colonel. Fernando again shouted, "A*ll of you Jump out, take cover, bomb, bomb*".

Like bullet he sprinted towards the windows and smashed the huge glass. Huge glass pan and fell on portico and the panels one after another started falling in seconds. Rolling among the waiting loading trucks and buses he quickly rolled. He saw many commandos jumping simultaneously. Many were rolling along with him like a wheel. One RAF man who found that the Arab was nearing, opened the fire. The Arab fell down pressing his stomach.

In two seconds, Whole Air Port lounge suddenly witnessed a tremor and flame. Something hot, like a pie, fell on his neck. The whole hall was full of black smoke. Colonel Fernando froze a second. It was a pound of human flesh. He lost his sense for a few minutes.

We have lost our men-this was the only audio sound emerging form his brain. Fire fighters siren neared him. He stood up slowly. Left arm joint seems to have been dislocated or it must a bone crack. Blood is oozing out of wound in the head. No time to attend them. He limbed with burning pain to the lounge, after ten steps he fell again. The knee joints were affected. Two RAF men rushed and held him. The whole roof had cracked. Lounge is still with burning PVC materials and littered glasses. Emergency fire fighters were brought in by Airport security. The coffee vending machine on which he stood two minutes back is smashed and metal sheet are cut to pieces. It was thrown forty feet far off from its place. He turned to his left. Seven Buses and luggage vehicles were totally smashed and burning. By rolling in between them he escaped the pellets and glass pieces and splinters, which had rained on many of his colleagues and cut them to pieces. Perhaps three seconds or maximum of five seconds altered his destiny. Otherwise, he would have been as shapeless as the coffee machine, in a coffin. Several bodies are littered around. He has lost twelve of his men. How many have injured? His eyes were searching for the parts of the human Bomb which 10 minutes before walked straight towards him in that hall. May be a bit of clue, before the press or others swarm and destroy them. He was sure nothing but burnt flush will remain. Burning of human flesh gave an unbearable odors. How this man was able to smuggle such an explosive RDX inside that security area? How he was able to be inside with wrapped bombs all over his body? Why, he chose this location?

Fernando recollected the figure. By and large, he was rustic as any Arab portrayed in Afghan Desert. Was he an Afghan? Colonel's natural intellect again got activated. Some men brought a wheel chair and some first aid and bandage. Major Rampal, who was controlling the airport front came running. He had already ordered for Ambulance. Called the CCTV footage for three days. Airport authorities do know that these men will not leave, unless evidences are confiscated and security is restored. Now his brain opened distress management cells. Trained eyes searched rear side where his human scum might have be splashed. Pieces of Pathan dress lead him to that display rack. The cloth was struck below the big metal frame stand kept for newspaper display. When he got it pulled along with the cloth he found some more materials. It was a burnt two page note and passport with a few Dinars. The note contained some Arabic words. A piece of cloth, may be his bag. Some men were behind him. He found some T.V. group are taking video and they are advancing. Colonel was furious. *"Hold them there itself. They will destroy evidences."* He ordered others to cordon the area and move away from the debris. He notice a lone suit case. He signaled to his men. Anti-bomb squad moved forward and carefully lifted the box and softly folded in the rug. Without tilting the same they carried it to the other corner of the airport. By the time, the crowd in the front of airport started making a loud noise. No chance of taking risk unless area is combed. Security chief of the Air Port was behind him. Major. Rampal was told to take charge. Colonel told him to cordon the area with security and to attend men injured and dead. Airport Security Chief wanted to tell something, seeing the tough face, nodded and left to arrange for the immediate transit of injured followed by the dead. Rampal ordered all his men and other securities to form 15 crew and check all the terminals. Reporters' crew, surged to front showing their identity. But, were pushed back with one words "ORDERS". Rapid force is in full control as though they have done a palace coup. Somebody was bandaging the hands of colonel. Somebody moved the wheel chair he was seated. Slowly, he is becoming pale with pain.

"Sir, who has blown the terminal?"

"Which is the outfit?"

"How did you get the clue?"

"How many are dead?"

"We want to go in."

Colonel turned to them. *"Please, let our people complete the investigation. It is a planned attack. May be a different target, blasted prematurely. Suicider has no alternative except to blow himself as RAF traced him."*

Lady voice screeched

"Are you sure, Sir, No, but the power of the bomb give us an idea, that it is not for a soft target."

Colonel was feeble *"Yes madam, No terrorist outfit will lose its men and powerful explosive in these soft targets. That`s all, gentleman".*

"How many my men have died?" His words came feebly from his mouth.

"May be fifteen, mostly RAF men". One reporter told,

"Had you not acted so swiftly and vacated passengers at the terminal, human carnage would have crossed two thousand or even three thousand, sir."

"Sir, we salute you and your men. You fell in the mouth of death to save all of us, sir."

Colonel lifted his head to see the face. The speaker was literally in tears.

"Sir, do you expect some more attack, who is the mastermind"

"Naturally, involvement of international outfit cannot be ruled out, Why don`t you contact Home ministry?" weary colonel and asked his man to move the wheel chair.

"We can contact them sab, but we want to know the truth?" Even in that worst trauma, the inner meaning of that sentence is recognized by him.

"Yes, gentleman, my job over, thank you."

"Sir, last word," Colonel raised his hand to protest, but he could not lift. *"Sir"* called a senior passenger, who was witnessing the dialogues. Colonel slowly raised the head with pain. His body was shaking with anger and tension. What kind of animals these pressmen are? The Old man fold his hands, *"Sir, We are really proud of your valor. Our family is alive to-day, because you and your men. We all will pray for you and your men to get well, Sir, God has sent you to save us sir."* Old man`s eyes were drenched. Colonel was deeply moved. The old man raised both his hands blessing him from the distance.

"Thank you, sir" on the brim of his eyes a drops of tear appeared and he is crying. This is more than a Veer Chakra award. Colonel mobile stated ringing. Rampal took it.

"Fern, are you alright?" the melodious voice was almost shivering and almost crying.

"Yes, Madam is he fine, sure, clam down, he is safe. We are moving him to Military hospital, you come there". Fernando raised his eyes and Rampal pointed out his heart and showed it symbolically.

Ten to twelve ambulances appeared. The Colonel was gently lifted by his colleagues. Orders were issued to keep the ICU completely vacated in the Multi-specialty Army hospital and surgeons from All India Institute of Medical Science were flown by special helicopter across the city. *"Hi, colonel,"* the sedative given is already started working and he lifted his eyes with all strain. *"Fern, how you are now?"* A beautiful lady about twenty three or twenty four was close to him. She was warmly touching his cheeks, eyes were having moisture. His lips were paining and blood is oozing. She gently whipped his face, without touching his wounds. Perhaps, Fernando would not have resisted his temptation to kiss her at this proximity. His whole body is now completely energized.

"Hi, hero, I am now your nurse, your security plus doctor. I have special permission from I.G. I will be with you, colonel?" She held his hand gently. The lady is Mayuri Singh. Most beautiful model and press reporter of a mega magazine on fashion world and living style. TIMES man once told her, *"why do you waste your flash on several models, you put your photo on the cover page. 50000 copies will automatically be sold in the stalls".*

She quipped immediately, *"Hi, you are correct, my magazine monthly sale is 87000 copies it will come down to 50000. My half bald boss will just throw me out."*

She looked at her man lying on the hospital bed. Colonel, well built, with strong iron muscle, is six foot tall. She is having a dotage on this man. She is a hero worshipper, Fernando is someone special to her. Fernando lips with blood strain showed signs of smile. He lifted his wrist and held her hands. Turning to the doctor standing nearby he asked, *"I never knew in this hospital for sedatives they use devices other than tablets."* The whole environment was changed. Doctors around smiled. Mayuri was blushing.

"Office" he asked her.

"Four days leave and told them, I will be with my fiancé, I already told my future father in law, sorry, your dad. I am with you and you are fine." Fernando`s smiled, eyes closed. Even in the worst situation, she will create a cheerful environment. That is Mayuri. He was moved to operation theatre. Two pellets were imbedded in his back. Two pieces of glass on his shoulder. That too after he shot 40 meters from the lounge by rolling down after breaking the glass partitions.

Turning away from him Mayuri came out to visitors' gallery. CNN channel was running. . Some passenger was being interviewed *"My life is saved by our Anti-terrorism task force. Every soldier had who took part in this operation in fact pledged their life to save us. Colonel is really a brave solider, sir".*

Some nearby "We *and our children are alive. They saved thousands of family. Our salute those warriors"*

"Sir, we were in the flight, just landed and we saw whole horror. Hollywood movies are nothing before our RAF men in

this real action. When the bomb blasted, we saw the Colonel jumping like a batman and rolling. What a terrific scene. My whole body was sweating. Even our flight was shaken by the effect of the blast"

Mayuri was bubbling with happiness. Now her hero is a national hero. Curiously, she watched the latest live on the Air Port bomb explosion. *"Air Port horror! Intelligence failure. Investigation soon on Rapid Action force"*, says Home Minister for state-the scrolling was repeatedly appearing. A chillness in the nerve caused shiver. Mayuri was in a state of shock. She knows that Home Minister`s statement not is superficial, but intentional. "*Where the state is conceived and ruled by insane politicians, the government will alone speak and their announcements are official"*.

Time 8-50 p.m. Fernando must have come out of Operation theatre. She knows Press will respond such lunatics. She must hurry. It is the time to feed Fernando.

CHAPTER VII - SEPT 2014

18TH SEPT 2014

DIRECTOR
HEAD QUARTERS
INTERNATIONAL ANTI-TERRORISM BUREAU
CENTRAL INTELLIGENT AGENCY
WASHINGTON: D.C

DETAILED REPORT

HIGHLY CONFIDENTIAL:

Sir,

Interpol police traced a flight passenger with suspicious movement at Doha airport. Discription: a short man with Afghan rural attire aged more than 55 or 60 but very strong. He had landed there from Tehran. But his passport was having Syrian ID. He was making smart movement from terminal to terminal with precision. Interpol officers suspected that this man is thorough about every regulation of international airport. He was also receiving instructions through SMS. Interpol man identified the location of this person sitting at lounge. The image was immediately transmitted to Anti-terrorist cell. They recognized him in one hour as an accomplice of Barul Azeez one of the Syrian al-quad leader. Not knowing his mission, International terrorist cell alerted Indian counterpart as his destination was New Delhi. Surprisingly, he was not having anything in his hand bag except valid visa, tickets and some dollars. His non-portable luggage were secretly scanned once more: No RDX nor any damn explosive. Our wing concluded, if he has to act, it is in the destination only. We sent a report with his blurred photos taken at Doha to Ministry of Home Affairs Government of India. For three hours Indian Security force failed to take any measure. When the man failed to move out of Delhi Airport. Interpol suspected that the target is Airport itself. Or he is waiting for some consignment. Or delivery of arsenal from some other carrier. Delhi securities failed to act or make any move. Second warning was sent to CRAB that the target suspected is Airport itself. In between the time, the suspect procured powerful suicide bomb with in the security zone.

Unnerved by the information, CRAB contacted RAF. Indian Rapid Action Force was so fast and unbelievably blizzard in action, astonishingly they cleared the whole aerodrome in 6 minutes without announcement or alerts. More than 8500 passengers and 2400 employees were shifted out of dangerous zone. Before reaching the suicide bomber the terror suspect released the very powerful explosive. Colonel

Fernando and eight were wounded severely and in this operation 12 RAF belonging to action force were killed. Lack of preventive step to cover up the terrorist by CRAB and delayed deployment of RAF have caused extensive human loss, but for stormy action of RAF. Now RAF has taken over the investigation directly.

2. We have received information from our Pak counter intelligent sources that two international Terrorist have infiltrated into India through Pakistan border. CRAB is doing a search operation. Headquarters may send a congratulatory message to Colonel Fernando.

OUR OBSERVATION:

Government of India must be instructed to share all terrorist movements and information with RAF simultaneously whatever comes from International Anti-terror wing or from

INTERPOL.

DIRECTOR

SPECIAL ANTI-TERROR WING

AMERICAN EMBASSY

NEW DELHI

New York Times came with copy of this letter in the first page. Social Media and face book came with their hero in action photo in million. Condemnation level shocked the new government. Minister of state for special security silently resigned.

Time Line came with an offensive article third day condemning the minister's mindless criticism on Rapid Action Force. The reporter quoted the Home minister's appraisal in which he said, it is Central Research and Analysis Bureau i.e. CRAB, which always get Interpol information or other such high security risk information. If so, how come Director of CRAB collected the files at PMO and gave instruction from PMO office.

The reporter shot back for the argument that great disaster was averted by RAF. "How the minister can say? We have lost twelve valuable RAF cadres. 15 were injured. The whole terminal was damaged beyond repair. The delay caused to catch the suicide bomber given him sufficient time to procure his arsenals from some other terror forces, who were directing him to collect the jackets from a hidden source of the Airport." Sitting before the Director of CRAB, Major Rajpal commented that the whole ministry and Press are exceeding the line of control. He asked the director to request Home ministry not to give any interview or reply.

The Press report gave further information quoting New York Times. On excellent role of Interpol and IATB of USA he wrote, "*A special international Anti-terrorism alert cell established by CIA had traced the terrorist in Doha itself. Mails were sent to Indian counterpart. CRAB director was fortunately with PMO. Minister in charge of special security by directing officials to wait for his direction to transfer the mail to Director of CRAB acted foolishly or indifferently, which delayed the whole operation. Fact is that he wanted to please by seeking P.M. 's advice on this issue and waited for him for two hours is an inexcusable blunder. Nation has paid a heavy penalty by these cheap political gimmicks"* Time Line wrote.

"Blame on RAF anti-terrorism wing headed by Colonel Fernando- is intentional? He is the one who traced that Mumbai Taj terrorist group had some haven at Gujarat before landing in Juhu Beach. So for 17 terror cases have been dealt by him, including several Maoist attacks."

"There is a small psychic clan of believers in terrorism are among the Hindus, Muslims, Sikhs and Christianity. Mercenaries, contracts, arms dealers, drug peddlers do run many terror joints. Sometimes revenge or great ideal of martyrdom are the diagnostic disorders. So, the CRAB is keeping alert 24 hours, the movements, identity, terrorist method of operations and surveillances. It is unwise to leave such vital directives from Doha to raw hands to deal."

"RAF admitted that Director of CRAB gave directions to them from PMO office. That means INTERPOL mails have not reached him in the usual course rather reached PMO. It is clear that the suicide bomber in Afghan attire was completely twice checked by Interpol. He was not having any ammunition or explosive. He landed one hour before and was within airport area to collect his jacket with explosives and ignitions. New York Times which was covering terrorist strike at New Delhi also identified, it is the hand of unprofessional in CRAB who

intercepted the first mail." The report was damaging and directly assaulting the minister.

Home Minister called the Director of CRAB. He knows what his right hand did. He asked how all the information are going to TIME LINE. Director coolly told him, *"Sir, You please read the report. In fact half an hour back I collected entire dossier from Time Line which contains all the Interpol communications, photos and possible clues on the mode of delivery of explosives. New York time has collected the papers from their Office of International Anti-Terror Bureau. Please direct your ministers' officials not to discuss in Public. RAF suspects two or three more terrorist have entered India and I have taken personal responsibility to provide all back up. RAF chief and his co-directors are coming for discussion. Please ask your people to be silent. I am instructing all Z securities to keep informing us, all movements of the ministers in the top security zone. Please co-operate"*. Home Minister Nerves felt an icy shock.

Two more terrorists! Whose ass will be blasted!

Is he in the hit list?

CHAPTER VIII - MAR 2014

"THE VENOM OF A SNAKE IS IN ITS FANGS. THE POISON OF A BEE IS IN ITS STING. THE POISON OF A SCORPION IS IN ITS TAIL. BUT THERE IS POISON IN EVERYPART OF THE BODY OF AN EVIL MAN"

- ARTHASASTHRA

'YOU NAME TERRORISM AS A FIRE OF FANATICISM AND BRUTAL TO US IT IS THE MAGIC POTION FOR HEALING OF OUR WOUNDS, A MESSAGE OF REVENGE'

Rajdhani, the fastest connecting Delhi-Chennai train sped through the dark tunnels of Bhopal. The one eyed giant serpent stops in four selected junctions. Midnight it stopped at Itarsi and people were thronging around, as many had a dull day, travelling from Delhi. A few passengers boarded the Second A.C. and calmly settled down not disturbing the sleeping passengers, two among them pushed three luggage inside the third coupe and one went in search of the Ticket checker. Destination is still far off. New Delhi -Chennai express drivers changed. Many sleep lost passengers finished their hot Samosa and tea and boarded back their compartment. Nagpur, Vijayawada, more junctions and another 1300 k.ms, it has to travel. The giant car do not know that, midnight, at Itarsi three suit cases have landed on its II A.C. Containing powerful explosive materials with RDX and no passenger is accompanying the same in that garage. The people in the compartment are unaware that they are comfortably enjoying their travel on the silent volcano. Perhaps, it may be their last journey, if the RDX wakes up with a detonator. Two men were still sitting on the side seat and trying to Pearce through the darkness. Their small hand bags are only identity for their luggage. The three bags which they pushed were in the adjacent bogey. The train is yet to take off. Every minute delay alerted their nervous system. Every passenger who crossed them created an unnatural uneasiness and discomfort in their mind. Both are well built and looked trim, agile as military men. One man is much young, may be twenty or twenty two. The other one is middle aged. The slight balding and greying showed that he had crossed forty or forty two. Their faces clearly show even in the dull light that they do not belong to this region. There was no much of exchange between them. But, occasionally, the senior was telling one or two instructions and the younger one was simply nodding. Suddenly, beside them, two rifled policemen appeared. The young one nervously eyed them and the whole body reacting with a shocked activation, but no sign of fear. The man opposite was calm and was passing instruction in sign language. The boy turned to him and got his signal. Slowly he bent down as though he is sleepy. His hands were gripping the butt of the pistol tied at his gum boot. Two seconds, the police eyed them. The senior showed his ticket and told that TT has not checked. Nodding their head they moved away. In that cold, a few sweat drops seen on the face of the boy. In low voice the old one called in an unknown language

"Hakkim, Do not show a sign of nervousness nor react in any manner, got it". His words came from his deep throat and it was so chilling. Hakkim without raising his head nodded.

He looked out, train started moving.

Hakkim Surathuaisin Ali, an innocent mountain tribal boy never thought that his fate will be changing suddenly at the age of twelve. He was wandering at the Karakoram ranges with his herd of sheep, occasionally finding the military vehicle movements and many a thousand of his own tribal man moving with rifles and weapons. Living in a remote land away near Swat, at the northern borders of Pakistan, at the age of six he became a shepherd by toeing the foot prints of his father. At twelve in the nearby village school, Swat, he had his primary education. He loved the school because it was in that old ruin, he was able to meet his age group and talk to them. Tribal clash was regular, besides the influx of escaping Afghans from the American forces and Talibans. This will often result in clan clash or resistance fight for and against the invaders. Gunfire, rocket blasters and hundreds of weapons were available within the village, but not one piece of vegetable. Tribal fights and bloodsheds have become his favourite pastime tale. He slowly became a worshiper of the warring Taliban and Al Quaid not knowing what they are and why they are blood thrust. Otherwise, his life was destined to be among the sheep and cold hilly terrains with an excellent dream of a shepherd.

His father, Rahim Surathuaisin Ali took a rifle one day and went out with his tribal men. Someone told that he had gone to liberate his people at Kashmir. Before that 60 years back his grandfather whose name was also, Hakkim Surathuaisin Ali went along with a small army and Indian Military force brutally killed them at the Pak borders. Some people who ran back in that war told that his grandfather had seventeen bullets on his body, then he died. He knows that there are two places called Kashmir on his East. One Kashmir is with Pakistan. On the other side, he was told by his villagers, People were jailed by Indians and Kashmiris there, always live as slaves of those Indians. Kashmiris are in torture and suffering; it is imbedded in his subconscious sense. In school his teacher told that Pakistan is a holy land enslaved by India once. Some other teacher told it was white man who ruled the country and he divided this country into India and Pakistan. Whatever it is, Indians are enemies. When Hakkim grows up he will show the same valour as his grandpa and pa did. Hakkim do not know what is this word liberation and freedom often used. Going behind the war lord of Mastuj and hearing the tales of insurgency and shooting with weapons are his fanaticisms. Never, he had seen his mother nor his sisters spoke in front of men, but whisper to him that they are behind the purdah and silent all through their life or chained to their home, because men do not want them to enjoy the rights and freedom. Naturally, the inner image and local influence turned him as a violent youth and at the age of ten, he was feared as a growing ice leopard. Few days of schooling ended once he hit his master for his arrogant attempt for sexual abuse. His master took him to his home one day and started rubbing his part. His protest was not cared. Hakkim normally over built for his age slashed his master below his hips. The whole village heard master's cry. Shocked Hakkim ran out among the ravines. For a week, Hakkim did not turn up to his village. Local folks who knew the desires of the school master, made up many stories and finally conclude that the school master will have no more rousing ever in his life as all the nerves are crushed by one blow. Hakkim`s medico effect, they laughed, has created a medical miracle.

When he returned to village he expected fury and anger of his tribesmen. But no one showed any sign. The master was pale and avoided him. Hakkim has to earn his bread. His mother even though lost her husband cannot go for work. Their culture do not permit the widows to work in shops or in land among men. People were telling, Peshawar is rich. Guns, rifles, hand bombs to opium, Charas, all are sold on the footpath. Karachi people are really enjoying the wealth of the nation, Rawalpindi is a paradise to live. Lahore is rich with Nababs and dance parlours. Dry roti and some meats and goat milks, nothing beyond is available in his Karakorum ranges. Many times the convoy from Musheerabad will not come and people have to eat some meat pieces and neither wheat nor any other food will be available. His mother took him to Malakand and Mardar to his relative's house. Someone promised to pay his mother Rs.2000-00, a year, if she leave her boy under their custody. Hakkim, saw boys of his age group is working in a meat shops, hotels, shops and he heard them telling that they live worse than animal. He went to Peshawar with another village thug Shakil. Both of them walked ten kilometer and crossed the city border. Hakkim was promised that there was a good job for him and he can bring his mother too for better life and lively hood. Both Hakkim and his friend entered a rough road. To his shocks and amazement there were rifles, guns, grenades and bullets in heap on the road side for sale. Some plants, Poppy seeds, opium packed in plastic packs, a lot and brown sugar powders were also being sold in pockets. Both Hakkim and his friend were suddenly shoved off by someone. He was dazed a minute and his natural tendency to hit back the enemy was halted by the timely intervention of his friend. The ferociousness of the boy shocked the opponent and he raised his A.K.47. His friend told the gunman some name. All of a sudden there was change in the face of that man. He sought pardon and receded showing his finger towards south east direction. He humbly bowed and withdrew from the scene. Both of them reached a big compound, rather it was a fort. Behind the door, two armed men were standing in uniform. It was not the same that was being worn by the Pakistan army. There was a board at the door "Ilahi-La ilah illallahh"

Hakkim`s friend went forward to guards and talked to them. He pointed his fingers two times in the direction of Hakkim and told him something. The guards regarded Hakkim with a pride and smiled at him. Fort inside ran to several square Kilometres. Both of them walked inside. Hakkim asked his villagers what he had told the guards. Villager told that he narrated the history of Hakkim`s father and grandfather. Hakkim never knew that their names are known at Peshawar too. But mother used to curse both of them as barbaric Razakkars. Hakkim`s grandfather forced that lady to marry his son by threatening the parents of his mother. She was literally dragged out from her home ruthlessly. Hakkim was told that they are more brutal. He himself faced the crude man. His father used to kick around, when he saw the boy loitering inside. But these people respect the very name, which his mother defined with all animal origins. Many times when he come home with some wound and street fight, his mother used to call him as third generation wolf. Hakkim was in a state of amazement and wonder about the way the whole area is designed with so much security. At the distance a central mansion was seen.

He saw the roads were tarred and foot paths are neatly paved. There were hundreds of cars and military vehicles inside the compound. After a kilometre walk they came to a huge mansion. "ALPHATIHA" the entrance had a welcome sign. More than 100 security persons were standing with automatic and stun guns.

To Hakkim, the 11 year old boy, even though the guns and known to him, he had no occasion possess one. Last one his house remained was a .22 rifle and his father took that for waging war against Indians. Perhaps he might have gone too close to the enemy as the range of the rifle was short and not test fired much. His gun was returned to the family as they could not carry the dead body of his father from the war field. Life in the mountain is not a great fantasy or fascinating. If almighty allows, people will live beyond hundred years and if a slightest provocation takes place between clans, dead bodies will fall in numbers among the rocky ranges. Many times none bother to claim nor to tomb do those as both sides perish in large number and remaining run away.

Hakkim and his villager is now near a big building. Rather it is a modern palace, which he had seen in the movies only. Perhaps, it may be the biggest one in the whole of Peshawar, even though it is situated more than two kilo metre from the city. Hakkim and his colleagues were let in after checking, as soon as they entered, they were asked to go to a side room and asked to be seated. Hakkim asked his friend why we are here and what job? His friend's eyes gleamed and he smiled with an assurance as though Hakkim has come to a land of treasure.

"Ho, grandson of Hakkim Surathuaisin Ali, what a great fortune to our movement, the third generation of heroes has come to sacrifice for our Jihad" a loud voice heard as though a mountain is cracking.

Hakkim turned to look at that man, whose voice boomed across the room. Life cycle changed and 11 years boy grew as tough Jihadi among the Hindukush ranges. His physique formation was much suitable to run among the wide ravines and rough terrains. His team was named as mountain leopards. Often they will land on some Afghan and American camps, capture the strolling securities cut their throats and steal their arms and dresses. They loved British army outfits and moved with that disguise across the plains. His corporal was a Pakistani, who introduced some knowledge of Urdu in Hakkim and more knowledge of war tactics.

"Hakkim, your berth is ready go and sleep". Suddenly, Hakkim came to his sense. He is in the train that has crossed Itarsi. In a low voice he responded *"Yes, bhai, when it will reach Chennai?"*

Curt reply came *"To morrow, seven p.m."* No dialogue further.

Hakkim is now looking at the roof. Peshawar streets once again, the palace like building *"grandson of great warrior Hakkim Surathuaisin Ali ...jihadi."* He is tired now -slept.

Ameen Habbib Rasool, Brigadier specialized in urban conflicts is lying on the upper birth dead awake. Unimaginable for an Algerian, born for a French solider and Arab mother to be traveling in an unknown continent with a mission, nothing to do with his life and adventures. Jijel is the capital of Jijel Province. It is a city located in northeastern Algeria and has an estimated population of 1,10,000inhabitants.It borders near the Mediterranean Sea in the region Corniche Kabyle on the foot of the Small Kabyle Mountains. Due to the rugged landscape, Jijel is slightly isolated, but it is connected by road to large cities like Bejaïa, Setif and Constantine 150 km southeast. A peninsula lies right out from the coast and there is a citadel to the north. Life was pleasant and wonderful to the young boy of 5 to 6 years, Habbib Rasool. He was living with his Arab grandparents and some said his mother was kidnapped by a French solider. She lived with him for two years, while he was serving as a French lieutenant she became the mother of a cross race. It's all happened in the bitter social conflict between the ruling French colonial oppression and Arab resistances in 1960s.Rasool was later told that he had come to earth sometimes in 1968 or 70. No body remembered his birth day nor he cared as he was travelling and moving with fake pass ports in dozen with different date of birth later on. In the aftermath of World War II the French government revived attempts to bring Muslim Algerians into the decision-making process. But these were too little and too late to offset deep-rooted colonial attitudes and a growing mutual hatred between the French and their Muslim subjects. Algerian Muslim attitudes had hardened and an increasing number of nationalists were calling for armed revolution. By the 1950s revolutionaries were being hounded into exile or hiding and the stage was being set for the Algerian War of Independence.

In March 1954 a revolutionary committee was formed in Egypt by Ahmed Ben Bella and eight other Algerians in exile which became the nucleus of the National Liberation Front (FLN). On November 1st of the same year the FLN declared war on the French through a spectacular simultaneous attack on government buildings, military installations, police stations and communications facilities in the country.

The populist guerrilla war paralyzed the country and forced the French government to send 400,000 troops to try and put down the uprising. However, the courage and ruthlessness of FLN fighters and their tactical use of terrorism dragged the French into the reactive trap of bloody reprisals against the general population, which served to galvanize the Algerians and strengthen the revolution.

The French use of concentration camps, torture, and mass executions of civilians suspected of aiding the rebels, isolated France and elicited invidious comparisons with totalitarian regimes and Nazism. The French government was caught between a colonial policy based upon racism and exploitation, and its place as a standard, bearer of democracy. On the one hand, the French colonials were intransigent. On the other, the world community was calling for a cessation of hostilities and a political solution. Caught between the war, blood shed, terrorism, the new born Amen Habib Rasool, the name inherited from his great grandfather vowed to finish ruthlessly any whites, whoever it is. He was deported to France along with his mother to meet the shortage of menial labour. He faced racial animosity, forced labour, torture, murder attacks and deprival of all survival means in France. An American couple, who engaged them, treated them as their Negro slaves of old American states. French Neo-Nazis attacked them.

He and his mother, while returning from market, somebody stopped the lady and started molesting her and kicked her on the bottom. These skin heads did not notice Rasool was carrying a heavy luggage twenty steps behind. Gagged and kicked by those brutal, she cried something in Arab. A fatal kick on her chest shocked her and she fell dead. Habib Rasool lost his mental control. There is no fear of life in him. He pulled an iron rail from the platform and thrashed the whole rogue gang. He was beating and killing whichever the human he found in his reachable distance. In him volcano burst, seven demons were dead with torn face, broken skull and back bones protruding out. Four fellows were with broken legs and hip joints, groaning and howling for help. No public were dare enough to come near. Many were seen running away from the gory scene. Someone suddenly pulled Rasool. The man was black. He dumped him in his wagon and rushed out in five seconds. The entire police forces were deployed in every lane and every den. His dead mother`s photo was flashed and the American gave the photo of Rasool. That was the last flash in T.V. and no one traced him in France.

Military commander, Muammar Muhammad Abu Minyar al-Gaddafi, commonly known as Colonel Gaddafi, a Libyan revolutionary and politician. Slowly, he became the extended arms of AL-QUAIDA and Rasool`s photo in French magazine was sent to Al-Quaid in Saudi Arabia. Someone picked him up in Libya and after two years he reached Afghan Mountains in Pak border, Karakorum. He was much closure to Pak terror group in the camp and he picked up Urdu much easier and even started reading the same. Slowly, his expertise and ruthlessness attracted the Al-Qaida generals and was trained for an urban based terrorism as his mixed blood gave him an urban rich appearance. The partition horror told by Pak group and other 1996 masjid demolitions and Kashmir wars were the political education planted poisonous weeds in his brain about India. He learnt and learnt everything, languages, cultures and terrain life style of India to prepare for a cross border terrorism. The genetic mental disorder of seeking blood of an enemy as revenge or brutally attacking an enemy targets, shown to him by his Arab mentors without application of human sense, made him to choose the new assignment as an holy war. His extra ordinary brilliance and ruthlessness earned a reputation and they called him brigadier Rasool.

While the whole passengers were in deep slumber, the man who was holding the trigger of the gun, is yet to sleep. His total scheme of attack is very different from the earlier plan. He is planning to identify the Ultra-right wing groups in urban towns and train them to use the weapons. On his departure the terror war will commence. Any slightest provocation by the present right wing government with its communal agenda is the signal for triggering violence and this time explosions are going to be latest devises that were deployed by Americans in Afghan deserts to destroy one kilometre surroundings. Brigadier Rasool along with his troops captured a moving US convoy in the desert and killed 20 US soldiers. USA is the donor of the all modern arsenals.

His entry with ammunition kits and huge dollar currency through Kandla port and movement to New Delhi as a French Citizen gave him confidence that in this country, he can even walk in Parliament and place a bomb. He had a house at Meerut High way, belong to his armed trainee, whose terrorist adventure landed him directly in Jail at

Karnataka. With so much precision, he fixed his travel from Itarsi from Meerut booking agent. His French passport always remained handy for him. But this house at Meerut remained as secret den for Rasool. His test fire at Delhi Airport through his old Afghan mercenary proved to be a great victory. Excellence of operation stays planting the ammunitions inside the airport with so much of precision amidst tight security. If he succeed in his next mission of migrating hundred youths to ISIS centre at Iraq, he can return back and create an army for jihad.

Brigadier Rasool is heading 100`s of Indian Youth in Iraq border and his brigade was waiting for his order to “fire”. The train sound is slowly diminishing. After all beasts too need sleep.

CHAPTER IX - SEPT 2014

-'SIR, WE DON'T NEGOTIATE, NOR WE ARREST THE ENEMIES OF THE STATE. OUR ACTION FORCE JOB IS TO TERMINATE THOSE ATTACK THE STATE FROM INSIDE."-

COLONEL Fernando and Major Rampal were inside the chamber of The Minister of State, in charge of internal security. Minister was busy with his party workers. Appoint time 11.20 a.m. Minister was still talking to his party men. Major. Rampal looked at the face of Colonel. Both of them simply walked out of the room exactly at 11.32.

CRIME RESEARCH ANALYSIS BUREAU chief director Kanna called his PA and told him to request colonel to come to his cabin after his meeting with the minister. Colonel directly walked into the cabin of Chief of CRAB . Mr. Kanna ignoring all the protocols of bureaucrats got up from his seat and came ten steps forward and hugged both. *"Wonderful boys, wonderful, I was waiting to see you two".*

This is not Mr. Kanna to the world outside. This man is a most dreaded official in the government, known for his integrity and boldness. In fact many ministers hesitate to head this wing. Once, PM told his colleague that it is advisable for the ministers to keep away from him as he is crab holding everyone's horoscope. Minister for Corporate Affairs warned him for his investigation into the drug money. He asked the Home Minister to invite him to his cabin. In front the Home Minister, CRAB chief opened the file and told the Home Minister that he may charge sheet the minister also, if he continue to back the international drug trafficker. Home Minister was blankly looking at the roof. The deputy minister for corporate affairs silently nodded his head and walked out. $.75, 000,000 drug deal was exposed by CRAB in a week. Three blue chip big pharma corporates shutters were pulled down. CEOs along with nineteen others were arrested and put into jail for life. Minister`s close fund raiser, cousin were two among nineteen who went to jail for life.

Kanna ordered for coffee. Colonel out of courtesy told, *"No, no sir"*.

"No boys, no whisky in my room". CRAB chief seems to be in a jolly mood, which is rarely he displayed. Seating himself, he came up with the issue of leakage of information of the CRAB officials to Press group. Major shouted that it is a cheap sale of information by some crooks in the department but costliest error. Chief told that he identified three officers and he cannot prove anything against them. In a week or two will be shifted out of Delhi. Fernando also knows that nothing beyond can be done.

He refused to discuss about the statement of the Minister for the state. But, wanted to know, why it took four hours to instruct RAF about the movement of the terrorist from Doha to New Delhi airport. Chief told that the minister as usual took the mail received from Interpol as CRAB director was sitting with PMO secretary. Instead advising the secretary to call the CRAB director he took the copy to PM`s office telling the officials not to act until they receive further information from PMO office. PM did give him appointment after two hours and once PMO office got the papers, they called CRAB chief and told him, why he failed to act. Fortunately, he was also in other department came to PMO office in five minutes. Information was blocked to him by the minister. In two minutes instructions were issued to RAF. Airport authorities were given instruction that they will have to follow the RAF direction and no argument nor disobedience. Airport chief administrator called for two minutes meeting of the Chief Security, maintenance and staff supervisors. Oral information was passed. Once RAF landed, the whole operation was executed with absolute precision.

Fernando admitted that more terrorist have entered the nation and he is getting their details in a day or two from the international agencies. One among them might have crossed the video cameras in several occasions, but failed to be traced on crime scene anywhere. Major told that he is an events manager and not stage actor. Kanna asked *"What you mean?"*

"Sir, it is a code language between us. He is the one who draws whole plot, provides ammunitions and explosives, give directions, perfectly execute the operation from distance. When human blood sheds, he will be 500 km away from the scene. But, this man is a vulture and will conspire, structures and select men meticulously, train and complete the task. Very few

Terrorists had such reputation. Abu Nadal in 1970s, Bin Laden in 2000, Mohammed Abbas, Syria, Abu Hamza, Egyptian. Afzal in Pak. Similarly, Dawood Ibrahim, interested much on India, Sheikh Bakri, London, interested in Kashmir but they are gangsters by identity and not religious fanatics or caliphates. Ten to 20 master terrorists are in Interpol list. When actual explosion or shooting takes place, many of these events managers will appear in public functions in the full view of the video and T.V.Channels in other place or some other country itself. Who are dead, who are defunct, who are in jails, who turned to drug trade, who had changed the identity and living in some Latin American countries- we do not know. When their target is fixed and when their suicide bombers are ready to be launched, their entry to the target land will be so smoothly arranged as legal or illegal immigrant. The targeted nation may not be able to trace their entry. Just like small mouse, they join the main stream and remain as sleeping cell. Sir, we have four hundred and thirty eight classical papers as well demos collected all over the world." Kanna was attentive, RAF men have gone beyond CRAB`s briefing, usual exercises and doing actual research on Terrorism as classified thesis. He is also aware RAF men are undergoing class room training on international terrorism and department is often getting special lectures from Scotland Yard, FBI, CIA, Interpol ex-officials.

"You guys are you doing any doctorate in terrorism?"

"Sir, if you award that, it will be fine!"

"O.K, So, you are now behind the sleeping cell: any briefing orally?" Colonel explained that he is now tracing the RDX carrier in the form of coat and one luggage, who had

delivered them to the Afghan terrorist at Airport a few days back. His assessment is that the Afghan terrorist is nothing but a remote trigger to explode at a vantage point of the airport. Had he moved 500 meters unnoticed, the death rate would have exceeded 4000 to 5000 and internationally, all Indian Airport would have been considered as dangerous zones.

"Our technical teams are going through the visual investigation to find out whether someone had entered the Air Port, exchanged baggages and walked out perfectly assessing the vicinity, shades, pillars that will be blocking CCTV visibility. Or someone going out in some other flight smuggled this baggage. 12 persons are deputed to do this investigation. Crime arranger seems to be an international expert. More suspicion is on some internal employee. Expert group was trying to follow the movement of this Afghan traveller and many times he was over shadowed by other tall passengers. However two times he stopped to receive the instruction and he was having a light baggage. But, a few minutes later they found that he had to move his luggage of the same size and color with more strain. He was wearing a heavy grey coat which was not there half an hour before. How this bag and coats were delivered to him? One strong doubt is that one of the maintenance worker could have brought the same. We are more suspicious because one worker, who was moving garbage regularly did not attend on that date. His friend who used to pick him up, came alone to airport. But at airport muster roll an initial of the absentee is found against his name. All are provided with batches. Someone with a duplicate badge was moving cleverly.

Chief asked, *"Had Someone of the terror group replaced him in the morning cleaning? Unless we trace him, we will not get a thread, I mean some clue, is it so?"*

"Sir, we traced his body 20 km at Noida Corridor in a most horrible state near high way. On the way back from the duty, he was kidnapped and injuries are there in his body. He was resisting and attacking them. Finally was drugged and his dresses were changed before killing him. He was wearing some dress, not of his size. To hide his identity, his face was smashed. Since, we suspected in this angle, we took his contract ID forms with personal body marks. All his uniforms, ID card and caps were all stolen after he was kidnapped and drugged. A Professional killer seems to have averted fall of blood in any part of his original uniform. We have gathered some skin and blood samples of the kidnapper and sent to forensic laboratory to map them. We believe that the attacker was more than one and had travelled in four wheeler.

"Well, O.K Go ahead, contact me on mobile, communications are strictly CD-CRAB with code "Events management." The chief director meditated for 10 minutes. He brain was revolving around the report and he is trying to pace slowly over the whole episode step by step. Colonel knows his habits. He also expected some odd questions from the director. *"O.K., ask your team to take three to four days CCTV to follow the Contract workers. Someone in the Airport corridors before checking point must be observing his movement. Identify the non-moving observers toeing the movement of the dead worker".*

"By the by, why Hyderabad?" Suddenly CRAB chief asked.

CHAPTER X - OCT 2014

OUR FACES, OUR FOCUS, OUR POLITICAL CHARACTER, OUR IDEOLOGY, OUR COMPANIONS, OUR ENEMIES, their dimensions, THEIR MISSION, OUR ORIGINAL AMBITIONS- ARE SO CHANGING. IF WE DO NOT REALISE AND TRANSFORM, WE WILL LOSE OUR IDENTITY AND EXISTENCE IN THIS NEW SUPER RACE.....

20 days before the Parliament Election in May 2014 Deccan Muslim Party had a serious meet. President addressed the central committee.

"Politics shall be on the economics, on the social conditions and not on religion or culture. We are often provoked by irrational Hindu communal organizations, day and night, talks of ethnic cleansing, and an idea of barbarian's age with blood thirst. What you think of Muslims in India? We were the one to commence the war of independence against British in India. Ask those, who are masters of history from 1756 to 1857. To fight for our liberty and freedom, it is not difficult for us to rise again."

"You made partition and telling Muslims to go to Pakistan and Hindu to India? Did anyone sought referendum? Some Hindu leaders wanted their smooth capture of state powers, some Muslim leaders had the hunger to head the nations. British Governor general thought differently, even after leaving the nation they can run their empire and ruin the two enslaved nations. They gave a name as commonwealth countries of British Empire. Common Muslims, ordinary Hindu did not share the ideas of all the three conspirators. But we are punished for the sins of dividing the mother land. Even after that tragedy, lakhs of killing and death, we had peaceful days with our Hindu brothers. Jackals are hungry and impatient again and again. They commenced their evil game once again. Disturbing the social harmony turned to be the agenda of power addicted, social maniacs with barbaric sensitivity. It rises up more during elections. Some rotten elements among us played the same devil dance. Some idiot Muslim challenges that he will cut the hands of Hindus. Some mad leader NPP told that those who do not vote for PremnathMawa shall go to Pakistan. Government refuse the imprison both of them, that is the greatest curse of this democracy."

"Last election 18% voted his party, due to the blunders of the present ruling United Alliance it may go by 7 to 8% more. 75% including us will be not voting for their new godman. 75% of Indian population, will they be sent to Pakistan, Hindus, Muslims, Christians and Sikhs-all? Is there no law to seal foul mouths with worms? Election Commission says that they will take action. Everyone one is aware of the impotency of this Election Commission past 15 elections. They are buffoons in this political circus."

*"Every time a communal fire is lit, slums where we live, becomes the targets. Land mafia spends his black money, a crore or so, for this heinous crimes. Our dyeing factories, if they are capturing markets, our hotels, if crowded, our cloth stores have become bazaar competitors, our metal factories supply more to the market, the trade mercenaries, plant the political virus and communal chaos. They burn our shops, our factories, our hotels and our markets so that we do not come back in the market as competitors. These masked tactics of this underworld empires are branded as religious activism. They are courageous because, they are having the backing and security of the police force in many states."*Anjuman Baig, President, Deccan Muslim Party, was fuming and-fretting. His anger and pressure went up. *"If the police forces are kept two days in the barracks, we will rise up and show them what our Muslims can do in this nation. We have lost the fear for our life."* Party Secretary Dr. Ajmal Khan suddenly got up from the seat and gave him a cup of water and asked him to come to the seat. He knows that Anjuman is emotionally upset and breaking down. In the front row, some fifth column in Deccan Muslim Party Central Committee, was using their mobile to take video of his speech.

Mr. Jabbar Ahamed was sitting before the T.V. and witnessing the whole episode relating to bomb explosion at Delhi. Who is the bomb carrier? Is there more than one suicide bomber? The Delhi Muslim community will face ordeals. Something started perturbing him. Ten days before, area secretary wanted the President to meet some Dubai based men for commencing Islamic education centre. AnjumanBaig, did not want to entangle in this Arab nets.

Three or four times, the area secretary was called for the meeting and finally it was agreed that meeting will be in the Party office attended by Vice President Khayyam and party secretary Dr.Ajmal Khan.

The mystery had grown when in one conversation, the visitor told that his group appreciated Mr. AnjumanBaig`s speech, '*if the police is silent for two days, he will torch entire India.*' But secretary clarified that they are deliberately misquoted sentences by some Pakistan Press. Mohammed Jabbar was totally confused, he switched off the TV. After a deep thinking, he called SameerBabu of Time Lines and told him the conversation. The false propaganda that some youths are joining war at Iraq under ISIS from Hyderabad is also causing a lot of tension. He told Sameer President Speech has been quoted differently in Pakistan press. *"Sameer Babu, these foreigners were quoting lines from Pakistan press. Actually, party secretary told that we shall call a press conference along with the visitors. But strict instructions have come from the contacts that they do not want anyone to know about their visit unless all contracts are signed. I and Anjuman have rejected the meeting. We feel that there is something fishy!"*

Sameer talked to Colonel. Colonel told him that Jabbar`s suspicion is correct and the team may have probable connections to terror groups linked to New Delhi blast. Colonel called Jabbar and told him that he will also be at Hyderabad and wished to discuss with their President AnjumanBaig and then to others. He also told him that party office area will be put under security surveillance.

Colonel reasoned that brutal terror elements used to destroy their trails, if they lose trust on their contacts.

Jabbar was happy with the response of Colonel and told him that he will tell the president about his discussion with him. Jabbar knows that colonel RAF is one of the trusted chief, who helped them in such crisis. In 2007, bombs triggered by cell phone blasted near Mecca Masjid in Hyderabad. Immediate reaction was to identify Jamaat-ud-Dawah and Lashkar-e-Taiba and some local extremist as culprits. RAF did independent investigation and they first time identified that that this also done by extremists group from Hindu organizations, that too some ex-army men. Like Samjhauta Express bombings in 2007, Malegaon blasts 2006, some other Hindutva extremists' involvement was exposed. Jabbar met Colonel and his team after that and expressed his thanks for giving a new dimension to terrorism in India, ending the concept of only Muslims. Now, Jabbar is afraid that his party will be maligned and destroyed by these external devils. To-morrow is not going to be a good day, Jabbar mind predicted. President was furious, why colonel wants to come? Jabbar was clear that they have to accept the ideas of RAF, which is exploring the imported terrorism. Jabbar asked Anjuman, "Why you suspect intention of RAF, when they tell you that they want to discuss at your office."

Morning Delhi flight landed at Hyderabad at 10.30 A.M.

CHAPTER XI - AUG 2014

"WHEN YOUR IDEOLOGY ITSELF IS IGNOBLE, -WHATEVER DEFINITION YOU GIVE, IT WILL NOT TRASLATE IT AS NOBLE"

Top floor of a service apartment at Banjara Hills was rented temporarily by the Area Secretary of Deccan Muslim party former Member of Legislative Assembly of State of Telengana. Area secretaries are more or less control the affairs of the party in one MLA constituency. His contact at UAE had given an important information that some top ranking business persons are visiting from Dubai to discuss with the party Chief. Date was informed, but how they are going to land at Hyderabad was not disclosed. The state of Telegana is yet to take shape structure its affairs with the new government. Deccan Muslim Party is one after a long spell left with two Members of Parliament, who were elected with wafer thin margin and six to eight MLAs were swept out of in the euphoria of new statehood. 37% of the Muslim voters had cross voted to this new Telengana People`s Party. First time, Mullahs and Moulvis roles had ended in these new states. Shocked by this reaction the fundamentalist groups were perplexed. Mixing religion and politics has flopped. Party leaders also understood that every Muslim will respond when others cry "there is no god but Allah". But not going to hear the moulvis if they cry, "vote for

Deccan Muslim Party". Former M.P. Jabbar sheik received a call. Along with him another party secretary received the call. After hearing all the phone conversations finally he told, enough is enough. We are not willing to attend nor meet these men. However, to oblige, he will visit party office by 11.00 a.m. when Colonel was supposed to reach.

Jabbar's mind is feeling a kind of uneasiness. Already political calculations are showing hundred blunders. Hindu parties too now found that their communal war cries are thinning in the air. Corruption, focus on development, jobs and food security seems to be catching people`s imagination. Muslims are not going to be polarized or isolated by dwelling on communal issues. Main stream all over the nation consists of 80% despite communal elements have captured the popular votes. New generation shall be diverted to fight on higher education, technology, better pay scale and market economy. If Muslims mingle in that, in India, the communal forces both in Hindu and Muslim will be defeated. The pseudo-secular forces, which are keeping them as vassals will see the end of serfdom. How to change the direction of the people in that dimension is a challenge.

He discussed with Party secretary Ajmal Khan. Party secretary told that he will attend the meeting and report him. Ajmal Khan is more a believer of human rights and secular ideas. Hundred times he faced direct criticism from some fundamental elements in the party. Party secretary knows that Mr. Jabbar is one of the high level intellectual in party and his thinking many times gave a right direction to party. One more Vice President Khayyam was intimated and he agreed to participate

Morning 5.30.a.m. two travelers landed in darkness. The area secretary Rahamad was waiting with his car driver. As soon as they landed he was instructed to send back the driver. Both travelers were in the Vijayawada compartment. Well built, tall and with masculine features, really looked like boxers. Rahamad reached them to greet. "*Adab*". Immediately one of them warmly greeted, "Aslam *Rahamad*" and started speaking in chaste Urdu.

Many times party had warned Rahamad not to entertain, men from Arab countries or give them any political platforms. In the past, several old Arabs married young Indian girls and abandoned them after keeping them in hotels for one month or 15 days. That was a humiliation to the whole community. Rahamad was condemned in such low profile business. But, big money and political ambition of Rahamad never deterred him from entertaining some external contacts. Party is controlled by AnjumanBaig and his continuous 14 years of presidency is unchallenged. Rahamad`s innate ambition is to capture the most powerful post. Party has got accounted money of Rs.1200 crores and properties worth of 19,000 crores. It is most unfortunate to have a president who remained as ghost protecting the whole assets, than devil that enjoys so much of public wealth. In fact, party President wanted to end foreign links of Rahamad. Vice-President after half an hour discussion agreed to discuss the matter at the meeting. He wanted meeting to be at party office itself openly.

The visitors had a heavy luggage and Rahamad thought it is all dollars. The moment the visitors greeted Rahamad, the first thing was to hand over $10,000-00 and wanted him to convert to Indian rupee. Three lakhs cash he wanted and remaining Rahamad can keep for meeting their expenses. They moved to the Land Rover of Rahamad to the guest house. On reaching, the visitors stood before the service apartment and told Rahamad that this accommodation is crowded and disturbing and asked Rahamad to find out where they are completely free of city pollution. Rahamad after a few minutes of silence, told that he has a farm house, in Hyderabad Warangal High way. The car reached the destination. The first visitor, without entering the farm house, went round and made a through check. He told Rahamad confidentially that they have come to discuss deeply about the future of Indian Muslim. Out of two, one man spoke more in Urdu, he praised Rahamad for his first bomb blast at Qudip minar. Rahamad's Decani Urdu could not match in the flow of conversation, nor was able to understand their accent many times. However, he started nodding his head for all.

His guest expressed his happiness. Before entering, he told Rahamad that he shall see that Vice President and party secretary shall be picked up in his car and no driver nor any assistance, shall come. Rahamad collected their breakfast on the way. Sharp at 10-00 A.M, the other two were picked from their houses by Rahamad and stopped at his farm house. Vice president was told that the guests are in the farm house and they can be picked up from the place to party office. Vice President refused get down from the car. Two men were watching from the farm house and one had his grip on the semi-automatic pistol.

It was almost 11.00 a.m. Fernando and Rampal landed in Hyderabad Airport and reached the office of DMP. They drove directly to AnjumanBaig`s office, which is three minutes away from his home. Anjuman was totally irritated with RAF landing in his office. Especially after his reporting through Jabbar all the development. Fernando called Jabbar. Jabbar was a little embarrassed and asked him, why he had hurried up. Fernando told him to discuss not in the phone. AnjmanBaig, with his royal background came in. His was looking all most 40 to 42 only, well built with mild behavior. His charm and affection to his party men is well known. In fact, many of the family problems were brought by women folks very often as his words are final as he will render justice without any gender bias or to favor anyone. He is a large followers and hundreds of youth used to organize, whenever he gives a call.

But, the press and media described him as villain of the Telugu language movies, with all brutal violence, murder and specter of terror. Colonel and Major introduced themselves and wanted to talk to him on some terror connections of his party officials. President blew up with rage and started shouting. *"So, you brought this venom of terror talks once again. Why do you insult us and behave as chelas of those right wing fellows at Delhi."*

Major Rampal got up and told, *"Mr.Baig, we can summon you to our headquarters, by issuing a notice, you know our powers. But, we came here on our assignment to save you, first."*

Baig retaliated, *"Jabbar has made a wrong decision. Your bosses are those unadulterated communal morphine. Under their influence goat headed administrations had done lot of nocturnal arrests, taken to destinations unknown, terrorized our women, recorded no FIR, spread concocted stories with pseudo-complainants. Habeas corpus Petitions and state denials, concocted evidences, fabricated documents, camera hearings and distorted recordings, predetermined guilt and predrafted judicial orders and finally predestined punishments. Goes to High court and Supreme Court to find that whole tales are fictitious after jail for 12 years, come out clean and weak. Tell me the truth colonel is it not the tale every arrested by state? So you are one among them? What you mean by terror connection?"*

Colonel was angry and also sympathetic. *"Stop it, Mr.Baig, two options are left, either you discuss or you fall into to their trap and end your political careers. For your information, some unknown elements are spying your movement for the past six hours. Our entry into your office is being conveyed by these agents to somebody. You want to see. Go back to your first floor and casually see the west. Just in front of the third yellow building one black guy with green T shirt is there. In east two yellow shirt fellows are sitting in a jeep and watching through binoculars. Green jeep with AP registration only. They are standing from 8.30 a...m to-day."*

AnshumanBaig went upstairs and found the loafer holding his mobile and sending message to someone. 200 meters beyond, he found two or three police in mufti and again just opposite in the east three or four police in civil dress is sitting along with rickshawala in a tea shop. Some jeep was 60 feet from the office. "*Why all these police in plain?*"

Colonel responded, "*We have another forty police force on all the directions with wireless. Another, ten minutes we are going to round them off for investigation. All are local guys. We have told to trace their background and local CID are tracking.*"

The situation seems to have cooled down.

"We do not want that prey to escape. Jabbar told that your vice president insisted that meeting shall be in your party office only. Good idea, that is why our security arrangement. We may get a lead once we capture your visitors".

Jabbar came. He told that his mobile is not responded by party secretary and vice-president. Some uneasiness and depression in the mind of colonel. Major, ordered to capture the three spies without allowing them to use the mobile further and bring them to Party office

"I am sorry, Mr. Baig, I do not want to take any risk. I feel that there is something wrong. Tell others not to come inside your office till you say."

In two minutes, the street pries were pulled inside and their mobiles were snatched. All the numbers they had contacted were noted down and Major told his wing to find out. He asked Jabbar to contact the numbers of Rehamad and others. He told the department to find out, whether their mobiles were contacted by anyone. Major asked that fellow, whom he is informing. That fellow refused to talk. Major put the hand in the pocket and found a role of dollars.

Suddenly, major kicked him in his stomach so powerfully, that fellow went four feet far and made a loud noise like an animal. In fact, his right shoulder cracked. The treatment shocked even Baig.

When he was picked up by collar, he begged and started blabbering in Telugu. Jabbar told him to continue. Jabbar told that he was paid by Rahamad in the morning a few dollars and he told him to wait here and report to a mobile number by SMS, whoever comes to office of DMP. Other one who was along with him, in his land rover gave him a photo print of a magazine in Hindi and told him to give information if he happened to see him anywhere near DMP. Number is not of Rahamad. The Sim number is from Delhi. That man produced a magazine. It was Colonel and Major, whose photo was published six days back after Delhi incidence. It was a color copy.

"How this man looked like"

"Sab, *Tall stout, foreign person from Europe, but spoke Urdu. The other one with him was young, but well built- Some north Indian or Kashmere dress."*

Khayyam vice president was stubborn that he will discuss anything only in party office. Standing at the entrance of the Farm house, Rahamad looked at the face of party secretary. Party secretary was not willing to differ from V.P. Rahamad went inside and told the visitors. Came outside two well dressed men with business suit. One addressed Ajmal Khan politely

"Good morning gentlemen".

The language and mannerism were of West. Within half an hour, these ruffian Arabs have converted themselves Westerners.

"Yes sir, Can we spend a few minutes and go. I have used the system of Mr.Rahamad for sending some mails. I expecting some response from my office. It is very important."

Reluctantly both of them went inside. Ameen Habbib Rasool, one of the two visitors told that he is running a training institute in French town and Spain and he is willing to open an educational institution for Muslims in India. Slowly subject of training changed to militating the Muslim youths and he stated spitting venom against Indian state, stating that Muslims are living in fear and subhuman conditions in India. Every evil things that are happening all attributed to Muslims. Rahamad was nervous. He did not know how to answer. Both secretary and vice president did not open their mouth. Mosques are desecrated, Muslim women are humiliated, their independence challenged. There is a fury of intolerance, phobia against all Islamic rules and this country is humiliating Islam. Rahamad wanted to interfere, but secretary showed his hands to be silent. He understood that things are going to be worse and he started sweating. Rasool told that he and his organization will induct funds and train up young forces.

"Why a nation alone shall train its army, why not religion or race to have its own militant force," He asked. Rahamad

found his Urdu expressions are more of Karachi or Sind or Lahore and not of Dubai.

For Secretary Khayyam, pressure was mounting up, *"Have you already contacted anyone in India, or are we the first".*

Question seems to be irrelevant to Rasool. Hakkim Surathuaisin Ali, the henchman of Rasool was able follow the conversation partly as he is less knowledged in Urdu. Rasool shook his head saying *`No`*.

"Had you ever met some Indian and discussed with him about Indian Muslims?"

Same negative reaction from Rasool.

"Had you gone through good Urdu Indian magazines, which are discussing about Indian Muslims?" Rasool shook his head.

Slowly, he started, "*Mr.Rasool, we do admit that we face the onslaught from Hindu fundamentalist organizations periodically. Siva Sena type of political parties live on the insulin or capsules of assaulting minorities. Amidst a section of diseased mindset, in their fanatic regimes 20 to 30 lakhs Muslims are leading royal life in construction, Movie world, in diamond trade and hundreds of business at Mumbai. When political organizations runs short of ideology and people support, they resort to all obsolete gimmicks and pseudo-religious fireworks. Of course we suffer insult also. But what is the solution you advocate? Militating a few? Creating civil war condition? Bombing and shooting like Taliban war lords? Again running away to deserts or jungle, live a dog life? Had you advocated this against the churches in Spain, how may came with you? Had you talked in France, when they banned Burka? Had you talked to Swiss people, where they refused permission to build Mosque? Did you talk to Australians who refused to allow Muslim to practice their religion? Under which Sharia, the Muslims were acknowledging and living with main streams there? Did you ever asked them?*

"You expect us to rely on our Arab friends? Who are our friends? Can I call Saudi as our friends? Where day in and day out our boys are beaten for small errors in jobs, twenty or thirty are punished and beaten for some street fight with locals? Indian Muslim boys are having no proper home in spite they had gone on contract work? Can I call Afghan our friends, Egypt, UAE, Iran friends, Lebanon as friends? Were they not Muslims? Where, you all had gone - when 6, 50,000 civilians were shot and killed mercilessly as dogs in Iraq. Did you not see the naked photos of our people who were kicked, hit by rifle butts and treated as stray pigs? Where your army, when 10, 00,000 Afghan civilians were mercilessly killed in remote villages by US? Searching for one Bin Laden, how many carpet bombs had been dropped? How many had been killed in the cave homes. Thousands were left with broken limbs, grievous wounds and starved to die? Have you ever read a news that more than 160,000 young children are suffering from Blood cancer or Leukemia in Afghan? In GAZA annihilation, Palestine Muslims are murdered and bombed from the roof. Your guns and bombs, you used there? Mr.Rasool, from 1948 mass extermination and ethnic cleaning is going on. You can destroy Israel in 48 hours. Still, you were not angered? You did not try to bomb one prime minister one army general in

Israel? What happened to Muslim brotherhood in Arab? If we create a civilian conflict here, who is going to take us as refugee? Do you think we can create another Pakistan here? Which is much worst place to live to-day? Is Pakistan peaceful, is there guarantee for life in Peshawar or Paktoonistan or even at Lahore or Karachi? You shoot a girl on head for going to school? We have millions of our daughters who are now our dreams, our future, vision in colleges and technological jobs, doctors, software engineers and business magnets in many positions. Do you want to bury them in graveyard?" Vice President stopped one minute and again thundered. He looked at the face of those two. Hakkim was curiously hearing this debate. These people sitting in some corner of India, talks widely about every Islamic country? How they know all these things? These guys are speaking truth. Every Muslim area schools and colleges are found in Delhi and one or two he saw in Hyderabad on his way. Some Nizam university was very big and he saw that while crossing the city Centre.

"Tell Me, is one Prime Minister Safe in that country? What crime Zulfikar did when you hanged him? What his daughter Benezir Bhutto did to shoot her down? Remember both of them assassinated by government agencies only. What crime Barak Kamal at Afghanistan did? You hanged him, why? USA was pleased and cheered your act of cruelty against your own blood. Now ISIS, a wing earlier funded by USA. Have you come to recruit from Andhra Telengana states? Is there a democratic government for 10 years continuously in any of your Arab state?"

"We too have lost two PMs in the militants attack. But democracy survived. Any Government will think hundred times, before creating another political confrontation or lifting the guns against people. History has taught them the lesson. We are more fed up with our external friends, whose houses are full of human blood, which they will never wipe out. We are happier with our country. Please get away"

Kayyam was silent a few second. No body among them spoke. Rasool wanted him to get exhausted. *"We will win: We have no doubt about our shining future. The ink of the scholar is more holy than the blood of the martyr" -Koran says. We will win by building our youth as a powerful movement, by education, by aggressively moving to capture more employment, more business opportunities, more by our hard work. This is our motherland. We are betrayed by our sympathizers, we are provoked, insulted by our rivals groups, we are threatened by our enemies, all have become not our weakness but our strength. We have lost the fear now. Our past pains, agony, insane responses, looking for sympathizers, advisors from remotes like you, all are coming to end. Our fear has gone to dust. We will survive. Let the dogs bark, let darkness surround, the caravan will march among the dusty storm. As Mohammed was guided by Gabriel, we will follow Mohammed, the messenger of Allah in the right direction. We are moving towards His light only".* Vice-president looked at the face of Rasool. It was red, growing cruel and brutal than any wild beast. He was afraid that this man will do anything. Before this man-eater reacts, it is better to leave the area.

Rasool`s whole body was shaking and he was about to walk out without exposing his anger. SMS suddenly clicked in the mobile of Rasool.

"Warning, that two Delhi army men in photo are with AnjumanBaig, President DMP." Rasool got alerted. Bastards, these fellows are traitors, they betrayed us. He ordered his man in some other language. In a sparkle of a second both of them drew their guns and point blank shot all the three. Vice president turned a bit and threw an iron vessel on Rasool. It hit him hard on his head and he started bleeding. But bullets were piercing his opponent till he become lifeless. Rahamad was shot mercilessly by Rasool, This is the man who called them all the way has betrayed. His temper did not end, he told Hakkim to pack his entire luggage and place it in the Land Rover. He was bleeding a lot. He washed his face and bandaged his wound. He untied the baggage and checked the explosives. After a few minutes he move out. While rushing out, he saw the all three lifeless bodies scattered in the hall. He drew his pistol and shot the secretary with a rage of an animal and shouted loud, *"harami, harami, traitor."*

Now Baig is clear that terror elements are behind him. What happened to his secretary, vice-president and the area secretary? Phone rang up. Colonel told that message was delivered to that number 18 km from Hyderabad in Warangal High ways? Rahamad had contacted Vice-President by phone from that location two hours before. AnjumanBaig was shocked. Was It Rahamad`s farm house?

*"Who knows that location?"*Jabbar had the number of the driver of Rahamad and further shock awaited for them. Driver dropped Rahamad in the railway station and waited. In the early morning Rahamad was advised to send the driver back. Driver moved away and went to a tea shop. From the distance, he saw the persons, tall and well built, foreigner and the other one was carrying a huge luggage and wheeled trolley box. AnjumanBaig got up and told, *"Colonel, I am very sorry for my hasty outburst. Let us move to the farm house. I sense something wrong. Please tell your police team to move ahead, we will pick up the driver on the way."* RAF men did not respond, their instinct was correct.

Driver of Rahamad was waiting at high way hotel entrance. The moment they reached the hotel, Anjuman moved to the other side and driver took the wheels. Two Police vehicles sped along with that Scorpio at the speed of 80 to 90 km. Police siren gave a clear road for the vehicles to move. 14 minutes the vehicles reached the turn to mud road of the farm house. While approaching the building the driver told that his boss vehicle had come on that route and returned a few minutes back. When he Major asked him, he showed the tire mark ahead of him. Colonel directed all the vehicles to stop 60 feet away from the farm house and asked the police to take the position surrounding the building. West side wall was not having any window. Both Colonel and another police inspector discussed about the mode of attack. Colonel did not want to take a risk unless he is sure that there is no bomb, as the criminals had left the location a few minutes ago. Tension was mounting, he was not willing to go near the building as there was something mysterious around. Especially some gunshot chemical smells, blood in the parking place of Land Rover telling not to go.

In tenth minute, there was a powerful explosion. But by that time, all were 20 to 40 meters away. Involuntary reflex made the entire battalion to drop dead on the ground. After 30 seconds, Colonel lifted his head. Scorpio car glass was smashed by a brick flew from building. 30 meters that piece had flown. Timely ducking below saved Inhuman. A small piece of glass pierced the shoulder of AnjumanBaig. First time sensed the threat of death. He was few seconds away and by the grace of Allah. His destiny rewritten. But, what about his men?

Bomb detecting squad reached the spot. Colonel was very much careful. This enemy is not a new adventurer. Well trained, with a skill for neat execution. He moves away leaving no trail, nor identity. Tracking is like running in Land mine region. Forensic experts took a sample of fresh mark of blood from the location where the land rover was actually parked before moving. There were two or three drops of blood and a piece of paper with blood strain. Terrorist have moved out of the area.

The driver of Rahamad and the small time spy were taken to CID office to draw the identity of the man whom they had seen. The sketch was immediately sent to Delhi. At Vijayawada station, CCTV saw two men were found running to the Hyderabad train, with heavy luggage and a trolley bag. That picture was mailed to Hyderabad and the driver identified that these were the persons, whom he saw at Hyderabad station, while they were boarding the car. First vital clue - man and his DNA.

Bomb detection squad cleared the site. Police inspector, Colonel and Major alone went inside. The whole room was smelling with strench of burnt bodies and flesh. The bomb exploded in the passage. But damaged the human bodies that were lying in the room. Police photographers and forensic experts entered. Anjuman Baig begged the colonel to permit him to see the bodies. Colonel told him that he is not going allow him as the bodies are in almost charred and he cannot sustain the scene. Colonel felt that both Jabbar and Anjuman may not sustain the horror inside. After one hour large tarpaulin bags were brought and all the bodies were wrapped separately and sent to post mortem. On seeing the human debris Anjuman swooned down. Ambulances which came to carry the bodies, one was diverted to take him to hospital with police escort.

Colonel was sitting before CRAB director. He lost the track of the terrorist by one or two hours. Mode of conveyance or track is not able to be identified. But, his identity is now traced and CRAB has alerted all its branches to trace back the two. Colonel has told the inspectors and Baig not to answer T.V.Channels and allow them to brag as they please. The petty criminal and the driver of Rahamad were kept in police custody. Driver`s father came with a bail application form. Knowing fully well that he may face the same fate of his boss, driver told to leave him in custody of police for a few days. Inside the prison he is safe. Next day news media carried stories of their own.

Southern Cornicles

-Leading newspaper from Hyderabad-

`BOMB EXPLODED WHILE DMP MEN TRYING TO MAKE HAND BOMBS.' `THREE DMP MEN CHARRED TO DEATH IN BOMB MAKING EXPERIMENT'

'ACTION INITIATED AGAINST DMP PRESIDENT.' 'RAPID ACTION FORCE LANDED IN THE CITY TO INVESTIGATE.' TWO LOCAL SUSPECTS WERE ARRESTED MORE ARE ABSCONDING.'

Third day Anjuman Baig called Colonel directly on the phone and told that he cannot go on holding his public statement as the party image is being tarnished. The NPP was holding celebration everywhere telling that Anjuman future is perished. Colonel told Jabbar to withhold any response for one day and he will give them an official letter and it can be publically disclosed in a press meet. CRAB chief told that issuing rejoinder or giving any supportive statement will be displease the government.

Fernando told that he had got the lead because of the dead DMP leaders. He told the Director of CRAB, if any excessive disclosure is made by Anjuman Baig, in his defense, it will completely spoil the lead they have got. He told him that Anjuman Baig will be directed not to exceed the draft of RAF. Terrorist are on their way back to North. Home minister was given a detailed explanation and CRAB Chief told that they are going to give a copy of inter department communication to Anjuman so that it will limit his public exposure of whole conspiracy. It is unwise to give more uncensored information to media and public at this stage as terrorist are on their way to execute their next crime. HM got nervous and silently told Mr.Kanna to handle the matter through his department- he will brief all information to P.M.

Next day by 11.00 a.m. AnjumanBaig called for a press meet. Hall was over crowded. Suddenly some press members started raising their hands. Jabbar got up.

"You please sit down, we want president to respond"

Anjuman was completely broken down and his eyes were dark and deadly sorrowful. He asked his assistant to distributed the copy of a letter from signed by Colonel Fernando chief of RAF addressed to CRAB director copy to Anjuman Baig, President of DMP and Jabbar, Ex-MP. Jabbar told tersely, "*we are not answering any question. Please go through the letter.*"

"Why, sir, why you invited this press meet?"

"We are acting on the directions of the government in this terrorist attacks. Please go through the communication."

To

Mr.Kanna,

Chief Director,

CRAB, New Delhi

Dear Sir,

-ON THE ASSASINATION OF THREE OFFICE BEARERS OF DMP AND BOMB BLAST AT HYDERABAD-INTRIEM REPORT

You are informed by our wing that some foreign terror groups were trying to contact Indian Muslim organizations, individuals luring with foreign funds for terror activities. One such Group, which we are yet to identify the origin, contacted a week back, Deccan Muslim Party. Mr.Jabbar, former Member of Parliament, who also helped us in the Masjid bomb explosion at Hyderabad, contacted us and reported to us. Reaction of his party president was also against such foreign contacts and refused to allow his party officials to meet.

As a second thought, they consulted our officers and we held a discussion with you in this regard. We finally advised that we will rather trap these terrorists, so that we can send a blow to the terrorist headquarters. On our request and to oblige our plan, a meeting was agreed upon at their office premises of DMP, a public place, even though it is dangerous to entertain the terror elements in public offices.

Our meeting of Mr. Anjuman Baig commenced at 11.00 on reaching Hyderabad. 11.10 a.m. we suspected that some foul play and with the help of local police officials and CID and telecom service providers, we found out a location at 11.25. The location was a farm house at Warangal Highways. In 20 minutes we reached the location in three vehicles and 11.50 we faced an explosion. All the evidences, links and movements are being investigated and we will furnish the same by mail.

We believe that the terrorists had changed the location/ venue or at gun point and three office bearers were taken to an isolated location to coerce them. Unfortunately, the kidnapping of the DMP office bearers took place, even before we landed at Hyderabad. By call detections, we found that it was Warangal Highway. It was the farm house owned by Rahamad one of the victim in this blast. What has caused rift we do not know. Two terrorist suspected that they were trapped. All the three officer bearers, unarmed were brutally shot dead on the spot. They also planted a powerful time bomb to wipe out the evidences. The vehicle of Mr.Rahamad was taken by them and dumped in River Godavari near Rajahmundry. We traced this after 20 hours. Farm house is surrounded by 100s of acres of wet land and only one mud road is connecting the same with main road.

OUR OBSERVATION:

The assassination might have taken place between 10.50 to 11.30 p.m. i.e. within 15 minutes of their reaching the farm house basing upon the last call of VP of the Party to office at 10.45 a.m. ., But his voice was not heard by the office assistant even though someone was conversing on that side .

We suspect that the terrorist had changed the place of meeting at gun point. We found that the altercation in the place show that DMP office-bearers had gone without any arms, seems to have antagonized the terrorists. In defense, one vice president had attacked with an iron vessel on the head of terrorist and the vessel had hit his head and dashed on the wall making red mark with his blood. We were able to see the evidence of brave fight put by the DMP office bearers against the gun wielding terror elements. Sixteen bullets were shot on V.P. And other two office bearers. Semi-automatic pistol model 809 was used by terrorists. We can deduce from the angle of shots proves that two pistols were used. It is also seen that Secretary of the party was moving to the entrance and bullets were shot more in his back. We found 11 bullets shot from another pistol. Rashaad was also mercilessly shot in the head three times.

1. We report that on our request this meeting was initiated.
2. We are following the terror trails and we will catch the terror forces soon.
3. Sir, we deeply mourn for those three martyrs, who for the cause of nation lost their life.

4. Government shall recognize the sacrifice of the three members of DMP in our effort to capture the terrorist. We will place our RAF report in details in ten days.

Sd/
Colonel. Fernando
Chief of Rapid Action Force.

New Delhi

Anjuman Baig was in tears and the whole press team stood up. Totally, it was an unusual environment. Every reporter was in tears. One senior reporter came and caught the hands of president and told, *"Mr. Baig, I openly apologize for our yesterday's headlines."*

Without a word, he went inside and he fell on his sofa and eyes were swelling with tears. No one was dare enough to go near him. Reporters had seen such tragic episode but never seen a president of a party cry without minding that he is being observed forty to fifty public men. This man is terrorist, rogue, blood thirst fellow, anarchist, raising the rage and communal fire- all notorious titles were attributed to him. He is an ordinary human with unshed tears reserved for his loved colleagues. Man who agreed to take a collateral risk at the request of RAF, in national interest and lost his valuable men in that battle against terrorism.

But, how many will write about the unsung heroes. **Southern Cornicles** came out next day!

"We wrote something wrong about you my noble friends-

We seek apology standing before your holy graves".

CHAPTER XII - OCT. 2014

"WE INHERIT LOST CAUSES AND UNPOPULAR FAITHS OR OWE OUR LOYALTIES TO FAILING BARBARIC CULTURES FOR CONTROLLING A STATE. ULTIMATELY, WE WILL BE THE VICTIMS OF OUR RUTHLESS LAWS."

Not far off, in the border of Gaziabad and Delhi a huge farm house covering nearly sixty acres is buzzing with activities. A biggest stone structure stood among the groves. This massive three storied structure spreading over 7 acres, constructed with all amenities, including hugeRs.42 lakhs worth dish antenna other towers **RASHTRIYA RAKSHNASAMITHI** Training Centre is a registered non-political organization. But this is the nerve center of their political research, publication, analysis and training. Prime Minister`s prime political decisions are formulated by the THINK TANK and followed up by the TASK FORCE. Files moving to Cabinet ministers were often scanned here. Many ministers who's announce certain policy decision in parliament do know that the birth place of such documents are in this delivery home. To-day, the hall at the third floor is houseful with top ranking cadres from all over India. Totally sound proof and centralized A.C. Stage was with one chair and table and with a mike and podium. The chief of RRS, BAJI RAO was the lone occupier on the dais. Proceeding commenced. Chathuvedi Acting President of UP got up. BajiRao was immediately irritated. While everyone serves the R.R.S, in U.P. RRS serves for all his evil designs. Biggest land lord near Noida, silently developed a Special Economic Zone from the Barathiya Congress government without adhering any regulations. Six MNCs are his clients with seven million dollars annual payment. He is going to talk about Barathiya culture after refusing to accommodate any Indian corporate in his SEZ, as a policy. His children have gone to USA for education. One million dollars he paid for their education. All his payments were made in USA, so that he can avoid Indian tax regulation.

Now he is at his peak, *"Eighty long years, we had waited for the right opportune from1925. The visionary Shri. Keshav Baliram Hegdewar dreamt of a Hindu Nation. Poojya Madhav Sasashiv Golwalkar wrote that other communities must lose their separate existence and merge in the Hindu race or stay in this country as subordinate, claiming nothing, deserving nothing-not even citizen's right.' Words are not mine. Friends, I quote this from `OUR NATION DEFINED`. Not overnight, it is the life time of two generations, we were waiting. While intolerance to other religious faiths explicit in Sri Lanka, Saudi Arabia, and Pakistan and in many Islamic countries, why we cannot take them as our forerunners. Time has come. Our patriotic responsibility to lead the nation has come. Our great heritage and culture shall be reenergized. Manmade frontiers are still haunting in our ancient dreams; yes, our dreams to create the Akanda Barath is not dead. Hundred times, RRS* *spoke and you also heard. Yet, it rings as holy mantra. For this, we shall conduct Jihad and not them."* His finger was pointing out the direction of Pakistan.

"Our mission, we preach to men who share our vision in the Army. We have had lot of bloodshed in the Kashmir border. The Pak occupied Kashmir need annexation back. Indian Partition in 1948 was an unpardonable act our past rulers. We lost it at the time of our national independence. We have to redraw the border line. We were observing with lot of anger against the growth of terrorism. We determined to make it a holy war. Terrorism is no more the sole proprietary of Pakistan, Taliban, Lashkar-e-thobe, Jaish-e-Muhhmmad, Harakat-ul-Mujahedin or Al-Qaida. Nor those men can continue to think that they have no border for them to walk with their guns and bombs. They act as though there is no authority over and no law to control them in this undeclared war. We will strike terror in their land. We have our men. We explode the myth about their heroism. Bertrand Russell said, "`patriots always talk of dying for their country and never killing for their country". His thinking, we follow. If Pakistan wants us to de-annex a state, Kashmir, we will not say anymore that we will give our blood and not Kashmir, we will take their blood and take back a part of Kashmir now under control of Pakistan." He stopped looked around. The whole hall resounded with clap and renting slogans, *`Bharathmathaki, Jai`*.

"If anyone in Kashmir demands an independent state or interference by International agencies our answer is no more tolerance. Last two Indo-Pak wars, we won in the battle front, we foolishly lost in bi-lateral settlements. The leaders of the time

had a political delirium. Error cannot be repeated by our bold lion, Prime Minister PremnathjiMawa. Our actions will be an undeletable carving in the history of Asia". A loud applause greeted him from U.P. contingent.

"Now the idea that people across the border were once our blood-being repeatedly spoken by our intellectuals and left. These orators shall be silenced. Enough, we have heard them and they had mislead our people. They are supporters of terrorist and they are anti-nationals. Lefts are experienced jail birds, they will not feel any discomfort to be inside as better comforts are available to them in Tihar jail. How long we can tolerate, is not an issue, why should we tolerate?

Our national economy is under serious threat now someone spoke. We actually inherited a bankrupt economy. People may show their resentment and anger against our government, if we do not give result. We have no magic wand to revive them. We had given hundred hopes and thousand promises during election. Call back, we have promised Ganga water to Tamilnadu. Whereas, the water flow in Ganga has come down from 15 lakhs cubics to 5 lakhs cubics year after years. We cannot airlift it, 2500 km, we have to draw this water across the plateau? We have promised huge investment in Bihar. Seemandra promises crosses one lakh crores to build their capital city. With promises we have captured the power. We have to survive in power, either we shall generate wealth or we shall slowly erase old promises with new one. You are our most trusted core group hence you shall think, how to divert the mind of these 1000 million people. We shall create a party force of 10 crores and 50 lacs core groups to manage the politics of the nation. This not my word, this is the ambition of our Messiah.

Create alternative ideas, change the political streams and speak to people. Create debates on state level failures and put them on defense. Unless we have a hold on all the states, we will continue to be worried about of future existence. We shall paint the misdeeds of the neighboring nation in the most garish color create an ill-feeling towards them in the minds of our people. While attacking them, we shall identify their religion more and not with their nation. Against them, we shall create an eternal hatred in the minds of our Hindu majority. It will generate a permanent fear in the minds of the minorities. Our agenda, we are going to carry out with three faces.

Our outwardly or official utterances, NPP will adopt a soft posture, always speak loudly about justice, more democracy, obedience to constitutional sovereignty and harmony amidst communities. We shall be silent about their scheme of action. We RRS shall openly launch our campaign on Hindu rajya, temple construction, religious conversion, common civil code, border provocations, minority pacification by other parties in public debates. Our militant wing organizations like Hindu Parishat, Sakti Sena, and Vayuputra sena will raise histrionically cry and show the power of Trishul.

Let me say friends, we cannot suffocate much longer under this parliamentary democracy. We can't construct a powerful nation with this fragile system".

He stopped a moment, "*We need a President, directly elected president of India. Yes a constitutional change-President shall be directly elected by the People of India".*

The whole hall is stunned by this announcement. President is highly perturbed. He got up from the seat and took a seat in the third row. Some members asked Chathurvedi to stop his speech.

"Guruji please come to the dais, please"

Baji Rao got up, *"When someone impose his agenda on RRS without our permission, then why we are called policy making body the CHINTAN BAITAK. We are partly removed from the posts even before the election. I don't think, this post carry any respect, if so, it is no good to adorn that seat anymore."*

Chathurvedi is one of the PM`s trusted man. What he is talking, not the part of to-day`s agenda, he knows. Chathurvedi looked around. His message is conveyed. Approval or disapproval is not his business. His untold message is-RRS your next agenda is defined. Baji Rao stepping down is not an issue for him.

He continued, *"Seventy years, we were building our militant force with different mold and name. British was not bothered about us because our prime task spelled out by our PojjyaGuruji. It was to establish the supremacy of Hinduism by converting this as a theocratic state. Eliminating the minority out of main stream and the specter of communism, which is anti-religion, remained as our unfulfilled mission. . With our total dedication and political strategy we have captured the power. To realize our ultimate goal, tactically, we shall change the path of present strategy.*

"People will not believe slanders initially, but repeated, repeated mass campaigns will seduce them and they will slowly assimilate and their distrust will slowly vanish and finally will accept our versions in future times. The more powerful rhetoric we are, we will find more acceptance from major section of the mass. Some professor told that, our people love to believe lies wonderfully framed and excellently presented. They need an intoxication for their brain. I too started believing in that theory. We had a trial run in parliamentary election. Never, India had seen such a mega, wonderful political campaign. Never our success rate was so high. It will be our spring board for our campaign for Presidential form of government. Our campaigns, actions and approach shall be on the soil Lab test basis. Our cadres will first identify the weak spot and clean them with our saffron brigades. Fortunately, we are backed by a large number of Indian corporates. Our campaigns are scientifically modernized. Media has become our day long campaigner even long after the election is over. We shall appreciate our Prime Minister. His astonishing electronic campaigns triggered a new wave of mass contact, silencing and trampling all the opponents' election strategies. He invented an American Presidential campaign and made both ruling and opposition spoke for and against only one person. All other leaders lost their luster, space and images. First time a PM candidate has become a marketed product by the sales team and in this super brand race, he had toppled all others." The audience did not like this expression. BajiRao showed his restlessness. This is not a political or samithi dimension. This will damage the real cadres' image about the RRS and ideals. In long term this will destroy the basic ideology and trust on the party. Who taught them, the new

vision? RRS with its meaning of protectors of nation seems to be changing as Rakshasa Rachana, protectors of demons.

Chathuvedi continued, *"Now our task has commenced. Good language if it does work fine or our natural slangs with heated slogans, intimidation threat or coercions whatever people do understand, we shall adopt. In that process, some gruesome act may inevitably cause political problem. There will be disturbance to peace. We will take care. Our goal is nearer and nearer now. Our time has come."*

He stopped a minute to observe the reaction of the members. The sermon, the language, the mission is meant for spreading horror. He continued in a booming voice,

"Our THINKTANK has already drafted our projects and methods of campaign. Police, central Reserves will be implanted with our men in every level, so that nothing is spoken against us nor evidences will allowed to exist in its true form. To create a nation of our own, a society of our own, any amount of sacrifice is less. Bold decision shall emerge. As our beloved P.M. says, time has come so also our celestial fortunes too. Are we going on action or suffer with inaction-decide."

He took a sip of water and looked around. He looked around he realized that many were distancing themselves from the very approach itself. Some were trying to swallow. But, a major section seems to be infested with the call of revival of the salute "Hail Hitler" Chathuvedi studied. This crowd shall be provoked. The words now he turned to spit of venom and fire,

"Burn the red flags. Foreign born ideologies cannot be allowed to be implanted in our soil. The reminiscences of Arab invasion on our Hindustan still burning in our heart. During 1947 partition, millions of Hindu had come from Sind while 30 million Muslims were to leave to Pakistan. But still a major junk stayed. This time it is one way traffic. People have to go to Pakistan and no one is there from Pak to move to India, crossing Waga Border." Shocked over the histrionic speech of their UP President, the whole Samithi dropped dead for a few minutes. There seems to be deep conspiracy in the mind of this man, to incite communal war once again. Baji Rao face became hard as stone. Devil is playing its evil game and our silence will burn us to ashes. He looked around. Purandar who was sitting four seats away, smiled and showed his hands to be calm.

It is not unusual for Chadurvedi to provoke communal fire. Similar game he will play in some corner of Uttar Pradesh or Madhya Pradesh then fly away, sit at Germany at his daughter`s home and watch TV or browse net to find out what is happening in India and give a press statement through his vassals. Sometimes he will select areas to move the villagers from the location. He will create a communal problem and burn the huts of both Hindus and Muslims and create a refugee camp and thus villages will be sold to industrial houses or land developers. This is his inbuilt business quality and he had done this ten times and continue to be President of a state Unit.

One senior member, Tulsiram, secretary, Ram Sevak Samithi got up and shouted, *"Stop your barbaric rhetorics*

Chadurvedi. You campaigned at M.P in 2001 and there was a big communal clash. 97 people were killed and we RRS lost 49 people because of your provocation. Without any permission from us you organized the whole morcha 2003 at Jodhpur and you were sitting at Singapore flight to USA when the city was burning. We know, you spit fire at Muzafarnagar in 2004 and went to U.K. for 30 days. Muzafarnagar Burnt and 178 people were killed in the clash.20 RRS are still in jail. President Guruji please come to the dais. RRS will not discuss on the presidential form of government. We do not want any ghost speakers to carry their agenda without the permission of the chair? Enough of devils sermons, If you do continue, I will not bother to seek legal action against you. I pass a resolution that Chadurvedi shall be suspended from the RRS and a full-fledged enquiry shall be constituted to remove him from the Smithy. Before the end of the day, the drafted resolution shall be tabled. I place this on behalf of M.P state."

Chathuvedi knows that one more word will burn his ass. He shouted *"Vande Matharam"* and got down. He has to send hot news to his boss Madan Vyas that RRS has well received his announcement.

Slowly, rose Prurandara Vittala An old warrior, who served 42 years in this Movement. BajiRao sensed that internal war has commenced. Purandar raised both the hands and saluted his President. Leader of culture and history wing Samithi members has got a great regard for him, for his deep knowledge and courageous stands. History of the nation from Vedic period till date, he can authoritatively speak on culture, social life and wars. He is an authority on four Vedas and Upanishads the ancient religious scriptures. Privately some used to call him Vidhura, the most brilliant scholarly brother of maharaja Pandu and Dhrithurashtra in the Mahabharata epic. RRS has retained him with revered position for his knowledge and saintly life. His noble views are unpalatable but no one ever contradicted him. He joined his hand and greeted, *"President Namaskar. I do not want to speak on Chadurvedi`s speech. His name means that he is perfectly knowledged in four Vedas, the holy scriptures of god. Unfortunately, he represented the ideals of devils. RRS is not the organization for devils and evil spirits. I stop with that, leaving his views to your fair judgments. But what is our future line, we shall debate, not one day nor one meet, the whole nation shall participate. Our time has come, celestials are changing someone often quoting. Celestial stars are changing us and we are going to choose a new path to restore the glory of RRS."*

"Before our eyes the world is shrinking to a village. What is happening around us, we are yet to cognate and mold our brain to the changing situation. Changing our perceptions is essential before we emotionally send message to our cadres. We are in a different time zone and with different brain wave. RRS is termed as one of the most intellectual organization. We hold that rays in our brain, while we talk, that will transform our words into a glitter of a diamond in the sun ray-says noble scripts of Upanishad. We shall fit our thought process to that objective state of high wisdom.Trend shows that we are slowly denaturing our qualities. If it is written in our destiny, we shall also fail and fall under the changing planetary positions. Yes we will fall, If our movement turn to be an evil empire of one crore members. I believe in the writings of super nature.

I have no power to alter. So I have no fear of seeing the dance of devils or howling of vampires here. A few minute back you heard music of the devil." Chathuvedi gang rose up. When the cadres turned their face to look at them, they sat calmly.

"Indian population is reaching 1250 lakhs. It is a mad imagination to drive 1/8 of its population either to Pakistan or Bangle Desh or to have another psychic war. 21st century wars are with remote arsenals and atomic weapons and not with hero and martyrs with swords and shields. No Bhishma nor Arjun are going to be in this Gurushetra of Mahabharata war conducting war of death with bow, arrow, sword and spears. As Dirudhurashtra, the blind king, we cannot sit at home and hear where bombing happened and how many are dead. Invasion of technology like micro nuclear instruments called suit case bombs, bioterrorism are on the way and they have changed the power balance. Not that it is new, Chanukah's Aretha Shastra tells that how the ponds and water bodies can be poisoned where enemy forces are advancing. But bacterial war spreading through air is latest danger. Our boys are explaining that drones, automatic pilotless flying object of any size can be done at a workshop, one of these days. Robot war boats are on the lab test stage. Nobody is safe from the sky nor from sea too. So, hold all war cries in which none of us martyrs nor warriors. Especially, Chaturvedi type of cowards with three tier security compounds, ten gun man around, shall not speak of tales of Ranapradapsingh or Shivaji maharaj." Chaturvedi got up, Baji Rao shouted, *"Sit down"*.

"What is it you have achieved now and why is this euphoria? Apply your sense: You are aware 31% voted for NPP. 12 to 13

crores votes? Out of it 50% are anti-incumbency and allied party votes? How to dissect and study the mood of a nation? You learn first! When major junk of people are not with us, war mania, idea of creating one way exodus are acid test, most potential danger: Again it is a height of 21st century stupidity. Think alternatives. My words may look as rising protest. It is not any revelation of any prophet too: Mere common sense of an ordinary thinker. Our face, line of movement, our political character, our ideological path, and our companions have all changed. Corporates are our new partners or bosses to our friends NPP. We commenced our journey with feudal kings as our mentors. We have lost the original path, mission and direction. We do not have a generation with us, who read sastras, Mantras, holy scripts and talk to us on the great culture with its deep sentiment and fervor. Modern Hindu mutts,Madrasahs of Muslim, churches, bible societiesare religious enterprises, largest real estate agencies. Wealth, abundant acres of land and political power, if you trust, going to save you and your religion-shamelessly admit that you lost faith in god. All the heads of these institutions have not become holy priests, Moulvis and Bishops. They are CEOs now. They hold control over your religious faith, now vast land wealth, partly on corporates and they are trying to capture political powers too. Who they are? They claim that they are the incarnation of the holy god. Without true faith in almighty, where religion exist? This 28 acres, we took with a plan to convert it as holy land to talk about world of religion. Swami Vivekanada`s Chicago meet is 125 years old. Have we changed this to a research Centre for world of religion? Go home and sit in the sanctum and think, think deeply. Are we on the right direction? We need a new light in our path. We shall clean the algae and slippery strains on our yards. Our holy *river Ganga is polluted and desecrated as our religion, did you tell those who did this, you are a profane and a blasphemer? You could have stopped 60% pollution overnight instead of spending several thousand crores of people`s money in the name of cleaning in that river. Here too, we shall block the polluting elements to enter, that planning for depollution's. Guruji, lead us to the changed mission and path before we perish.*

I shift to politics. Previous government in its last days merged government with corporate powers and fell victim to the crony capitalism. What they did in the end, NPP leadersare doing in the beginning itself-remember. Before, this election we know many a millions of honest cadres worked not for nationalism with patriotism. But, the one billion rupees came from the darker side of the economy, swallowed by our pseudo cadres. Suddenly some eighty to hundred got up and started shouting. "*Narendrabai, how much you got?*" Narendra smiled and stood silently. He knows that he has to face these fund eaters and corrupted elements in RRS.

BajiRao got up and moved to the mike. "*This is RRS meeting. I as the president allow or disallow any statement by the speaker. Not any other person here. Tell truth, keeping your hand on your head, how many have not touched that money. Pomander till date had given several million rupees to this RRS. Never taken one rupee from our RRS. He prohibited me from revealing this to anyone. All his earning from royalties for books and lectures were remitted to us. That hand is habituated to donate and not to touch any dirty money. If anyone make on wrong allegation on his character, I will remove him from the primary membership. This is RRS discipline. This is my final word.*"

"He is here not because he wanted, But because we wanted these learned and noble leaders in RRS. After 45 years of total dedication and sacrifice, he need not hear some rogues to call him traitor or corrupt. Please sit down, I allow him to continue. "Guru's whole body was shaking with anger.

"Poojyaji, our shakas are becoming rituals and place for business discusssion. We are actually losing cadres with a political commitment and with emotional involvement. We can boast today, this Government is our own creation. But not those who are in the seats of power going to ack. Our claims are not acknowledged by super media and campaign managers. They require that credit to get their bill cleared by NPP and corporates. Not an issue, we never bothered about our brand values. If we take fanaticism as basic agenda, the adopted strategies as the cause to bring the change in the destiny of the nation, we are committing one more major blunder. We created more communal fire in the past elections and faced worst defeats. Again, to-day, converting our growth and favorable environment, a monster in the making, lead the nation to bleed once more, it will not be tolerated by our own voters. . No god will bless us for our endless psychic ambitions or a brutal massacre. We captured the power, we assume, not because our people responded to the Clarian call of our Hindutva new avatar for call on the faith. We were voted as the previous rulers were in a decomposed state and state was ruined by the long rule. Think of those moments, when tribal and slum dwellers saw us as their beacon lights. In natural disasters our cadres were searched by people to rescue and help them. We were seen as human god in calamities. Nation demanded our RRS attention when it was in political and natural disasters. Will

we be able to reconstruct the lost glory? Study, the mood of the nation and draw future plans.

First read the people of this nation, their anxiety, priorities and changed visions.

Did you observe the body language of people in every occasion? When Pakistan President visited, our P.Ms spirit was much higher-why? More people showed eagerness to meet him why? If Pakistan is your enemy state, why this reaction contrary? Why we were anxiously waiting for his consent for eight days? Why the premier of Republic of China is getting a special welcome at Ahmedabad? Even Bill Clinton or Tony Blair received not much importance—Why Nawaz? Inside Pakistan Bilal Bhutto, PPP tried to provoke Million March to Kashmir and he is heckled and empty plastic battles were thrown at him. People treat him as latest buffoon. You know why?

Mark my words, truth is, People of both nations are fed up with the Kashmir or Cargill wars. People hate wars. Warlords' temperament and human barbarism are vanishing. Their ISI and terror outfits are to be met in different language, isolating them and finishing them altogether. We bend before law and reasoning and not before brute force. Enmity at borders are now a days a bane to civilians. Capturing Territories of enemies are considered as lunacy of their own government. No more psychic war cry nor victory celebrations are now fanaticizing people. If any primer or president are talking of war and aggression, people feel that it is a preamble for huge arms trade. If their language continues arms purchase crosses trillion dollars! Our coffers are being emptied. Should we not apply our mind?

Creating enmities among communities or religions or violence in the frontiers are going to fatally damage to our party. We wrote and told about Gazini, Timur, Babur and Aurangazeb. After hearing all the history people asked us why more than 100000 Hindus and Muslims, especially of upper caste went appealed to an old Badhsha, Emperor Bahadurshah Alam to lead the first Indian Independence war. The last Mogul is the first leader to Indian Freedom movement at North, you know? SirajUd Doula in Bengal, Hyder Ali and Tippu Sultan were the warriors who waged war of independence in South. Tribal whom we kept as suppressed class fought the war of Independence. Chakmas, Khasis, Naiks, Kolas, Gonds, Coorgs, Santals, Nagas, Sanyasis and millions of peasants, were part of independent movement. Did we ever recognized them and made them a part of our national reconstruction later. Is there one here among those tribes? Hindu kings who served as serf of the British were honored and revered by us in those days. Most of our great leaders adorned the palace of Maharajas, who were British vassals. Now, we glorify the kings who fought against Moguls and sultans and not those who battled against British. Am I not correct? I am sorry about my post mortem report. Am I wrong in telling in right time? It is a radical political review."

Hatred and venomous thoughts we wanted to plant, we resorted to Goebellism and distortion of history many times to counter the opponent. Our sins are not washable. A few fanatics among us with blood churning languages, lies, half lies and some truth are able to create sense of revenge against Muslim. Muslim fundamental groups does the same on their part because it is their profession and not a religious duty. Yet, we were not able to isolate 90% Hindus and basket them in our fold even in voting! Muslims are decisive to go with every party, ignoring their brands and green color flags. My speech may be poisonous. I realized our past sins, whence I collected materials for 150 years of freedom struggle. Whom we call our great guiding lights were not in the national movement

Because of our caste system and feudal control, we had bowed before a venerable super caste, the white Brahmin of the Nordic race. We obeyed them. While we practiced untouchability in our own society, we were untouchables for the British. The apartheid existed. The shame, we refuse to record in our pages of history. But we wrote in our BUNCH OF THOUGHTS 'Actually, caste system has helped to preserve the unity of our society- Are we justified? I am sorry I am hurting, but to-day my expressions are to assault your subconscious side of the brain. Do we have to preserve the hate politics with advancement of civilized education? For my harsh terms, I apologies. I advocate a complete transition in our path. What I seek is permission of this house. I will place a paper soon with the permission and consultation with our top think tank. We will end the racial and communal socio economic system in every form. RRS will adorn the new role in the new political system. See all humans equal before society, god and law.

I again appeal to you do not quote some foreign lands with atrocious governance. Barbaric governments are not our role model. To build the future of SAMITHI as well as party which we want to save, we shall choose alternative strategies. We cannot inherit the lost causes and unpopular faiths or owe our loyalties to failing missions. Let there be no cloned Talibanism in our organization. Afghanistan is not a far of land to learn, what fanaticism is and political mania means. Fifty years, if we failed to read the transformations in political history and learn, we are blinds or we are political illiterates or we determined to continue the old hoodoo practices. Unfortunately here both ruling and opposition had bowed to U.S. and G-5 supremacy and publicly supported all their atrocities in Arab land. Terrorist group found another enemy at their door entrance to revenge. Warnings we failed to hear. They came to parliament house. I honestly believe that our blind American relationship and terrorism are inter-related. Please note, Arabs are lifeline for our petrol and fuels. Our offenses against Muslim will, at a point of time, will force them freeze their oil supply. Religion, in peace noble and holy: In hatredness and war most untamed wild animal. I initiate the debate over our policies and alternative path to the past. I know I deserve a big condemnation for seeking a complete U turn in our strategies. Time has come. We shall boldly say that we capable of drawing new lines and laying of new path. I express this not at the time, when our destiny is weak, forcing to take a decision. But politically we are strong and now we are going to shape the destiny of a nation with our power.

Pracharak, teachers of the movement, shall know, we are Hindus. Our faith is mother of all religions. We lit the light and path the many a new born religions. Tell one noble ideals of some other religion, I will dig and quote you the same from our holy scripts 2000 years before. Our Temple shall be built by our devotion to Him with mortar, sand and cement not with human blood. Our nation shall be built by the wisdom of the sages. No one on earth can erase our past and blind our future. Fear not the fire flies because we are children of Agni.

My prayers will not go unanswered by god. My mission will see the light. Our one crore cadres will hold their Sathsangh, their holy meet and rewrite our future to the changing time. He stood silent for a minute recited some prayer and started moving to the seat.

A deadly silence suddenly engulfed among the whole PRACHARAKS. Is the entire RRS is launching a new political mission?

Suddenly, the whole meet attention was turned to the last row. Two of U.P. vice-presidents furiously rush to the well and shouted. *"Purander, traitor and political agent, throw him out". "RRS betrayer"* "poison, *throw him out or we will finish him"*

Some members tried to stop. Violently they advance towards Purander and smashed his face. Blood started pouring from the nose and mouth of Purander. Whole hall got up. BajiRao raised his hands and asked them to sit. Something magic occurred. Responding to his appeal the crowd stayed in their place. Calmly Purandar took out his kerchief and whipped out the blood. Folded the same and kept it on the table of President. "*Yes, the first drop, and here I shed. How many million drops of our people will be on the altar, we do not wish to count now? God sake, cross the firewalls of barbarism. If not, remember future will not pardon us. We will be the curse of our god."*

CHAPTER XIII OCT 2014

THERE IS NO HUNTING LIKE THE HUNTING OF MAN, AND THOSE WHO HAVE HUNTED ARMED MEN LONG ENOUGH AND LIKED IT, NEVER CARE FOR ANYTHING ELSE THEREAFTER. --ERNEST HEMINGWAY

Road Rover was speeding at 80 to 90 Km. Rasool knows that at any time the check posts will be alerted by police. That bastard colonel might have given directions by this time. The whole project of creating a Terror Sleep Cell is destroyed by that son of a bitch. RAF full history and its functioning has been read by him. He knows that he cannot confront. They never wait to respond your guns, they shoot. Otherwise he would have waited for a day to inject at least ten bullets in the chest of that colonel. His whole body is sweating and his anger was mounting. Hakkim was terrified by the body language of Rasool. He did not understand, why he should be afraid of this brute. Hakkim himself is a trained cold blooded murderer. After seven heartless killings in Afghanistan, he was chosen as confident of Rasool, whom everyone called Brigadier. His whole Brigade was not more than 190 people in the Hindukush region. In that, four or five are lame soldiers and hundreds are opium addicts. There everyone is Lieutenant or captain or major. In an ambush, Hakkim killed a major and a captain of US army. His whole terror group, the liberation army, was so happy, they arranged a separate function to honour him. He took the cap and shoulder rank strap of the dead and told his leader that he killed a major. In the celebration he asked, why he shall not be called Major Hakkim as he had killed a major of US. Someone told him, if he kills the president of USA, they are willing to call him President Hakkim. Hakkim sheepishly admitted that it is easy to pronounce the word Major than Lieutenant or corporal or President. But the brigade was not willing to raise him from the level of chaprasi as it will deprive them of an errand boy to carry out their personal jobs.

They reached the flooded Godavari River and started moving on a river side road. Rasool stopped in a no man's river bank. He reached side of the river and started moving on the muddy land. No human being was visible. He parked vehicle 20 feet near the bank and asked Hakkim to unload all their luggages. Hakkim could not understand and told him that they are in a remote place. He received a hard slap. Fearing more kicks, Hakkim took all the packs and rushed out. Rasool started the vehicle in full speed. The vehicle rolled fast towards the river. As it touched water Rasool jumped out of the rover. The vehicle simply went another 20 feet inside the water and turned around. Rasool watched the vehicle floating in the flood and turned back. Both of them came to the main road and stood in a village bus stop. That was a high way. They saw state transport bus was rushing fast. Rasool stopped the same and told the conductor that they are urgently rushing to Nagpur and he is prepared coming in standing also. He paid Rs.500 for two tickets and the conductor told him that he will drop him at Warangal and he can capture a bus to Nagpur. Next three hours both of them had a deep sleep. In the middle at a stop, Ramgundam, the conductor told them to have their lunch as the bus will stop for half an hour. Rasool went around and signalled Hakkim. Both had finished their lunch one by one. Warangal they got up in the Nagpur Bus and reached the city by mid-night. Mid night they were told that there is apassenger train between Nagpur and Indore.

By 11.00 A.M, train reached Indore station. They waited 15 minutes till the crowd move out and slowly got down holding their luggages on their head. Their luggage were covering their face. Coming out, Rasool went to a saloon. Both of them had a neat shave and face wash. There itself they changed their dress and moved out. Ten minutes after they reached Sadar Bazzar and Rasool stood before Hotel Rain Drop. Hakkim was stunned by the huge palace like hotel and asked Rasool, *"Are we going to stay here"*. Rasool silently nodded. Rasool went to a public booth and called the reception. The receptionist took the line. *"Has Mr.Rasool sahib from Dubai checked in?"*

"No, sir, he is supposed to check in to-day morning"

Rasool continued, *"Any of his friend came or visitors?"*

"No, Sir, none"

"Madam, I am picking him up from Station, will be there in five minutes. Will you tell me his room numbers?"

"Sir, 277 suit second floor corner sir."

Rasool eyes were moving around to check any unusual alert movement or sharp reaction in the security area. Ten minutes he closely observed everything: No instructions and normal activity. He moved to the gate.

Lying in the luxurious cottage, Hakkim was enjoying his grand lunch. After ten to twelve days and that too first time in life, he tasted the most exciting dishes in his life. Raoul did not mind him. He knows that this ruffian has never seen such exotic foods and luxury of royal hotels. Cottage is Rs.22, 000-00 per day, Hakkim heard. He was sad that he could not give Rs.2000 to his mother for her lively hood, twenty two thousand, he can send for eleven months to her. Rasool ordered two sets of suits for him and Hakkim. He gave an instruction that Hakkim shall not move around. Hakkim also wanted that. He ate all his chicken, mutton, turkey likes, enjoyed TV and slept hours together. Next day, Rasool received signal that his contacts have landed in the hotel.

"Mr.Hameed, we will be meeting in your cottage by 9.00 a.m. o.k." somebody called him in the phone in French.

Hameed invited a tall fair lean guy with iron muscles, *"Hai, Maxinence."* He shook hands with him and anther one came forward, *'AmauryLaurance.'* It was sharp 9.00 a.m. Two tall French men came inside with a heavy bag in their hand. These guys by the very look seems to be ready for any kind of brutal conflicts. Spending half of their life in travels internationally and shawling huge income in million dollar illegal arms sale. How arms enter in every nation or how they are delivered in their destination, even Interpol or spy agencies do not have clue. Because, sometimes governments are involved. NATO directions to move weapons are there. Hundreds of shipments are regularly moving military wares from factory to large cargo vessels and these vessels do not come under any regulation of any nation. They supply to smaller regular cargoes in the mid-sea. Arms reaches the ware houses of the purchaser or supplied directly to the warring rebels. Here are two agents of this mid-sea emperor ships. Two minutes both of them showed their passport, a business card and Rasool his Dubai I.D.

"But are you not from France?" exclaimed visitor as they suddenly got wild and turned suspicious. Rasool took out his French Passport and both of them exchanged a glance and took out a Valet and checked the number. They shook their head as a sign of approval. They took out tiny projector and mounted it on the table focusing the lens towards the white wall. Amaury told Rasool to put off the light and screen. In one minute, they started displaying the latest arms starting from Bofor guns, Westland Helicopters, tanks, sniper rifles and short range missiles. Then they told Rasool to see the medium range missiles which can be guided and accurately targeted beyond 6000 meters and short range missiles upto 4000 meters. Rasool has already his own choice in his mind, yet silently heard them to explain in their own way.

Finally, He identifiedM4 Carl Gun star latest version and checked the manual for effective range and functioning and operations. Three missiles and 2 sniper rifles of long range, ordered. He told them that they were given orders for Suicide bomb coat. One man opened his baggage and produced a fine designed coat and reversed the same. The whole coat was neatly packed and evenly stitched with RDX bomb tubes and batteries.

Rasool called Hakkim to remove his coat and to wear this weapon designed coat. Mr. Amaury explained how to operate each power source, battery links and RDX ignition as then to press the button. They gave a small needle with iridium head and told that no operation will be activated unless the needle is inserted. First time a small chill drop of fear ran in the body of Hakkim. He could not understand what they discuss in French. But, he knows, what this coat is. He had developed a suspicion that he may be asked to be the suicide bomber as Rasool was proud of his early success. His death warrant is signed by this gang. Rasool asked them to explain three times about the triggering of the bomb loaded in the coat asking Hakkim to wear the same several times. Maxinence explained and gave him a clear guidance on the operation of latest version of the rocket launcher. Rasool asked him, whether he had done to any sale to Indians. Max who was biting some cheese finger chips replied, "*Mr.Rasool, we are not doing any illegal trade. Unfortunately, the buyers are not applying for legal possession of all these lethal arms. We purchase from Lockheed, Boeings, Noble, Westland, Ganstar and several Israel corporate. They are the suppliers of largest Mass Destruction Weapons to small blue pistol. Government of India is the largest arms importers next to Saudi Arabia. Some time we ship some extra thousand pieces, retain that in the same ship and sell it in the illegal* *market like yours. We have enough buyer clients with lot of advance payment. Our personal arms up to rocket launchers are irreligious; I mean people of all religion do buy here. Our trade is reaching a target of 77 million dollars and more of guns. One AK-47, we sell at $250 and a hand grenade at $20 to huge orders. If I find a guy little bit desperate and ignorant the same I will sell for 1000 dollars per piece."*

"O.K. What about the payment. No Bank credits nor international transfers. Some kind of monitoring is taking place in this country."

Hameed took out rolls of dollars and they shook out saying that it is difficult to transfer the same in such volumes. Hameed knows what they are wanting. Hameed brought his large suit case and cut the rim. He drew a long, thin tube and slashed the same in front of them. Diamonds of 10 to 11 carats slowly fell on the table and sparkled in the room light. He made a paper work and gave three stones. Frenchmen were so exited and astonished on seeing the pure lights of the cut diamonds.

"So, you want this?" Without looking at his face, they were turning the piece leftward and rightward to check their purity. They took a mobile photo and typed some information. Hakkim was looking at them without understanding what they are doing. Three pieces of stones only and not bundle of dollars?

"Kimberley, Gold reaf?"

"De beers! Certification is already in your mail, you can check up Mr.Amaury."

"Not a problem, our men are there to hunt you, if it is fake."

Terse and stony response came from Rasool. *"If one missile do not hit its target, the other two will knock your home at Marseille, 33. Quai de pont, Mr.Amaury. Sign the missiles for identity and go. The blast will cover 17osq, meter, with a small grenade head, is it correct?"* The Frenchman looked at his colleague and smiled with a seeping anger. They know that Rasool is a ruthless brute. No doubt that he will do what he now said, if his first missile fail.

"Shall we have our lunch, Mr.Maxinence-you get lot of French dish here," Rasool is calm now. His hatred to French is well deep rooted, however, it is easier to deal with French and Italians, who say too hoots to international laws and regulations.

The lunch was served in the room with lot of Royal Salute and Signature brandy. Quick finalization and payment made the Frenchmen to relax. During Lunch Raoul asked them about the world arms dealers and how they market. Maxinence was sharing the spicy tales of arms sales in various countries. As the whisky passed in, the mood of the dealers much more relaxed. He elaborated how the international arms deals work. *"The major trade was done by CIA and USA itself spending government treasury. They were once spreading the fear of communist invasion all over the Europe and Latin American countries and huge arms were dumped in many countries under the pretext of security. You know Raoul, these countries spends another billion dollars every five years calling the old weapons as obsolete and useless against the advanced technology. If, in a country, if any official in the defense ministry reject the pressures, Arms lobby used to fund mercenaries or contract killers to finish the obstructers. The cost of these death squad will be borne by the arms manufacturers. If not sex entrapments, sexual assault propaganda, false bribery cases, charges of drug hoardings, LSDs Opium consumptions, all kind of black mails will go. Take India, it was forced to buy Lockheed Martin F-16 at 40 million dollars to counter the air power of Pakistan. Pakistan got few planes first at less cost and whatever the loss, Lockheed shifted to Indian bill. Pakistan in the meantime came with a shocking information that it had lost two F.16 while their pilots were going for training over Himalaya. The two planes were sold by ISI to China and they landed in an unidentified airport in China. In ten months F-16 equalant war planes were produced by China and sold to African and South American countries at eight to 13 million dollars, which is one third of F-16 US sale price".*

Mr.Amari told "*Our lobby has recruited lot of advocates and paying them for continuously to propagate in Public platforms and political circle that India Shall equip itself with latest version of some Lockheed's, Boeings or Westland helicopters, air force jets, arm wares and tanks. Many of these guys are ex-generals and military arms depot in charges. They, somehow see that government continue to procure arms and defense budget is fully spent.*" Rasool looked at the watch. It is the time to depart. The Frenchmen will check out in half an hour. .

One hour later, Raoul and Hakims got into a luxury van with some large packages of imported goods and the van moved towards, Kota, Madura, and reached Meerut. Even before reaching Meerut, they relaxed at way side hotel. Rasool took a large brandy from his handbag and asked the driver to have one glass along with him. That man took three pegs of free offer. Rasool asked Hakkim to take the wheel. The van driver told that he can drive. But Rasool told him to sit in the front seat. The evening light has gone. Suddenly the driver made a sharp gagging sound. Hakkim thought that he is going to vomit. But his hands and legs fluttered and violently moved, knocked on the sides and try to grab Hakkims hand. Hakkim turned to look at him. But stern warning came from behind,

"See the road and drive".

Suddenly, the man sitting beside became all of a sudden silent and he slided down.

"Park the car on the side of the road".

When car was parked, now Hakkim saw the driver is dead and Rasool has used a Nylon black thread and chocked his neck. Rasool was seriously checking the pockets of the driver. *"We shall leave no trace of our movement to any one."*

Hakkim shook his head. But in heart, he did not approve senseless killing. To him, these are not heroic acts of a Jihadi but a cowardiceness of the psychos. But if he open his mouth, the rope is still with Rasool as well as his neck is in front of Rasool. The van was slowly moving. Rasool found a marshy bush and he pulled that man, carried him on his shoulder and threw him twenty feet away from the road. The Body was dumped inside the semi liquid sand. Rasool came out and sat on the front. With his eyes movement he told Hakkim to move the van.

Meerut 17K.M. the mile stone once crossed Rashool asked Hakkim to get down and sit beside. He took a left turn in the next curve and entered a by lane. After Half a kilometre he took another left turn and entered a village road. There was lone house with high compound. Rasool came left and right of the house once. He told Hakkim to open the lock in the gate and he handed him a set of key. The van slowly went round the house and two time after moving like that, Rasool parked his van in the back yard. From the back door they entered. Rasool told Hakkim to do security job up to 3.00 a.m.

Rasool, in two minutes, slept on the floor. Hakkim opened his bags and brought out a large plastic cover. He remove the seal and spread it on the table. Eight pieces of fried chicken legs, three mutton Briyani and four omelettes. His guard duty began.

CHAPTER XIV - SEPT 2014

"HOLY ROBES ARE MORE ENDANGERED BY ITS OWNBUILT IN UNDERWORLD EMPIRES NURTURED WITH AN EVIL DESIGN TO DEAL WITH THE ENEMIES OF CHURCH AND THOSE WHO COME INTO CONFLICT WITH THE AUTHORITY OF ARCH BISHOP"

Purandar was slightly drowsy and he was gently held by two of his members and he sat in the front line. Tulsiram looked at this noble man, who was attacked a few minutes back. Most scholarly man who had published several research papers and books on ancient religious scriptures of various faiths. He was revered by every cadre of RRS. Tulsiram was in closet with Purandar and Baji Rao two days back. Purandara Vittala was in a deep discussion with Baji Rao. They were interacting over the political winds and directions.

"Guruji, NPP victory will have shorter life as it is not people`s euphoria on great dreams, or a liberation from total oppression. Wish of the people was to get rid ofrotten ruling front. Secondly, the hopes of the people were raised too high. If the people find that the promises are not carried out, the party will be another color balloon in political sky. In the matter of exposure money laundering and money in secret accounts in foreign banks, NPP

has failed in the honesty tests. Problem is financial integrity of a nation is an anathema amidst Indian corporates. The corporates lacks social responsibility and moral standards. Government will soon indulge in three anti-people programme. One not interfering spiral price rise by corporates, two labour reforms to reduce the cost components of human labour, three denial of due shares to agro-products and withdrawal of subsidies. This government will lose its vision and purpose as corporates are going to hold their power over the rulers. Survival of government can be decided, how they resist the monsters. If they fell into the trap, the government will face political unrest soon.

Purandhar related to Baji Rao, his interesting conversation with Mr. Panikkar a theoretician on Communalism. The striking reality is, as long as fanatic communalistsidentify an enemy to their ideology, clan, religion or race, they will go behind their vision leading a major junk of people. But those illusionary images will vanish the moment the clan lose interest its conflict, or develop suspicion on their own movement, or their state falls short of economic revivals, or creation of no job or no business opportunity or sense of passive reaction by enemy. This will create a frantic situation. The communal or clan leadership alternatively try to SEARCH FOR AN ENEMY or to develop a new propaganda art, tale or platforms to keep the flame alive or at least ashes over them. They will try to hunt conflicting groups among their own tribe. Ultimately, they will create the virus of enmity inside their own religion.

Purandar narrated how Shia-Sunny conflicts are taking a bloody war shape. Catholic-protestant conflicts are popular tales of Europe. How, Islamic state in Iraq and Syria, a new rival organization to Al Quaeda are organizing a barbaric conflict of bringing all Islamic states under the control of Caliphates. These groups with their imaginary empires of year 1250 or 1260s kill more of their own people. He told that this movement ultimately will destroy the existence of oil rich Arab nations by internal war. 20% Arab oil wealth were destroyed by the war within.

In olden days, Shiv –Vishnu worshippers beaten each other: Hindu-Jains conflicts resulted in battles. These are reversal of civilization to barbarism. 60% of history of war if read with an alternative theoretical focus, it is all clash of ideologies of two faiths. Religion was laced wild animalism. Animals launches bloody war on territories, on protection of species, preserve identity of their own herd and finally to be the head."

Purandar laughed and told Baji Rao that Panikkar asked me one question. *'Are all our politics activities resemble that of animal world or not?'* Baji Rao mockingly responded, *"These Malayalees and Bengalees are strange thinkers, Vittala. Be careful, they will always present a different perception to any issue or subject in the world. Remember my talk with EMS created a major jerk in the British Empire."*

Purandar told, *"As long as you follow the masses of saffron without inducting your ideas of transformation you will worshipped as man of wisdom by a conformist section. When you opens the skin and shows how things are rotten, you will turn to be the prophet of Devils to them. But if RRS does not change, it will wane and melt, it will slowly ruin, moral values will be lost. It will rot in the hands of pseudo nationalists, business interests, who have percolated in large number. Already gang war is noticed in some states."*

Purandar`s was highly perturbed by the muscle power tactics of NPP secretary Madan Vyas and his men. NPP will not hesitate even to knock their men if they do not follow the boss obediently. Violent attack on Purandar vittala was the message to Baji Rao`s bitter antagonism over financial packages received by NPP before and after election. Especially his attack on corporate funding and his wild attack on the bribing of Rs.10000 crores to RRS state units to meet the election expenses has exhausted the tolerance limit of NPP against the old aged rebel.

Tulsiram attention turned to the meeting hall. RRS meet turned to be chaotic and cadres were started yelling at the thugs. Purnadar again got up from the chair. With blood oozing from the nose and forehead, Purandar walking out. The crowd menacingly advanced against KaitharTripathi who attacked Purandar. But Purandar pushed them back and indicated to the stunned president to control. He knows that Kaithar will be sent out as mass meat for his act. One after another walked behind him. President Baji Rao eyes are drenched. Never, a conscious lofty ideals of Hinduism was politically surmised. Never a rogue sevak applied such brutality in meetings. Never a major section walked out. Steel discipline he preached- now a broken bits of glass.

At lawn, Purander was surrounded by a section of admirers. If RRS is divided, it will be a worst blow at this juncture. President a conformist, did not have the old courage to have a radical transformation, for the fear of facing a massive resistance from the old guards and new fanatic entrants. New middle class and rich RRS cadres are dragging the movement into the idea of creating an artificial unrest in the name of communal conflicts. The agenda crossed the barrier of religious sentiments and turned to be a brutal business strategy by many trade groups. They wanted to buy this organization for their political edge or business promotions.

Bajirao took his car and he asked Purandar to accompany him. He wanted to take him to hospital immediately. The car moved, Bajirao called back some press debate.

"Guruji, you condemn that Muslims and Christians are indulging in religious conversion, but under Hinduism, have you ever built any passage to the Muslims and Christians to come back? Even in Hindu temple, those who from other religions come to pray are prohibited. Shameless anti-thesis! From which script or Veda these idiots had derived these ideas? Is god anybody or groups' sole property? To-morrow, Shiva worshippers will be prohibited in Vishnu temple. See, churches are open to others! How do you tolerate when thousands of swamis claims that they are gods, does all religious blasphemy?"

Baja Rao, *"Most sensible questions. Who did these insane regulations, I do not know. I purely agree with you, Hinduism do not require baptism. Faith and devotion are enough. We are one who believe that everything born on earth are god's creation. Why someone build gates and compounds. When I worship a cow, purchased from Muslim or Christian, why men shall be distinguished by me?"*

A Press reporter raised a question to Purandar. *"Some swamis are performing religious purification to those who are coming back to Hinduism-is it correct?"*

"Hinduism a noble path of life on earth-religion tag does not fit to this holy path" Purandar answered *"How one can go out Hinduism and returns? When a soul is dead and when it takes birth- is it not eternal? Hinduism is like the soul of all faiths. To us religions are like different sareera, a body with blood, skin and bones. Hinduism which you see with religious mold and frame is also a body like other religions to create identity. The soul of the Hindu faith is full of the eternal rays of holiness and nobility. We are not able to reach those ideal state of mind, that wisdom, the inner flames. So continue your pursuit to learn, understand. You may get the answer. All rituals are superficial and a few for the survival of the performers. No one can be your teacher nor you be their disciple, when you go in pursuit of the truth. Sit and mediate, do not ask how long, you will realize the depth of its real existence."*

Someone asked Baji Rao what is his next agenda. *"I wait for Him here"* and smiled, *"He waits for me there"* pointing his finger to the sky.

Baja Rao`s total isolation from the NPP Propaganda activity after the insult he faced from Vyas already debated by NPP. Some senior leaders restrained NPP leaders from debating as they are not holy cows and that man with Spartan quality has hundred good reason keep away from NPP. Headquarters of RRS refused to involve in the distribution of Rs.1,00,000 millions to RRS shakas. But more than 34,000 shakas received the funds for election work directly. Guruji privately called senior party leaders and lambasted them. He understood that they too were facing untold humiliation inside by new middle class second lines, which is using RRS as their brand image. After the election the breach between NPP and RRS is noted everywhere, but NPP felt that it will be good to keep RRS out of governmental deliberations.

That night four or five were discussing on the RRS future line till midnight. Draft document was written in hand by BajaRao. The theme was for isolating the RRS from political parties and rededicating their movement for nation integration and political integrity.

Midnight call woke up Kaithar, vice- President of RRS, UP. He did not respond to the long discussion from the other side. Finally he laid down the phone and rang to Madan Vyas. Madan Vyas shouted,

"Idiot finish them, otherwise they will pull down the government"

Morning 7-00 A.M. all the electronic media suddenly stopped all their regular operas and News. Mourning music started flowing. Breaking news flashed:

ACCIDENT OR POLITICAL CONSPIRACY OR TERRORIST ATTACK?

NATION PLUNGED INTO SORROW! PUJYA GURUJI BAJI RAO KILLED IN A CAR ACCIDENT!

More than hundred people say, the goriest assassination of Baji Rao, President of RRS and his vice-president Pundit. Panduranga Vittala was by a fake accident on the High way leading to Gaziabad. Maruthi Swift car in which Baji Rao was travelling, seen completely crushed and thrown out of the high way by 20 to 25 meters. The accident resulted in fire and the whole car is burnt before fire engines reached the spot after one and half an hours. Though, police is claiming that it might have been accident, some higher ups confidentially told that it is a planned assassination, executed by a team of professionals with all precision.

NNP headquarters some men discussed whether this can be called terror attack! Kaithar nervously got up and shouted, "*No, do not do that?*"

Madan Vyas exclaimed, "*Why?*"

Kaithar shuddered, *"Madan sab if you call this terror attack, the investigation will be entrusted to CRAB and Rapid Action Force. That brute colonel is waiting to pump some bullets in our ass."*

Every channel started giving a different tale of conspiracy. The attackers used a high powered truck to crush the car from behind and push it exactly in a location, where30 feet depth is noticed in a U turn road. The car was being followed by two trucks. Witnesses have seen that the truck running in high speed on the main track suddenly crossed to left and hit the moving car in the third lane and took a U turn on the side road and vanished. Surprisingly one more truck which was coming behind the car slowed down and blocked the traffic flow from behind, for creating gap to the killer truck to change the lane and crush the car. Some channel released a truck with Pakistan Flag painted on that. Crime Branch called them to hand over the footing. The channel withdrew the flashing. Witnesses did not come forward as they will faces too much ordeal than the perpetrator of crimes. Bajirao`s driver in the front was also dead. The whole nation came to a grinding halt in two hours. Time Line made a stage by stage inquirers headquarters was in the state of shock and the tragedy is unbearable. Many who know everything were not in a state to speak. RRS tears had no sharer from many NPP leaders.

Time line tried to contact Panditji mobile. His daughter`s line, no response. Somehow or other, Sameer did not digest the death of Panditji. Sameer was associated with Purandara Vittala in the SOCIETY OF INDIAN CRONICLES. He used call him affectionately as Panditji.

Sameer knows that Pundit from 5.00 to 7.00 a.m. will be practicing yoga and meditation. After 7.30 a.m. he will be available for the world. Earth will not stop, nor will sun melt, if I do not respond to any call before 7.30 a.m.-often panditji used to tell. So his chances of accompanying Baji Rao is remote.

Timeline had published many excellent write ups of Panditji 'Mahabharata-reflections of Vedic cultures'. Several literary programs were attended by both. Many times Panditji used to admire Sameer for his political conviction and vision at his young age. Sameer`s personal number rang. SMS was sent to him, using some international number. Sameer took an unlisted number and called, *"Panditji, May I see my guru, it is Holy Thursday"*.

Pundit Purandar got his identity, *"Yes Sameer, my boy, my blessings to my disciple."*

Usual exchange which they use when they often use, is now used for identification.

"News has reached you Pundit?"

"What?"

"BajiRao is killed in a car accident and the whole car is totally pushed in a slope by a powered truck. Petrol tank busted and the car was completely charred. Panditji, some other leader who accompanied him has also become a carbon in that accident. The media says that it is you".

"*So, they, they at last killed him*", suddenly, the other side line went off. Some lady took the phone and told that Punditji has lost his consciousness. Sameer Babu knows well about the intimacy and affection between BajiRao and Purandar. The voice is of Mrs.Purandhar.

"Maji, I have to talk to Punditji, very very important. I will give a call after 15 minutes? Or you call me in this number, I will wait"

It is Baji Rao, who brought Panditji and gave him freedom to write and speak in most rigid organization. Panditji respected the contribution of BajiRao to the Hindu community. Purandar refused convey his personal views on RRS and its political line. Sameer called the personal number of Fernando and asked him whether there is any terrorist involved in Mr. Baji Rao`s car accident.

"Who assassinated him and who is the one accompanied Mr. Baji Rao."

"Sameer do you have some vital information. You are telling that it is assassination?"

"No colonel, I am asking you, whether you have verified the identity of the one who accompanied Baji Rao,"

I know Sameer, you want to know, whether RAF or police has got any clue and identification to prove the other one dead is Purandar- is it not your question?"

"O.K. that is my question, even though you have framed it".

"I know and you know that Purandar is flying in an Indonesian flight from Singapore."

"How the hell you have traced?" Astonished Sameer.

"What you think of RAF, my friend? For the past 15 days, we have engaged an excellent private team, who are individually reading the names of various passengers who are politically famous, financial top ranks, terror activist, army officials of various nations in Asia, so that we can also identify the terror troops or VIPs in endangered or death zones. Purandar Vittla name was accidently observed by one of our scanning team and when I asked each one to report the VVIPs, Business tycoons, suspected terror elements and politicians. Major Rampal told

me four days back, that PurandharVittala, Guruji's friend is flying along with his wife by 3.45 a.m. by Singapore Air Lines. In fact, Guruji's movement is in our scan as we felt that he will be subjected to terror attack at any time. We had engaged a huge machinery to extend surveillance on VVIPs, beyond cabinet ministers and some opposition leaders. Is the report enough?"

"At 8.00 a.m. when I read the name of Panditji, I told Ram pal not to reveal, as mystery shrouds in the death of Guruji. The killers will follow Purandar, once we reveal his existence. Again it was police enquiry and issue is who perpetrated and not who died at present. We have shut our channel. Did you talk to Purandar."

Sameer said *"yes colonel"*

"Colonel, can I ask you a question?"

"Yes, you want to know who assassinated Guruji, any terrorist involved-correct."

"Fernando, please stop scanning the brains of others through mobile radiation therapy? Yes, that is exactly my question"

"Sorry man, state is handling this and we know that this is not terrorist game or external conspiracy. We do not know, whether it is palace assassination. Please try to investigate man, whether any foreign agents were paid to do a neat job, bye editor sir."

Sameer waited for ten minutes and called Mrs. Purandar once again. He told the lady to hold the line for a minute and hear his instruction. He asked her, where from Panditji contacted now. She told that as per original schedule by 4.00 a.m. flight they flew to Singapore. At 6.30 a.m. they reached Singapore. His friend has come to take him home as he is planning to complete his morning Yoga and pooja. He is leaving to Indonesia to study some historical papers in Sumitra. Sameer, told her that it is wise that Panditji remain at Sumitra and stop contacting anyone at India. He told her that he may be given an information about his where about as soon as he reaches Sumitra.

"Madam for god sake ask him not to attend any public meeting or talk to anyone in India at least for ten days". "What about his friend`s channel".

His wife said he is a naval officer from Singapore and more confident friend. He reported about the car accident, Gurujis' assassination and media information. He assured her that he will pass on the information about their safety to their daughter and ask them to maintain silence. Sameer sat on the seat. His mind is still with Baji Rao. *"So, they killed him!* "Fernando's last words *"This is not extremist act, external conspiracy, palace assassination, investigate any foreign assassin involved."* Bloody colonel knows who has murdered Guruji ! Purandar knows why he is murdered!

Baji Rao remains were placed for public honour at Gaziabad RRS national centre. The body identified as that of Purandhar was also kept along with Bajirao. Lakhs of cadres and public visited and paid tribute to the mortals covered by Saffron flags and flowers inside the freezer coffin. .

One crore RRS members shaken the nation by a national bundh. More than two crore people poured on the roads in every city and towns. The whole nation came to a halt. NPP hoisted the flag in half mast and party workers joined the mass processions. Among the million cry, two men were happy that their plot succeeded.

"Good job, Kaithar", Madan Vyas praised him.

Special service from Israel were in their flight to Dubai. One million dollars highest paid two truck drivers returning back to Tel Aviv.

GRAB chief was in high temper. What kind of criminals are these people? Importing Professional killers to kill their own leaders. Government is giving a cover up: Horrible!

Fernando was in closet with CRAB chief. *"Are you sure colonel, in your statement if one word is wrong, our heads will be chopped?"*

"Yes sir, two days back they came to India. They are in the Interpol lists. Ex-Mossad men but mercenaries with job assignment. We lost the track after they landed, because we were checking at the entry points and it will take some hours to identify. But, when they were allowed to cross the security with One Million dollars two hours back, Airport security chief told me that it is 'directions'. Not to hold them for investigation. At the same time he also obeyed our direction to report about the suspects leaving the country. They are landing in Dubai and taking a flight to Milan and again back to Tel Aviv."

*"What they think, are we impotent?" Kanna was bursting with anger. Killers walk through the security zone and we are telling bon voyage! Wait bloody shit, I will tell who we are, bastards."*All vulgar spellings came from his mouth. Colonel had never heard such dirty words from his boss.

Like wounded tiger he was walking his room. Colonel knows that he is digging graves. Suddenly signed to Colonel to come to his table and opened his lap top.

TOP SECRET

"Flight No. 244 New Delhi to Dubai Two passengers, 1. Jabez, 2.Sadriro seat No.C34 C.35 are reaching Dubai 13.45. Have crossed our security zone at Delhi Airport with three heavy trolley bags. They were identified as international mercenaries in the Interpol list. The file shots attached. They hold drug payment of One million dollars in cash and chances of drug parcels. Detain them and interrogate about the sources of stashed dollars. Please inform, after completing the search and independent investigation. Funds destination Iran or Tel Aviv via Milan."

Sd/

DIRECTOR
CENTRAL RESERCH ANALYSIS BUREAU
INDIA
TO

INTERPOL OFFICE-DUBAI INTERNATIONAL AIRPORT

INTERNATIONAL NARCOTIC AND ILLEGAL DRUG TRAFFIC CONTOLLER- PARIS

Colonel got up. Kanna, " *What is your next job, Where you are moveing?*"

"*You have done a brilliant job, sir. I am going to check up how many are pissing in their pants in Delhi Streets*".

CHAPTER XV - NOV 2014

EVENTS HAVE PROVOKED US TO WRITE: OUR WRITINGS ONCE AGAIN WILL PROVOKE EVENTS.... BEWARE OF FALSE PROPHETS, WHO COMES TO YOU IN THE SHEEP CLOTHING, BUT INWARDLY THEY ARE RAVENING WOLVES....New Testament. (St. Mathew)

LIFELINE Nov-2014

"NO MORE PRIME MINISTER."

"I WILL BE THE PRESIDENT OF INDIA"

PREMANTH MAWA MOVES AHEAD FOR ALTERING THE CONSTITUTION OF INDIA

WATCH PARLIAMENT MELO DRAMA— LAST DAYS OF INDIAN PARLIAMENT

A heated debated rocked the political circle. Publics started arguing that it is political excess. Prime minister instead of solving the existing problems now diverting the national attention with a new issue. Some NRI wrote that India requires not even two party system, it also requires one dictatorship regime to repair it. Irritated Indian commented that the writer is living among the slave citizen of Hatti, where thousands of people are dying under dictatorship. He does not know the meaning of democracy. MPs started realizing that their play fields will slowly shrink. Some M.P. commented to his ruling party friend,

"By the treachery of your leaders, your freedom will be in peril".

Another article appeared how in the name of terrorism, President George Bush altered the provision of Bill of Rights through US Patriot Act. Even now several thousands of people are as under trials for years in Indian Jail without charge sheets or proof of crime. Under Patriot act, *"Unreasonable searches: Jail Americans for indefinite period without trial"*. If applied in India, more will be in Jail than in their home. In India, insane leaders will endanger their own party men first. Powers do rule the law here.

PMO was totally shocked over the range and dimension of this debate. Even before the debate reaches to a disastrous level or an explosive stage amendments process shall be completed. PM never thought political activism will be so much against constitutional amendments. He called for a Cabinet meet and PM spoke so elaborately and abruptly concluded after his dialogue. Press headlines appeared with a large fonts *"Cabinet unanimously approved the constitutional amendment bills"*.

Till date 98 amendments have taken place. Telengana amendment alone had some political debate. In Andhra state division, parliament had a good real show of tearing of shirts, violence, punching on faces by opposing and supporting members. A demoralization among the ruling party M.P's threatened the NPP. Members of Parliament started debating within themselves. This collateral damage, if not reversed, the presidential ambition will crash. Only one person, who is not a parliament member and a minister not under any oath, MadanVyas is confident that the bill will be introduced and passed with majority.

Nobody was really aware that a constitutional amendments bills will be placed before the parliament. One among them is amole, the bills were leaked to press. Damage is done. Law ministry is suspected. Law ministry showed its finger to Parliamentary secretariat. Parliamentary secretariat never cared to react. In government, you can fret, you can fume, you can suspect any one, you can bite anyone, you can fire anyone, and all are immuned viruses. Each finger will point out every other person from secretary to chaprasi. The chaprasi will point his finger to the tea shop boy, who will be delivering hot samosa on the important government communication sheets often, not knowing much hotter informations are there in the paper than the hot, hot samosa. Ultimately, a week after, all will end with a silence of a grave yard. Government will move around with pain, with broken leg for sometimes. When another limb is broken, previous injury will be forgotten. That is the beauty of the gigantic mechanism of central government.

Whereas seventeen TV Channels were covering up this subject at 7-30 A.M., the ministry was not informed how to counter this. When they asked what is wrong if the country follow American system, with two parties contesting for the post of president, Sameer Babu shot back, *"In U.S. both Republican and Democratic have no visible difference in their political ideology or in their vision with regard to the brutal foreign aggression. Don`t back up some political lesbianism that delivers no change in the socio-political system.*

If you want to trim you democracy, better remove the dammed corrupt money and muscle powers. Seal their entry at the nomination stage itself in all the three pillars. Pillars, I mean, legislative, executive and judiciary. You will not be able to do because 50% MPs are jail birds, sitting in parliament instead of prison."

Parliament, that day expected fire crackers. Minister for parliamentary affairs sent a note to Speaker that Prime Minister wants to speak on important agenda. Opposition shouted that notices have already been given for various agenda. Speaker told when Prime Minster wants to discuss some important agenda, other issues be postponed. Senior leader Rajasimha got up,

"Speaker, you please read house regulations before passing such order."

A doldrums followed. Rajasimha again got up, *"What I told is the regulation of parliament. Neither this shouting brigade nor speaker can overrule."*

Home Minister Kanoj understood that, it will further damage and back fire. Once media gets the guideline, their present debate language will be corrected by them. Jagad Singh, Punjab, from the opposition unwisely commented that the house shall discuss the constitutional amendments published in TIMELINE. Ruling party member Sharma got up and told that the information of press need not be answered by PM. Immediately, 20 opposition members got up and shouted, how Sharma can block the opportunities of the opposition. PM was waiting for this wrong move. Speaker told if PM is willing to make his submission on this issue, regular agenda can be deferred.

Speaker turned to Rajsimha. Rajsimha simply said, "*Nice move, you win Sir.*"

Prime Minister got up. In his usual style, he commenced his speech. "*Honorable Speaker, Yes, we are placing amendments to Presidential form of government. We have reasons and we have our mission. We spoke about radical changes in our manifesto. People have voted not only NPP but also its manifesto. We change our agenda accordingly. We are now setting our time frame and agenda to complete the promises we have made, the hopes raised. We are the choice of the majority Indians.*"

AAP member Vardan got up "*PM is misleading the house.1250 million-Indian population. Out of the total population, 840 million are with voter I, D. 540 million actually exercised their franchise. In that, 171 million have voted for NPP that too all their 28 allies in India shared their votes in NPP constituency. And it is also counted as NPP candidates' mandate. 171 million minus allied parties is not majority voting*"

Home minister Kanoj murmured, *"New broom, trying to show that it will sweep well."*

PM waited as the speaker asked that member to sit down.

"Living happily in harmony is much wiser than creating calamity by seeking clan and communal identity. Yes, we set new track with beams of light for the disillusioned people in our nation. Many policies of the previous rulers have damaged the system, the nation, the future. The nation need builders of a cohesive state, but they survived by dividing the people. We have decided to break the blind tradition and build the bridge for them to meet and mingle into the main stream of the nation. Existing democratic system do not give us a fast track. More blocks are there than roads. That is why we want a presidential system to take the nation in the right path bulldozing the road blockades and road blockers sometimes."

"Pacifications without rationale had squeezed the system. Previous ruler's intensions were not to bring tranquility but keep the enmity ablaze under ash. I am for persuading people who tried to impose separate identity. I am asking them to see their brethren in Australia, France and European Union, where the cultural unification with local people has taken place. Those who tried to create breach are silenced by the government. People of that nation tolerate less on non-issues like religious divisions or communal divisions, because, the country you choose to live is more important than your personal faiths, passions and freedom. I invite those who aspired for separate entity and existence, now to merge and find oneness in this new democratic vision and ambition of majority. We have no intention to keep a section as sub-ordinate, claiming nothing,

deserving nothing and not even citizen`s right. Those who were instigating a section to keep their identity and claim some concession, damaged their growth and national participation.

Read sixty years of history, you will agree with my observations, they inherited the British legacy of divide and rule and kept you all in the state of poverty and they grew fabulously rich and remained power for too long. I invite you, the Hindu, the Muslim, the Sikh, the Christian, the Buddhist or Jain-because we planned to take leaves from those nations which have moved, far, far ahead of us. When you ask for concessions and sympathy, your acts and demands are converting you socially weak, racially impaired and nationally handicapped. We want you in the equal plank or in the same plank. Difficult it is to adopt or imagine, because our minds are clogged with hundred fears, suspicions and political superstitions infused by our friends in the opposition. We have miles to go, taking the whole nation together, we have miles to go removing our mental shackles".

"Now, the will of the majority people must prevail over-that is the ethics of the social system. Our faces, line of movement, our political target now passionately move in the direction of our ideology and vision, remembering that we have lost too long time, a period, in fighting enemies within and witnessing the compromises with enemies beyond the borders. That is why mortars are still fired as daily greeting from the line of cease fire."

"Errors after errors committed by the governance damaged the national fabrics in 1947. Especially, one Jinnah dictated the terms of partition and nation divided. We still faces problem in

Kashmir because of special status. The king Hari Singh wanted a special status when his borders were flooded with tribal army. We conceded. But Kashmir is still left in Isolation, being an integral part of India. I agree, regrets are not going to redress the tragedies of yester years. At the same time abandon all hopes of building the future with old ruins of 66 years. Our doubts on the future vision are basic trauma we face. Whoever try to blacken that vision, instead of sharing the glory, are traitors".

Opposition got furious. Saalva, the opposition leader stood up *"Mind your language Prime Minister, remember, your are not addressing your paid audience at your constituency, to shout, to clap and whistle with your specialized laughing brigade in the front ten rows. You are addressing the parliament, still opposition is alive."*The opposition as a whole got and shouted at the prime minister. Premnath smiled and waited one minute.

"I fully agree that opposition is still alive with their paralyzed body in bed and eclipsed future. This nation is destined to shape its glorious future, where, their cursed faces will slowly disappear from the political arena. They deserve no future."

"Speaker Sir, every country has got a great pride about their historical past. Even USA with its 600 years of history proudly display its ancestral relics. Old Testament provides the legendry epics and heritage continuity for Judaism, Christianity and Islam. All of them share that noble past. Abraham, jacob or Gabriel appear as godly creations by all the three religions originated in Asia minor. So, Old Testament gained the continuity in two new born faiths. So being Indian, can he disown just because he has embraced a new religion. Why we

shall be deprived of our golden era of Vedic period. That is our origin of civilization. He is a Buddhist, he belong to Jainism, he is a Paris, he is a Muslim, he is a Sikh, or he is a Christian-he is a child of this soil and religion is an intermediate incident of history of his human life. Can he say my heritage is dead? Something many do not want us to question. Many do not want to answer, why?

This holy soil has given birth to revered sages, prophets, distinct civilization, literature, epics, philosophy, culture, science. Are you not its rightful holder? It is associated with one religion as pages of Hindu history, you are told, why I am also made to believe. But, that is a narrow version of the interpreters. It had the glorified altruistic ideals of receiving, embracing, assimilating and spreading a noble blending of various rays of thoughts. It is the tributaries of hundreds of clans that existed and invaded and claimed the right to settle. It is the sagar, the ocean of noble thoughts. Rig Veda said "Let noble thoughts come from all sides". When our minds are so broad like ocean to receive, why a few try to hold their ideals and identity without merging and mingling with us? None born in this land can disinherit their past. If you still say that I have no historical identity, then you abdicate your claims over this mother land. Do you concur with me?"

There is loud shout echoing his call, *"Yes. P.M, Yes. P.M. You are right"*

"If anyone say that, Ancient wisdoms be rejected, because I changed my faith: Ancient and literature cultural heritage is not mine, if you say so- you are insulting your motherland or you own mother? My words may hurt you, but it will not fail

to wake up your consciousness, that is buried fathom deep. You have psychological perversions. I ask you come out of that maya world."

"My friends! How noble culture we have inherited! One example! Even though we had lost river Indus to Pakistan, we did not rename the name of our nation Ganga Desh or Yamunastan. We still keep name as India, in the memory of our holy river Indus. India can never lost its vision of secularism as Hinduism never was defined as a religion but a way of life. We have hymns on gods which speaks of no shape, no color, no emotions nor visible existence, spreading everywhere, being nowhere, nether origin not end. It says god- I am all pervasive, I am without any form, I have no hatred or attachment of the world. I need no liberation. I am everywhere, in everything and eternally. I am an infinite kindness, eternal knowing and bliss, Shiva, love and pure consciousness. "Prime minister looked at the house with a look of a philosopher and took a deep breath. Ruling party drummed the benches showing its appreciation.

"This one religion has infinite expanse of embracing hundred faiths or can extend the hands of pure love to everyone irrespective of all beliefs. That is why Indians can culturally live, mingle, spread knowledge and transform those societies all over the world. Give one reason, why my vision is erroneous. If you say mine erroneous, have the courageousness to go to Mecca or Jerusalem, Bodhgaya or Vatican and tell the people, that their heritage claims are like worshiping of false gods. Peacefully think! I speak to your matured and sub conscious state of mind. Think, the answers will come.

If your religious identity are sacred private affairs and demand no concession nor legal classifications, nor branding or social isolations, we honour your cultural advancement and social pride. Then, we feel that you are a valuable citizen to lead this nation along with every Indian. You recognize that you have a heritage bondage in this soil and owner of the noble ideals that exists. Yes, you will be ensuring your right place to lead people and nation. Feel, you as Indian born is a shareholder of that mythic and mystic treasures. The epics and noble ideals of Upanishads are from the wisdom of your ancestors. Because, of temporary aberrations, your beliefs and faith has changed by default. Or changes caused by certain miserable destiny or necessitated for your forefathers' as incidence of survival. Do you want to disown the treasures of your ancestors? If you still say, yes-Let me ask you frankly- why? You have no answers, I know, your old fear still haunts you for generation. A foreign heritage you adopted under compulsion of time, had transmitted a psychological meningitis, which our friends conveniently used to keep your condition as bed ridden and which I want to permanently cure. Decide what you prefer!

We know that it will be possible for you to rethink, if these old political brokers are kept away. They exploited you as their vote bank. It is now possible if these pundits, I refrain from using the word bandits, who grabbed the name and fame of freedom struggle of million and converted those volumes as their family holdings- are exposed. They erased the role of hundreds of martyrs of struggle for liberating the nation and built their family epic. In their conspiracy they held our political future in their shackles. Time has come to reframe your role or radically rewrite them with truths.

He turned to the communist bench," *Ask them, they will ventilate their historical grievances. They were banned 30 years by British, they were jailed even after nation got freedom. They fought against Nizam of Hyderabad to demolish his cruel feudal hold on the poor landless. They rose against British. But none of them were seen in the pages of history of Independent struggle. So, the ruling party in the past erased all the chronicles and poisoned the Amritha of our Bharath Kanda".*

Communist member Siva Menon got up, *"Thank you for the compliment to communist, which is unprecedented and never expected in future too. We are rather afraid to acknowledge as words are emerging from the tongue of a man who every hour planning to wipe us out of the political map of India. Our objective attack on your mission will not be diluted as for communists are concerned. Your languages are fine as flow of honey, but we know they are nectars of poisonous plants".*

PM`s lips showed a smile. *"Your support will be there even to us. We both are treating each other untouchables, still when we sail across your path of struggle, you will come. Admit, were you not with us in the past parliament tremours? Memories are short Menonji, I am sorry. You supported them and they betrayed you. Still you refuse to learn whom to trust and whom to discard. That time will come.* "A ripple of laughter greeted the house.

"Speaker sir, I continue with my primaries. I do not have the genetic qualities of my predecessors to adopt more silence than coming out with open debates. Past governments have kept you as separate clan in ghettos and demonstrated their love to your state of poverty, miseries and treated you all sick patients in

hospital with pain killers and sedatives. My appeal goes to all minorities, as you are branded till date. Join the main stream! We are showing you a new path to march along with us. Keep them away from fishing in troubled waters any more. Have a conscious turn around join, in our march or be lost in the storm of drainages. Time has come. Choice is yours. If you miss, another hundred years you will regret.

Now, my call to everyone is explicit and open. I have a strong faith that we can change the path of destiny, than succumbing to it. For this we need more power and strength to your government. We need to have strong executive power to break the hardened and stoned bureaucracy blocking us to reach our goals. We call you to be with us for the changes, we bring. We determined to change the form of government, which are prevailing in 43 countries from USA, France to Maldives. Your future we will safe guard.

I come to the major threat. The threat of aggression and terrorism. We faced wars three times from a smaller nation Pakistan and one time from a major nation China. We have determined to equip our nation with more weapons and more war heads. We are now buying arms and modern war air crafts and submarines more than 50 billion dollars. We are the second largest buyers from USA and Pakistan is also landing in arms deal with 15 billion dollars with its collapsing economy. They shall know their strength and silently take a few steps back in the frontiers."

"They shall also close their Peshawar to Musheerabad terror camps. If they carry the terror preaching beyond the borders or send intruders, or harbor them in their soils like Dawoods

and his chelas or recruit here, our government is not going to tolerate. We will cut the roots with evidences or without evidences-without minding, which human right organization cries or weeps. We need to lead the nation with iron discipline to crush the elements that has caused blood to spill." Ruling party members rose up and clapped their hands. Home minister after two minutes got up and signaled them to stop.

"Members, I am distressed to see the condition of economy. We have more closed industrial sheds than running-Why? In industrial sectors, Investment without returns made us to lose lakhs of crores. How much we have lost in public sectors? Policies are wrong and industries have become disastrous. Concessions with no limitations had thrown us in the whirl pool of financial ruination. Too long absence of strong alternatives in parliament resulted in the ruination of a nation in the hands of corrupt ruling political alliances. Our industrial isolation from the market economy and non-inviting and disgusting response to International corporations, crude roads for free flow of global finances- placed us far behind hundreds of nations. Error is in the decisions of group of ministers and gang of alliances. Red tapes were kept alive for the gate fee collections by the persons in power. Ten years, there was a government with highest impotency and unbearable inefficiency. We are now offered 3 trillion investments, by one country, unparalleled record in the history of our nation. We are placing the red carpet to them, who will make our nation another Western nation. Our take over itself gave this confidence. If we show the consolidated power of legislative and executive in a presidential form, we will be the destination of wealth of the world.

We, the government is determined to change. Change to a different administrative set up to make the nation strong, to make decision fast and undeterred by too many power centers, too many bodies existing with too less performance. We bring a change with a strong CEO, a presidential form of governance. Somebody from the opposition got up. Speaker told rudely, *"sit down".*

He look around. The whole ruling party members were thumping, thundering and awe struck by phrases and language their leader. One of the ruling party member got up, "*The house has heard the ineffable and infallible speech of our PM, and still you feel that you have counter. Graciously accept him as our supreme commander to change the fate of the nation, there is no shame or sharp fall in your position sir.*"

Rishi Bararth an independent member got up, "*Sir, no doubt Prime minister spoke well. Had he spoken the same before a mirror or among his sycophants, none would have questioned nor disagreed. Unfortunately, he is addressing a parliament today where majority members still use their brain.*"

Speaker with red face, "*Mr. Rishi Barath, P.M.is yet to conclude and your indignations are unwarranted. Please take your seat.*"

PM, pointing out casually the AAP members, "*Some body remarked we are only 171 million voters strong. By our deeds and vision we will reach the 740 million voters. Thank that member showing so much interest in strengthening us. I also invite them to join the main stream. Only 4 of you in this house of 543. What you are going to achieve? When you started as movement, you were with us, you went away from us. Many of your leaders joined us. You contested against to defeat us. Fortunes did not favor your leader. No hard feeling sir. I have invited everyone in this house to be with us in our march. Why you are hesitantly thinking. Tell our leader at Lok Sabha, accept our ideals and join the bench. I am not asking you to defect, because my government is not in minority as the previous one for 10 years. Nor any crisis haunt us to save my majority. It is not horse trading too. Honorable merger of two good corporates makes our market strong. Every member now has a decision to make. Either you are with us or you are with the anarchist and defeatists. My advice is change the name, all your future tales will be decorated and laminated with golden lotus" Ruling* front rattled the whole house with their continuous drumming of the bench for two minutes.

"No future president of India will be rubber stamps of the ruling party or their ministers. We, with the existing order, failed to eliminate corruption and bribery. We have not found a good statesman in India to prescribe a right alternative solution with the existing order. Sixty six years, we have lost too long a time friends, too long a time in the life of a nation with one generation gone without tasting the fruit of their hard labour while building their nation"

"To-day, USA is able to tackle the terrorism because, the President is able to take fast decisions and implement them with his executive powers in an unparallel speed. We had government which celebrated a bahrath procession of terrorist at the entrance of the Parliament. Our soldiers died, but one

more terrorist live to say, you have no right to punish me for my human hunting in your nation"

"Shame, shame"

Tables of ruling party members received a thumping and they booed the oppositions.

"Let me share more of owes and sad past. Lakhs of Bangladeshees have crossed the borders and settled here in the tea estates, agriculture and as coolies in cities. They endanger our securities. Not one step was taken to stop the inflow or to drive back the intruders. We will end the influx now. We will close the borders. We need unbridled powers to end this national disasters. We shall the strike the targets just like American war plane F-16"

"Honorable speaker sir, Indian Parliament is a laboratory with the delivery of 98 amendments to constitution and hundreds of laws in its law lexicon. Two more amendments are proposed with one reason that the present parliamentary system fail to answer all its anomalies and sickness. Our governance with other alliances caused several failures and cancerous corruptions. The number games often caused frictions and fall of parliaments. Stop this menace and start with governance as corporates do.

By putting forward the will of the people in front and election of their president directly, we can regenerate rays of democracy with its powerful image. New election results are decisive for a change in the legislative and executive power. Let the people vote and say whether they need a president backing us or let them reject us in the presidential contest. Now the house shall validate the bill. We place our bills to amend the constitution.

Your copies will be before you in a few hours. You debated the bill without official copy before, a welcoming change with the changed times. Changes are inevitable. Accept them with a sense of pragmatism and intellectual perception!

Hon'ble Speaker, the time for lunch has come. Let me talk later.

From the ruling party member side, there is a roaring and applause. All are awe struck and gazing at their Demosthenes of Indian parliament.

Session close for Lunch. Member after member went to their lord of the ring and showered songs of praise. Home Minister Kanoj hugged the PM.

PM does not know how long his magic potion will lost long.....

CHAPTER XVI - NOV 2014

OUR VOICES MAY BE CHOCKED
OUR LIFE MAY BE SILENCED
OUR FOOT PRINTS MAY BE ERASED
BUT TURN BACK TO SEETHE STROM WE RAISED
THAT WILL THROW YOU OUT
OF YOUR POWER.

"Hon. Speaker, a motion on two bills on constitutional amendments are being discussed rather debated. Copies were being sent to us through newspaper. Extraordinary brilliance is seen in the performance of 16th Lok Sabha. 'To move the bill or not to move the bills?' 'To be or not to be'- who is the Hamlet here in the ministry with a hesitancy to table? I do not go for that research. My observation is that ministers themselves are displeased to breach the constitution. Hon. Speaker, I speak opposing the bill? Will it be part of the proceedings of the parliament? "Rishi Barath, an independent member stood up to speak.

Parliamentary affairs minister PromodSa got up, *"Honourable speaker, cabinet is firm that this bill be passed. I understand that most of the opposition are turning silent by welcoming our amendments, leaving some independent member symbolically to oppose."*

"Hon`member shall know that the discussion on this already initiated by Prime Minister, the copy of the bills has reached the members through the office of the speaker. Please proceed"

Rishi Bharat smiled, "Thank you sir, I am thankful for three parties, permitting me to use their allotted hours to me. I clarify to Home Minister, all the three parties wanted to fight the diabolical game of the ruling party. They had given their responsibility to me. But I assure sir, I will still save valuable time of this house as I am not here to deliver long speech for justifying an ignoble cause. Or inserting an operation theatre knife smoothly inside the human rights and national harmony, as my predecessor."

"The truth is" he looked around for a minute and continued, *"The constitution of India has itself invalidated these two bills. In a hurry to carry the political reform, as they call, they failed to see that constitution makers had put the nail whereas our ruling class thought that it is the latch. Sorry, we will take it in the last, quoting experts in constitutional law."* Entire opposition smashed their hands on the table.

"So far constitutional amendments in the past, came for a change in the frame of law. Now these two amendments are drafted to change the status of this house and power of an individual above the constitutional bodies. This parliament with its wisdom shall not allow amendments that will ruin its existence. I speak not on behalf of some opposition members".

He stopped and looked around, all faces were looking curiously at him. *"I speak on behalf all the 543 members including the Prime Minister of India".* Some ruling party members sprang up from the seat. Prof. Rishi Bharat calmly showed his hands to sit down and continued his speech.

Treasury bench is really shocked, how this man got the permission to speak. The independent member is known for his brilliance and political excellence and capable of mesmerizing the house with his lucidity, clarity and authority on the subject of debate. Three parties have shifted their allotted time with a confidence that he will tear down the bill before it is placed.

Vasudeva from Bengal rose from the seat and asked for a clarification, *"Sir, If on a technical reason or erroneously if the drafted bill is to be rejected or to be referred to the technical committee, which item, of this parliament, you will reject and refer?"*

Speaker simply waved his hands and asked him to sit down." *I know the rules, please do not raise unwanted debates."*

In anger the member said, *"In the regime of Ghosts, Unholy Shastra's will debate about eating of human flesh."*

"I expunge the remark of the member", Speaker was shaking with anger and he knows most of the members of Parliament are capable of turning him a buffoon.

Prof. Rishi Bharat continued, *"Sir, I am not going to discuss about the technicalities of parliament but I would like to deal with the core issues of the amendments primarily. I may also be permitted, I repeat I may also be permitted to rebut the extensive political analysis of our Hon. Prime Minister and his honorable colleagues. I suo motto, take up the copies of the bill placed by, Sorry sir, published by TIME LINES and parliamentary proceedings."*

"Prime minister in his lengthy speech referred 'earth is degenerating to-day. Bribery and corruption abundant.' So, I need the extraordinary powers to stop the fall of the nation. The essence of his speech, I am quoting from Assyrian Civilization tablet 2800 B.C. Political system has got a genetical disorder. I totally agree, but what cure is prescribed? Here, Patients investigated are people, diagnosis were done with our instruments the parliamentary democracy and Medicine are prescribed and consumed by doctor P.M. for his healthy future. What a wonderful game, it is sir? P.M. Instead of chaining the corrupt and culprit should he shackles a nation and its innocent people who voted for him? He, a great technical savvy, is for a morphed democracy or morphine democracy, I am yet to understand. Please note that our Honourable P.M. and everyone here fought elections entered this house of democracy- were and are the part of the system for the past 20 to 25 years. His party was in opposition in this parliament. Were they ignorant of scams? Are they not aware who did that and how they did that? Were they ignorant of billions of dollars exchanged? Was anybody having the audacity to deny you the information or investigation? Now a trillion dollar black money is in international banks and they refuse to release the names of the offenders. They say no balance accounts are there. Cannot they call for two years transactions and trace the cash flow? Whom they cheat? 125 crores Indians! They quote some bi-lateral tax agreement and deny us the information we are entitled to know. They refuse to reveal the culprits names saying that you have a settlement not

to reveal the criminals. Who introduced that obnoxious clause? Not the foreign governments, because their system do not scuttle transparency. So, the government of India is the prime culprit to include a malicious clause. And the present ruling party is an abettor! Assume such clauses exist, are they not void under any law? And the ruling governments are haven for the financial terrorist of the nation-I charge you! The group of ministers, your acts are against the national interest!"

Sentence was so provoking the whole government bench got up shouting. Some without capturing the meaning of financial terrorism, thought professor had accused the government as terrorist called the speaker to expel him from the house.

AnjumanBaig who was enjoying the speech of professor told his colleague, *"So a different category of terrorist without guns, I have never heard, professor is bringing new form of terrorism? I think, these terrorists will exceed thousands"*

Rishi continued, *"So, you will sign agreements to-morrow with Interpol and say drug traffickers names cannot be revealed. And will say sorry to the nation that we have signed secrecy clause with Interpol or US anti-drug trafficking agency! Are we imaging ourselves like Panama state where President Martinelli Berrocal himself tried as drug trafficker? With an agreement with Income tax department of India you may refuse to reveal the list tax evading Mafia? In banks you will not release the list of defaulters? In land revenue department you will not release the land grabbers and large land holders holding of thousand acres. What kind of legal and judicial system is this? Criminals Secrecy Protection Act-when you all have passed.*

What an insanity is this? Is it Demon Crazy state? The darkness is hovering over the very concept of state with a diseased midset. If you are totally blind, you are unfit to rule. If you remained as silent partners, ethics demand that you shall not run this government with the sulphur smell of corruption: resign."

"Mr.Rishi, you do not have one seat properly, you are asking the thumping majority government to resign. It is parliament not mental asylum to speak whatever you want?" Shouted back the Home Minister.

Rishi patiently heard and smiled at Home Minister, *"Yes Sir, you are correct, this is parliament. But do not convert this house as monument of national mental asylum just because you have majority here? Answer my objections: If individual hides an information from the state, it is termed as criminal conspiracy under law, if the state hides information about criminals to citizens, what you will you term that? Noble State confidentiality?"*

Home Minister Face turned red and he looked at speaker. Speaker was helplessly looking at P.M. He knows any comment at this stage will invite sarcasm and piercing response from this mad man who is turning the whole house as his arena of battle, with no fear nor error in utterance to call them unparliamentarily language, to stop him.

Sir, our PM regretted that we do not have one statesman in India to prescribe a right alternative that includes himself. I fully concur with him. By becoming a president overnight, will he be able to acquire the wisdom of statesman? Or do have we to create a presidential post to make him Wiseman. I believe both are unwise suggestions or ideas?" The whole opposition got up and clapped their hands.

Speaker warned, *"Hon. Member, No personal attacks, deal with the bill"*. Ruling party members were furious and they demanded that the independent member shall not be given time to talk. A large group started yelling at the professor. After, 10 minutes shouting and counter shouting the house came to order.

"My friends by chocking my voice, you cannot silence the millions, who will hear me to night as alive or dead, more forcible and with more freedom provided by the streets in India than the seat in this house. No matter I am allowed to speak or not here, nation will hear me in louder voice." The thunder of his voice shocking brought dead silence.

"First thing you shall learn, once this bill is passed and amends constitution, that day the parliament is paralyzed. The right to legislate is passed on to one man and we will be men in mortuary to dissect bodies for a post-mortem- referred by a President. We will be doing the anatomy rather operations on law. We will be dummies and not MPs from that day onwards. To hang ourselves, we are bringing not one but two thick ropes as 99th and 100th amendments. That is the end of our 66 years of parliamentary democracy and our power to legislate. Do you want this? Answer me my ruling party friends?" Prime Minister got up but without a word he sat back.

"Hon. Speaker, this is not T.V .Channel, ask that member not to speak cini-dialogues. He is wasting the precious time of this house." Parliamentary affairs Minister Pramodsa shouted.

He saw that his members are maintaining absolute silence, absorbed in the speech.

"Yes, every minute of this house is most valuable I agree with our honorable minister. Because you have placed two bills to end the life of this house soon. "Remark of Rishi was sparked with a loud laughter.

Turning to speaker, *"Sir, Hon. PM was condemning 66 years of economic and industrial policy as a failure and that was his main plank of condemnation. Did his party placed an alternative policy till date in this parliament? Permit me to travel a few centuries back and also to deal about the new world order. For Liberalization, and opening of market for global financial transfers-both present and past ruling parties were co-authors. Let them come with a balance sheet and cash flow of India. What is coming investment is looted back in different forms. Whatever our foreign debts are almost equal or less to the money stashed by our industrial and business houses and kept in foreign shores.*

I trace back the period of East India Company that had captured India. General Robert Clive, who later committed suicide and warren Hastings, the first governor general of British India, who later was impeached in 1794 in British parliament for treasons, brutality against native Indians, loots and atrocities-I recollect. First Governor General was termed as blood hound and beast in the British parliament. During their period, they were transferring 3,000,000 pound sterling from India per annum. In a book Eastern India Vole III writer Mr. Martin 1838, quoted that "British India accounted in 50 years at the 12% compound Interest to an amount of

84,000,000,000 pound sterling! 1838 one man was able to monitor how much India was looted and drained in a period of 50 years? In 1990`s Mexico opened its gates for US dollars and in 9 years it paid back 12 times more. Hon`ble Prime minister referred the industrial sickness of public sector. When they constructed the nation, we went holding the begging bowl to the Western Investors. Nobody came. Indian capitalist, they refused to invest, so much patriotism! Still the nation, saw the blooms of industrial gardens and many a private industries started as its tributes and as its branches. Who laid foundation for heavy industries, steel, telephones, aeronautic, boiler and electronic industries- is it not the government? Was it golden or gloomy economy? When they had grown giant, finance ministry declared a heavy dividend and tax bill from Public Sector Units: See the record: budget was financed more by public sector at one time than private. 10 to 12 crores of employment grew in the industrial sector. When the market economy opened they found the PSUs are biggest giants affecting the interest of the private capital. So, government deliberately killed them and made them sick by curbing their funds flow, modernization efforts and competitive market entries. They ate when it was healthy and past few years the government started selling the sick units, lands, shares for meeting the budget short falls by Rs.50000 to Rs.60000 crores. Even in death, the so called sick industry became bloodline for Indian Budget. Honorable PM, the previous rulers were perpetrators and oppositions were co-conspirator." The whole NPP and the Barathiya Congress simultaneously rose up to protest. Undaunted by this, Rishi raised his figure and showed his left and right side and with a belling voice, "*Yes, thanks of the identification parade, please sit down*"

The house loved his instant sarcasm and all party members had a loud laugh.

"Next budget will also be healthy by sale of shares of some healthy Public Sector oil or steel shares. The whole government lives with mother`s milk and fathers wealth even to-day. Without having a penny for further industrialization, you cut their roots, trunks, sell and condemn the PSUs as useless dead wood. What a great financial wizards, you all!"

"It is a shame! Not one finance minister, I condemn, all those who have destroyed the nation's wealth for the past 25 years to promote this casino economy with Los Angeles luxuries for rich alone and converted poor beggars awarded with aluminum plates of ration. After this what you will sell? I tell you, Indian Ports and Airports, wet lands like Somalia and Ethiopia!"

"*Mr. Rishi Bharat, stop all unparliamentarily language*" Speaker shouted. He wanted this man to stop.

"Honorable speaker sir, please identify what are here unparliamentarily words and expunge that alone." Members understood, he is laying a trap to drag the speaker in to debate on issues. Speaker bent down and signaled to continue. There was a slight heckling.

"How much foreign money came in FDI, ECB and FII in stock trades and how much money gone in the drains in the name of transfer pricings, under valuations of export invoices and over invoicing of imports, profit transfers and other international repatriations? How much money had come on Luxuries of Five stars, gold markets and for hi-fi livings? One of our Indian

MNC has stored more than 9 lakhs crores of money in dollars in overseas accounts and under float funds, participatory notes and other instruments. Indian industrial houses are brutal bandits than their predecessor, East India Company. They have drained more blood money than the British. Many of our industrial tycoons and high network politicians and a few swamis shall be given a special award for the patriotism by keeping safe a fund equal to 50% of Indian GDP in foreign lands. If we say bring back, our Finance Minister furiously shouts that we are breaching international relations. But here is a PM turned preacher and saint teaches us on 'renouncing of all idea of possession and create thirst to enjoy and eternal bliss'. I am quoting great AdhiShankara's holy scripts 'Nirvana Shatakam' which he referred in another context. But truth is 90% of our population is stripped of possessions, livelihood and eternally with no hopes about next dawn. For them what is solace or relief you are offering? Prime Minister now made president-is that?"

"Tell us now, anyone member in this house did restrained you from enacting a powerful legislation to bring back the trillions of dollars kept by our unpatriotic traitors? If so, cut our hands for our treason. Swamiji, NPP, Member of this house, told that 35000 accounts? Ask me, I will give the video tape to refresh his memory. Money equal to half of Gross Domestic Product now outside- RRS condemned this a greatest treason, six months back. When you do not bring back that money as Prime Minister, how you are going to answer them in your camp? How the house can repose faith on you? With the a train of traitors at your tracks, how can we see you as our President?" The whole house roared with thunderous slogan *"Shame, Shame"*.

"Prime Minister is answerable to the house and directly elected president is not. That deletion of accountability of the highest office is the motive behind these bills and to turn as an Unquestionable monarch. After all, party ideology is synonymous with the legendary feudalism. This Party decades back wanted kings to rule us and we have to bow and bend before them, speaking nothing, protesting nothing and owning nothing, not even our self-respect. They allowed us bend before the Whiteman empires, ended in 1947. Now, here another emperor is bringing back the legacy in the name of President."

"Mr. Rishi will you avoid unnecessary dialogues?" speaker shouted.

*"Yes Majesty, but I am left with another one hour"*Rishi bowed with a sparkling in the eyes.

"We were debating about the devolving of powers from the supreme parliament to state, state to district and district to village panchaythraj level. I honestly put before all members including the great allies and members from the state of the ruling party-one question. When you are all debating about the devolvement of powers and critical of centralizing them, how come you will vote here to Pyramid it to one man. Is it not a great betrayal of your ideals and public postures? Please answer or go back and do a brain storming? You will tell that everything is wrong here. Stop this menace to democratic set up. Protest, protest whichever is party you belong to. Whichever is your ideology? Answer your conscience and conscience alone"

Parliamentary Minister Promod Sa was furious and got up, *"You need not advise our members, we know better than you"*

"Yes, Hon.Minister, I only appealed to the members to think, touch their conscience, and apply their brain? My appeal and language, to your members, if found democratically defective, error of human science, endangering your mission, please forgive me sir. I was not aware that you fear about your own shadows too, that follow you night and day. Sorry sir". He pointed out his finger around the ruling party benches.

He turned to speaker and continued, *"Sir, all government including the present government is also an agency for international financial capital and MNCs. Talking nationalism and patriotism and ending as abettors to the financial aggressions of MNCs, is their culture. To do a perfect the delivery of service, you do believe that Presidential format will be more helpful as that of USA? Even after 35 years of tragedy, the perpetrator of Bhopal gas tragedy is free. Anderson, he is dead I believe. Where is Enron and its rotten projects? What recovery came back after Harshat Metha scams? When Income tax dept raided the foreign firms, PM interfered and said that it will send a wrong signal to foreign investors. All present King's men also cried 'yes, yes'. Vodaphone CEO criticises India for slow decision after cheating some lakhs of crores in merger and take overs. All of you observed dead silence not to hurt the sentiment of CEO. Estimated loss is something Rs.110,000 crores or so. Hundreds of Indian assets are taken over by another company by a takeover and merger in different countries. We lost several thousand crores of taxable income and Indian laws are shut down their eyes and ears. You talk about national security hundred times more that your predecessors and you are on the process of selling defense production to foreign nations. We are the second largest arms importers in the world and now the remaining productions will also be under the control of foreign industrial houses. Excellent patriotism sir. Are you planning to recruit American armed force for border protection in India, Israelite Mossad for intelligence? Is that your contract undisclosed in your U.S. talk? We will pay unimaginable penalty as Afghan and Iraqis have paid, if your policies turn to be future programme of a nation."*

"Judicial nominations are now being brought under the government. Great, an ultra-right wing leader, why you want this presidential chair? We know, three pillars powers will be converted to Mono-block, try colour flag will be one- turn to be one saffron. My dear Parliamentarians, if the dictations to create a Presidential dictatorship continues 'the members here, you have nothing to offer but blood, toil, tears and sweat to protect the democratic freedom' as Vincent Churchill call during the second world war to British.

Angry P.M. got up and shouted, *"Stop talking rubbish, enough, wind up."*

"Your anger is correct, Prime Minister Sahib. I am left with another 52 minutes. Perhaps that may be the total allotted time for me in this parliament for my entire future. I may not be there or Parliament may not be."

"You're are not alternative, but an extension or continuation in that musical chair game. Just like Democratic and Republicans who alternatively hunted oil rich nations to add wealth to the debt ridden American nation, your ideas, polices are reprints. But you want a better shield from future falls and demands Presidential Powers."

'You did not want anything as a debate of the parliament to stop the financial calamities, political and economic squander. Most of the parliament hours were wasted or declared sine die. Now as ruling now your strategy continues to shut the doors of parliament forever. Your new BRAIN TANK, a body with ideas without accountability, is to replace planning commission. Your judiciary will come under you; committed judges with political bias are post honored on retirement. Day will not be far off, sir, in the streets the voice of dissent will be strangulated by your cadre army. "Opposition thundered the benches provoking the rulers.

Some ruling party members got up rushed to his table and menacingly attacked him. Members of the ruling knows that he is tearing of page by page the whole amendment proposed. His shirt was pulled and he fell down. One thug kicked him on his face. Other members came to his rescue, surrounded and protected him from being attacked further more. His glass was broken and his lips torn. He sipped a glass of water and took his notes. Some members rushed to the speaker and told him to call the marshals and rescue him. Speaker unwillingly reacted and called marshals and told them to remove four ruling party members out of the hall. House was adjourned for one hour. Speaker consulted the Home minister whether he can stop the agenda that day? The urgent cabinet group met in the lunch hour. P.M. was red with burning anger. Madan Vyas was in hyper tension. The opposition is forming large alliance and they had a meeting with some ruling NPP members.

The house met at 3.00 p.m.

CHAPTER XVII - NOV 2014

Harmlessness, truth, freedom from anger, Renunciation, tranquility of spirit, Lack of malice, compassion towards all living things, Freedom from covetousness, Tenderness, modesty, steadfastness, Vigor, patience, constancy, purity, Freedom from hatred, lack of conceit. All these are in him that is destined for goodness-Arjuna.

Hypocrisy, arrogance, pride, wrath, rudeness, and ignorance, these are found in one that is destined for evil-Arjuna.

Evil leads to bondage, goodness to deliverance. Have no fear, you are destined for goodness-Arjuna.—BAGAVAD GITA (religious script)

His lips slightly injured and were spilling blood. His face had severe black marks of lashes and beating. He came out of the parliament. Entire opposition surrounded him. NAP member told that they shall start sitting on the floor, dharna in the house. Other member suggested that we shall give public statement before the Press people. The whole press and visual media had a hot news and the whole nation saw Rishi being attacked by 2.30 P.M. His swollen lips, injury on the face and dirty clad dress was flashed across the country. A senior leader, NPP crossed them and came back to Rishi, *"Sorry, Rishi I am ashamed, sorry"* He moved back.

Basdev put the hand on his shoulder, *"Comrade, please leave the front row and come back where we and SNP party members are seated. I was really shock and wounded. These fellows are brutal, comrade".*

"No Basdev, they will be calm and fine fellows, if they are really confident of the success of their design. They behave like a trapped tiger, once their conspiracy seems to falling apart like ruined mud fort. See the drama in the afternoon. They may turn as wild bison. I am not the one to budge to all these musclemen tactics, you know well."

Basudev showed him a Viber message *"Dear comrade, I give you an authentic information and I will produce proof. Suicide bomber at New Delhi airport is a Syrian drug peddler. There nothing religious fanaticism. Who caused delay in passing information to RAF or is it deliberate?*

Two terrorists were held up at Kandla. Some Gujrathi minister allowed them to walk out freely. When they escaped from Andhra there was no response from AP, Orissa or M.P." Rishi asked him what exactly Basudev's friend wants to convey? Parliament bell chimed.

Afternoon the determined opposition moved in crisscross to surround Rishi Barath and he was compelled go to back to his seat so that no one can go near him without crossing the opposition fort. Speaker felt it as an indirect insult.

"Hon. Speaker, many a thousand pray to god to give them the holy death on the bank of Ganga river, many heroes in war front. My prayer is, I shall breathe for the last time, in this holy samvidhan, the great house of parliament of India. I thank those who now made an unsuccessful effort to fulfil my innate prayers." Speaker was about to react and Mr. Rishi Barath raised his hands and speaker was dumbed for a second. Speaker was totally upset. To-day, the member seems to be possessed and the whole house is totally hypnotized by his scurrilous attack on the government.

"Please permit me to continue where I have left before. You wanted a historical changes in the parliament. Let me touch the chronicles and tell, who you are. Do you have that historic sanctity to touch the holy scripts of constitution? Your grand old party Maha Hindurashtra failed to struggle against British Empire. That was the origin of your patriotism. When you grew as opposition you did not react against the evil policies of the past governance? Because you wanted to favour the big corporates and monopoly houses, which are corrupting the state. When the nation was suffering with poverty, hunger, homelessness, corruption, unemployment and suffering, you took communal as an agenda to cause bloodshed and hatredness. In 1996, government spent 12000 crores to meet communal clash alone. Rs.2300 for education and health care in the same year. You fed illusions and divert the people from their path of fight against the systemic disaster. You injured the nation with more number of daggers than curing the wounds. You scavenged for all faulty remedies, keeping growth and development of the party than of nation. Why as a ruling party Prime Minister, you did not react and reversed the policies of crony capitalism? Trillions of

dollars are now with Swiss or Bahama or Hong Cong Banks or 28 tax havens. You had no courage to force the previous government to pass legislations. You refuse to obey the directions of Supreme Court even to-day. You have no idea to retrieve as P.M., what as a President you will do? You will search for a position of the great dictator to solve the issues before the nation. Now tell me members, am I not correct?"

"Sir, what is the connection between foreign funding and Presidential election? Out of 196 countries in forty two countries Presidential system exist. Yes you are correct. But, 70% of 42 countries are not getting any investments from G15 countries, where your eyes are wandering. Tell me sir-Are you short of powers? 40 to 50 years veterans who worked for your party are no more power sharers. You ensured that there can no mutiny of elders in NPP. You are more than president in power to day? Why you want to impose the presidential system on us for your problem in your party?" House had a wave of laughter.

Home minister Kanoj shouted, *"Stop, irrelevant nonsense. Hon.Speaker you stop him from talking about our internal party affairs."*

"Speaker sir, yes, I am also concurring with Home Minister by telling, please do not meddle with the parliamentary democracy to control the tremor in his party."

"Sir, I am synthesizing various dialogues, the house heard and you allowed. They are all in support of imposing the same through an ordinance now. Some honorable member was referring about the poor Bangladeshi inflow as human herds or modern nomads. There is a split personality in ruling

party ideologies. Swami Nityanji, MP told four days back, in this house, that Akanda Bharath is a future mission and not a dream. The concept of Akanda Bharath of redesigning the borders from Afghanistan and part of South East Asia. Pakistan, Bangladesh, Myanmar and Shrilanka all in one compound. He commented in press meet that, if one Hindu girl is converted, he will convert 100 Muslims girls to Hindus. In this drama of violence of thoughts and public provocation he had forgotten basis of his abandonment of worldly pleasures and the search of a soul for enlightenment. O.K. let us forget that-noble ideals are reserved for true saintly souls. As sage Adi Shankara said, 'One ascetic with matted locks, one with shaven head, in his saffron robes– these are fools who, though seeing truth, do not see. Indeed, these different disguises or apparels are only for their belly's sake."

Swami Nithyan got up and objected, *"Speaker sir, member shall not speak issues irrelevant to subject debated here. He can discuss about me outside the parliament. I can answer him in different language."*

"Swami, for quoting the hymns of Adi Shankara, the saint, you get so much anger. Here is a great soul, in this house, renounced worldly things except his thousand square miles of wet land, several millions of trust funds, royal palatial huts, several Audi or BMW cars and hatredness and venom against Muslims."

"Sir, Swami instead of justifying the amendments, blamed that Partition was the conspiracy of Congress to retain their power In India. He spoke all in this House. You all clapped too. I retrace, in 1947, Mr. Jinnah lodged the same accusation against congress leaders as power mongers, when Congress wanted one

united India. Both Nithyanswamiji and Jinnah have showered blame on old Congress! Who is correct? In another website connected with Swami, it is mentioned that Pakistan and Bangladesh are disputed territories. So, what is the problem gentleman, if some of the illegal immigrants take your advise literally? Pakistani and Bangladeshi are your present or future citizens under Akanda Bharatha. Why do you want to build German wall to people, when you claim that the land they live is yours and there will be no borders. Perhaps you can talk to them now itself for futures vote banks. Is it not done by CM of West Bengal?

Ruling members shot back, *"you are talking like a traitor."*

Speaker raised his voice and told Mr. Rishi, *"Talk relevantly. Do not waste our time telling rubbish ideas provoking anti-national sentiments."*

"Hon`ble speaker, I sought your permission to talk on the pseudo patriots aimed at destroying the integration of a nation. This house heard, what you call as rubbish three days ago and it was honey drop for you. This house heard the same sentences which I quoted from their records. The original script writers do howl to-day 'I am a traitor!' If my recitals are anti-national quotes, what about the originals? Logic is simple. Lenders of ideas are accusing me-the borrower! P.M., he is their leader. Do you still argue that the nation has got to elect him as President?"

I do not blame them, a lone section, who are relying on the legendry tales for redrawing of the borders of the nations. To-day we have a new barbarism has emerged in the name of Islamic States of Iraq and Syria. These maniacs are taught about the largest Islamic empire commencing from Kazakhstan, Iran, Syria, Turkmenistan and ending in the east crossing, Gujrat, Rajasthan and Kashmir. They quote the Afghan Empire between 622 After Christ birth to 1250 and also 18th Century Durrani Empire. I know they misquote the histories and the territories, basing upon ancient invasions and looting done by some kings in in Somnathpur and other places in the olden times. Expansionism, talk on restoration of old empires, recalling conflicts between ancient kings with a communal colour, searching for an enemy to create conflicting groups and thus strengthening our identity and hold among our race or religion-are major political but sickening ideologies. These lunacies originated centuries back. For your political existence you have resurrected. You want us to be with you to imprint our name in the patriotic list maintained by your party. We boldly say 'No'. These black holes shall meet an end otherwise these conflicts will destroy national fabrics. Those who try to see every human relationship through their broken religious prism must be halted. Your vision and ISIS missions have similarity in their basic conceptions. Both ideologies cannot be sanctified by pouring thousand liters of Ganga water on you or hundred Hegiras to Mecca by them.

"Sir, Repeatedly hate speeches were heard in this house from the date of accession of government by the present ruling party. Some cheer girls are also dancing for these orators. Sir, we will not be silent spectators. Peace and harmony of my beloved Indians are involved. We can be dead than be mute."

Sir, with the permission of the house, let me recall the most tragic year of 1947. I recall, because this house dragged martyrs in bad light. In intentionally used the word tragic. Yes, Jinnah called for the separate land for Muslims. An absurd idea that religion constitutes national identity had caused this disaster. The same snakes are coming alive after 65 years-forces me to recall the mournful days."

"A nation with three hundred and eighty million population with 255 million Hindus, 95 Muslims, 6 million Sikhs, plus other religions suddenly got divided. Government of India was facing the pain of exodus of 6 million Muslims and 4.5 million Hindu and Sikhs. One million people died in this communal holocaust. Partition sword was cutting the human flesh everywhere. It was the days of hoodlums, hooligans, blood hounds. People died, children were thrown in roads, and women were raped. History has left us an incurable wound in our heart." His eyes were swelling with tears. His voice choked and he sat a few minutes. Sitting beside him another M.P. patted him and consoled him. Few seconds after he recovered,

"Sir, British cunningly declared that the Doctrine of Lapse of Paramountcy signed between princely states and the British Empire was repealed. Declared that 565 Princely states are independent on that date. The agreements signed during the period of Lord Dalhousie somewhere in 1850s lapsed. Announcement was made, If they wish, they can sign the INSTRUMENT OF ACCESSION with India or Pakistan or can remain independent state.

Hanwantsingh, the maharaja of Jodhpur, king of Jaishalmer, NawabMirapur of Bhopal met Mr.Jinnah, who advised them to merge their kingdom to Pakistan. Indian leadership had to

struggle to pacify them to sign the accession. Raja Hari Singh of Jammu and Kashmir, refused to sign the accession, whereas Dr. Sheik Abdulla, of the same state, gave an open call in the Kashmir valley to accede to India".

"Hyderabad declared independent state. In Hyderabad the brutal regime of Nizam faced a civil war with the landless peasants, led by the communist in Telengana region. 'Travancore Samastanam' a state in Kerala declared independence. People of Kerala rose against the government and forced the ruler, RajaChitiraTirunal Varma to sign the Instrument of Accession.

I recall memories of 1947, to this house with one reason- Sir, India would have been a torn shirt with hundred holes with thirty percent of land area under its control. We had no big army to fight. But, the whole crisis ridden nation was saved by those who are no more in this earth. With unbearable tension, attack, tragic tales of every hour and mental strains, those leaders were hospitalised several times as they were not able to bear the cruel state of the country. Their heart was bleeding over the innumerable miseries under gone by our people. Those martyrs is being condemned here by undeserving entries in the noble house of parliament. We used to quote that dead men have no enemy. But here are members still hold the venom of enmity and condemn those who lived and passed away for their nation. Some of you have insulted the people who lived, sacrificed and died in a situation of uncontrollable crisis and tragedy"

House was shaken and a dead silence rapped the whole house. Even the ruling party members were really moved by the emotional outburst of the Professor. Prime Minister turned pale. This man is killing my whole dream empire. He will end my future, my giant leap.

"Now sitting at the durbar of Indian parliament with billion dollar budgetary money, excessively spent, eaten and royally appropriated, present leaders have to magnify hundred times their image as heroes of fatal wars, when guns in border occasionally fire in Siachin, Kargil or Sialgot. While poor are being grinded between the millstones of taxation and inflations a large section of high fi network is sitting comfortably at the cost of government and planning to appropriate and misappropriate a huge flow of taxes and incomes as subsidies."

"Total central budget receipt to-day is Rs.17, 94,892 crores. Expenditure is more and that is our parliamentary budget in 2014-15. You know this country was running with a budget in 1947-48, Rs.171 crores revenue and expenses of 193 crores. Then, national current expenditure was to be met in a state of total bankruptcy. The two crores which you are spending to run the Parliament for one day is the same amount the government was crying for, to save the whole nation from hunger for One Day. Having faced so much crisis, having fought so many wars with China and Pakistan, having spent sleepless nights due to riots and volcanic social conflicts, the nation had surged forward due to the immense sacrifice of founders of the independent nation. I do not credit a few ruling members of that time. I talk about everyone in opposition, in center, in states, in villages. They were one in my eyes because they were living for this land, forgetting that they shall earn for the winters of seven generation. Hamlets of these people also sank in floods or scorched in sun. Families lost in the race

of time. This nation rose from the marsh to sky scrapers. Those martyrs passed away as unsung heroes. The undeserved are now trying to disgrace them and you are hailing these parasites as heroes. Shame on you!

You sport venom against them, whose sacrifice was unspeakable in those hard times. They did not name their ideology. But their heart was beating for every suffering ones. After facing misery, sleepless night, endless tension and so much of painful life as ministers and prime ministers of incurable regime, no Prime Minister came to this parliament and told that I want to nominate myself as President of India. Then I will meet the crisis of India."

The whole opposition raised from their seat and for more than ten minutes, it was almost a thunder. Managed M.P. Veeraj came to his seat and hugged him and his eyes were with tears. *"My son, your tongue didn't speak to-day, your heart, your heart, it is from your heart. I am very much proud of you. After a decade, I have heard a true parliamentarian to debate in depth."* Suddenly, Professor realised that man is from the ruling party, emotionally driven, crossed the bench. Rishi sat for a minute, turned the papers. Ruling party thought that he had switched of his mike. They wanted him to end the speech so that parliament can be wounded off to-day, till alternative plans are prepared.

He got up once again, *"with honey drops and fragrance of language, the Prime Minister has provoked a discussion to-day. Subject is, 'Are you a citizen with your devotion and loyalty to the pre-historic time? Or are you going to renounce your religious identity by denying your link to the Bharatha Kanda by disrobing yourselves from the past. This was the essence of analyses by the Prime Minister in a most beautiful manner and told that he will lead the idea of one nation, one culture and one identity, once Presidential bill is passed. I do not wish to see another holocaust. Yes, the language of Prime minister seems to be not drops of nectar but an extracted liquids from the teeth of the cobra"*. Angry ruling party members got up from the seat. Entire opposition suddenly stood up. Speaker anticipated a pandemonium. Rishi folded his hands to opposition to sit back in their seat. The ruling party members were shocked over the sudden reaction. They waited for the signal and sat once their party secretary showed his hands.

"Sir, you spoke of great epics, mythology and Shastra. I, as a great lover of the paramount literary epic work of Ramayana, yet we are not able to digest the treatment met by Sita in hands of Rama, the great emperor of Ayothya. In Mahabharata epics, Dhroupathi being publically molested in the king's court, that too with a strange logic. If, these two women were not there, two epics would have lost their soul, I concur. Will you agree, if the same logic is reinvented to day in real life of women in the present time? Will those curse of insulting and enslaving women be guideline for the women empowerment in your administration? Whether it is empowerment or enslavement of women-you advocate?

"Sir, Is Revival of Varna, the caste discrimination, your desire? Do you advocate the treatment met by the oppressed caste and tribals shall be revived in the social system? Will you advise us to follow these as ideals by our people now? Epics and Upanishads or Vedas are ancient treasures. The great values and directions

advocated in these holy scripts are not followed even by the great Swamis here.

"PM may request the speaker to delete those lines of P.M. speech on ancient culture and social system. If Four caste system is the frame work of this current government, our Prime Minister may be asked to step down no less a person than his own finance minister, Shri. Takurji, who being Kshatriya, the caste of rulers of the state. Laws of legends defines that Kshatriya shall be the natural rulers of the countries. Am I not correct?"

Nithyanji got up and told the speaker that Rishi Bharath is insulting the whole religious heads of the nation, the Hindu ethos and now the Home Minister. "*There can be no more tolerance. He shall apologies and stop his senseless oration, otherwise he will face consequence. "I do not know how people elect these cursed elements?"*

The whole opposition got up with a demand that the remark of Swami Nithyan a personal insinuation be expunged. Rishi Bharath nodded his head with a smile. *"Yes, Swamiji has the right to know the how this cursed element is getting elected for the past 18 years. Swamiji in my parliamentary constituency, in these 18 years as MP, I made 89% as literate and they vote for me. In your constituency you have allowed 18% literates: Others vote for you and you also get elected."* The satire created a hearty laughter even from the ruling front.

"Sir, *Marx said, "Religion is the opium of the people! "This what all others quote? I read his quotation in full,* ***'Religion is the sigh of the oppressed creature, the heart of a heartless world and the soul of soulless*** *conditions. It is the opium of* *the people.' Before touching the faith of minority, cure the ills of social system of oppression, convert it soulful. Remove the oppression and allow them to be equals- do this? Whichever the countries that had removed the oppression and socio-economic inequalities found that religion and castes vanished on its surface. The radical change is needed not be initiated in constitution but in our cultured brains, thought process and formidable actions."*

"I come back to your aroma of ancient Hindu culture and you want everyone to turn back to worship. I have beliefs, but do not sell that. I do Practice, I don't use it as political weapon. I do not preach because it is not my profession. But, you sell, preach, and use it as political weapon. You bring curse to the nation. What is your hidden agenda of touching the burning coal with ashy surface? When your agenda of progress and development now falls short, when your attempt to consolidate the vote banks are failing, your communal agenda, essential fire arm support, your party ignites. We know, why you touch, when you have absolute majority? Burning with your presidential ambition you want build the muscle power over the nation first. You want communal fire to pave a way to seize the absolute state power stampeding other political parties. To reach your desire, you want the society to be divided once again, by mesmerizing a few, instigating a few, coercing a few, oppressing a few, maiming a few, bringing disaster to the democratic structure."

"Neither the will of the god, nor destiny, nor any premonitions will change, the desire of our people to live in harmony. If with the predatory instinct, if the leaders operate sitting at the pedestal of high power and try to shackle the freedom of

people. Yes, Hon. Prime minister, the nation will witness and unprecedented up rise to defend our liberty. We reject your bill to your ascendency to Presidency. We also reject the all your preambles to do a palace coup. We are for a national referendum. We know our people will not surrender their liberty. Neither you nor any party in India had placed a manifesto on this fundamental change in this constitution, when they elected you. Let the people first give you the liberty to amend this provision. Then ask them to vote for your enthronement. This house has no inherent right to change the texture and format of the constitution. Even if you think, that by brutal majority, if you are going to pass the amendments, the people in the street are not going to allow you to do that. Before, being voted out by your own members with their enlightened consciousness, please withdraw the bills."

The demand for a presidential form of government shall once for all be buried in this house, deep fathom in our brain cells and from the platform of public lobbies. National poet Bharathi once wrote "Conspiracy will consume the noble dharma, But dharma will again win." We have a great faith that Dharma will ultimately win. Mr. Speaker, my last sentence quoting again Mr. Churchill. Our fight to close this undemocratic reform, "This is not an end, it is not even the beginning of the end, but it is perhaps, the end of the beginning". The debate on Presidential form of government shall be nailed and coffined by this noble house in the beginning of this debate itself. "Jai Hind"

Prime minister was glowing with anger and tension. His sugar shot up. He found that his own members are engrossed in the speech of Prof. Rishi Bharat. He knows that next two speakers are excellent orator chosen by the communist, Jayaraj M.P.and Deccan Muslim party president, Mr. Anjuman Baig. He sent a note to Home Minister.

Speaker told, "The next speaker..."

There was shouting and chaos. Ruling party members numbering 50 to 60 moved to the well of house and demanded to expunge the entire speech of Rishi Bharat. They threw the papers on the tables and pulled mikes. The opposition got up and was about move to the well. But Rishi Bharat stopped them. He saw the Prime Minister is rushing out in anger and ministers were running behind him. Speaker shouted among the pandemonium. *"House is adjourned for the day".*

Rishi was standing in the lawn with opposition leaders. Phone rang up. *"Well done Professor Sab, you have broken the great dream of a prime minister as a glass jar and turned it to 100 pieces."*

Sameer maharaj, I shall thank you. Your team provided the whole synopsis, back up and I myself felt the magic effect. Half of your notes is yet to be transcribed as speech"

"Don't bother, the snake that has encircled over our legs will not leave without biting- a Tamil Sayings. You will have opportunity once more to fight against this bill."

"Mr.Madan Vyas, the whole speech of Rishi Bharat is prepared at TIME LINE office. Yester night, 8.30 p.m. my officer saw the M.P. and a team of editors holding some papers and interacting

at the entrance of Time Line news office." Ravindra Pradan,IG Secret Intelligent Bureau was on the mobile line.

"Patak Katri, this is Madan Vyas'

"To-morrow, ash down- Times Line".

CHAPTER XVIII - DEC.2014

`SOMETIMES, DEMOCRATIC SOLUTIONS, SUSPENSION OF BILL OF RIGHTS CAN BE OVERWRITTEN BY EMPLOYING POWERFUL, INSANE, PAID MERCINERIES. THEY HAVE DIFFERENT LANGUAGE TO SILENCE THE VOICE OF FREEDOM THAT DISTURB PEACE OF THE RULERS OF STATE.'

Delhi................

It was almost 09.45 P.M. Police Headquarters of Delhi was alerted by the mobile police petrol that LIFELINE building is surrounded by more than hundred hooligans shouting, holding large sticks, weapons and lot of flags. Thousands of stones were thrown to break the glasses.

"Jai NPP. Those who clash with us will land in the sand". "See, our power to-day and remember ever in your life."

Indian type political vandalisms always will be rhythmic slogans and setting off buses or buildings in flame is the special effect for all the political arson and riots.

Patak katri, our local MLA is leading the group sir," Inspector on petrol called the head quarters and turned the police vehicle to that direction. While nearing the spot, stern order came from control room to the inspector to turn to Tilak Nagar as they expect certain trouble there. Inspector tried to explain that some goons are surrounding the Press and bombs are exploding at LIFE LINE. Some terror groups are carrying lethal weapons and hand bombs. They are waiting to massacre any one coming out. PatakKatri mobile rang up.

"Move back, before some press man identified your group. We are sending RAF in half an hour, to term it that it is terror action."

"The whole afternoon the RAF men were guarding the office and our plan was to finish the operation was blocked by them till 4.00 p.m. Again you are sending them".

"Home Ministry has told Central Research and Analysis Bureau to depute Rapid Action Force there. If Colonel. Fernando comes there, he will arrest you under Anti-Terrorism Act. Fool, you know that, court can alone stop your life in jail. He is given the power to shoot at sight by defense. We cannot take the risk of being exposed. You do what we say", order came sternly.

But the Police Petrol van in spite of high level direction, did not take a U turn. Parking the vehicle at a distance, the inspector signaled the policeman to respond the wireless and moved towards the spot. Inspector identified the gang Leaderpatakwas prominently controlling the operation violence. Fortunately, not a single human cry was heard from the building. After witnessing this hooliganism, officer silently returned to his vehicle. Policemen sitting behind questioned who these gangsters are. Inspector told his driver to go. Again, curious two police men repeated *"Who are they?"*

Without turning his head the Inspector of Police said, *"Bastards, rabies dogs of Delhi"*.

Suddenly one guy jumped put and changed his shirt. Ran fast to the building shouting and dancing. As he was rushing through the crowd, took someone`s flag and someone's head band and tied in on his head.

"Time line editor ko Maro, Maro dushman Sameer komaro"

He took his mobile and captured a close video of the burning building and also the MLA and his team, running here and there shouting, dancing like a mad guy and holding a flag. His drama was so exiting and Inspector was little bit worried. If this guy is identified and caught by this mob? In six minutes he ran back. Before nearing the jeep he looked back and threw the flag and ran to his squad.

Spitting and blowing hot, Pathak Katri ordered his driver to turn the van to Tilak Nagar and asked his men to run out of the scene. Three minutes the whole crowd retreated fast. One area leader was shouting, *"From the morning that bastard was patrolling here. Deadly bastard he will mercilessly shoot us-run, run away fast"*.

Another goon took his bike reached Patak and showed his palm. One cash bundle fell in his hand and he vanished in away from the scene. There was big explosion and a huge fire behind him. Powerful bombs were thrown inside and the whole building was turning to ash.

"I will get Rs.10000-00 to night without demanding bribe or regular hunting. My friend is running a local TV Channel. To-Morrow morning 6.00 am. His channel will flash this."

"Will I recommend your name to our higher up, for collecting valuable evidence" Inspector laughed.

That police was still operating his mobile, without lifting his head, *"Sir, It is already mailed to you and to my friend. I will collect that Rs.10000-00 and you take department award in full sir, please?"*

Mobile of Mr. Sameer gave a loud siren. *"Sir, videographer, Maharishi. They have burned entire press. One police petrol van came near and returned back. From distance, the inspector watched the scene and returned in the darkness. One Police man among them acted as the part of mob and took out close video with his mobile. Hundred to hundred and fifty local rowdies were around all paid mob. Three gang leaders were collecting their payment there itself from the MLA."*

Col. Fernando who was in conference call, responded, *"Tell me, were you able to cover up, whaoo,good" .Whole video must reach me. Now abscond or I have to arrange another mission rescue you too. Our force has received orders to go as bombs exploded. Go for cover, O.K.""Sameer, I am sorry, the whole press is destroyed. They unwittingly wanted to shift it on terrorist, and entrusted investigation to RAF. We have solid evidences."*

Secret Intelligent Bureau, Chief. Ravindra Pradhan, ranking special I.G. was almost in the second round of his usual Royal salute seventh peg. Someone called in the unlisted land line. *"Sir, whole Life Line office turned to ashes."*

"How many were burnt?"

"No sir, upto four p.m., RAF Chief was there in the office. So the gang which went there returned three times. Upto 8.00 p.m., they were fearing to go near the office. You know this bloody colonel, whole Delhi piss, if they see him 100 feet nearby, now. He must be the person who might have evacuated the whole employees. It was almost mystery to everyone. No body was able to trace how the inmates vacated. Our men says that only twenty or thirty were causally moving out after office hours and the vans loaded with papers. More than hundred workers in printing session were neatly transported. Usually much earlier by 4-00 p.m. onwards to-day. They had definite information, everyone escaped. Alive". S.I.B. Chief Pressure shot up .He shouted, *"Then what the hell you were doing?"*

The man on the other side was nervous.

"The man who is behind this escape operation is RAF Chief, Sir. We reported at 3.00 p.m. You replied wait till those bastards leave."

Mr. Pradhan shouted at the pitch, *"do not spit back, idiots, find out. Tell pressmen that the whole operation is Sameer*

Base's brain child. The press is running in loss and with huge debt. It`s all for insurance claims and to gain political sympathy, the directors themselves arranged this fire".

After a breath, Pradhan again told *"Tell, this is Kashmere Terror gang`s blast".*

The other man hurried responded, *"No sir, we will be exposed, Sir. All People watched this know that some Bajrang Sena are involved and they came with the flags and did all these hooligans. Some ten to 15 fellows were taking video in their mobile in that crowd."*

This man is happy and start walking to his home. Tomorrow Home minister will burn the ass of his chief. He imagined four inches whole in the twenty kilo bums of his boss. Pradhan gulped another large and shouted *"Go to hell."*

On his desk, the large photo of Colonel Fernando published in the paper. He poured the remaining Whisky in his cup on the face of Fernando and took his lighter and burnt the same. Now Sameer has escaped out of his hand. Where is his hide out? Pradhan`s private line buzzed. "*Yes Sir*",

Pradhan rushed to the office car. He forgot to close the whisky bottle. Inside the Home ministry office, there was a mid night Press meet. Press Secretary is trying to pacify the angry reporters *"No life loss. We are shocked that certain anti social gang had done with a vengeance. May be militants from Kashmir. Yes, RAF is investigating. We do not know where Mr.Sameer and his family members are? We have told Intelligent Bureau Chief Mr. Pradhan to personally visit. He had gone to the incident spot and at any time he is expected, Oh, He has come".*

Press secretary knows that he cannot further bluff and left the table. Mr. Pradhan tried to be poised and steady. Two extra pegs, to day, still steady. Whisky smell coming out and it is difficult for him to face the camera and light.

"Investigation is going on, it is premature to brief".

"Sir, did you arrest some hooligans, we had seen them burning the building and police was there? "Some reporter shouted.

"Who gathered evidences of the criminals, we do not know?" he signaled to his guard. Another civil servant who was standing, came to the front and announced, *"Press meet is over".*

One pressman shouted *"Mr. Pradhan, still ignorance? Go and switch on Webster channel they have repeated the telecast 11 times in the past two hours".*

Mr. Pradhan was lead to the back office. He does not know whether he will be blasted for his drunken status or his one line statement or for allowing Sameer and his men to escape. He shall go home immediately.

The whisky bottle, he had forgotten to seal, perhaps, he can go and empty the same. To-morrow, what is waiting for him? All these government will fellows get fucked, if these political fellows do not get what they want, including procuring of some prostitutes. O.K. Let them fire him on his burnt ass.

Superindent of police called him *"Sir, Renaissance corporate CEO called us and fired. I explained, but he is not willing to hear?"*

"*What, who the hell, why?* "His mental balance gone. Some shit job I can do than this I.G. service.

Phone from his Office desk, *"Sir, six months back, LIFE LINE installed all Proto type machines. Renaissance Capital limited gave the loan. Renaissance Insurance Corporation, in turn compelled LIFE LINE to have a comprehensive insurance for 11 crores, machines, building and transports. Insurance includes fire, earthquake, riots and arsons, sir"*

"Ask him to suck, Madan Vyas, yes, Madan via..." Another gulp of whisky went into his throat and he slipped on the sofa, in two minutes he was snoring heavily.

CHAPTER XIX - DEC 2014

HE, THE DEVIL IN ME IS STRONGER. ENDLESS, HATRED AND VENOM ARE BOILING IN MY BLOOD. I STRIKE TERROR EVERYWHERE, TO SAVE MY CROWN FOREVER …

"Under holy oath, I swear to risk my family, life and wealth to protect and safeguard life and regime of my revered leader, Shri Premnath Mawa, prime Minister of India. He is the leader of the Indian Reich and the people. Our supreme commander for our movement, our brave solider, our light in dark hours and the scorcher of our enemies………..."

Morning sun was bright over the Red Fort. This is the second day of their conference. Two lakhs saffron army raising the hand in front and taking oath. In Sanskrit language people will say prayers, not knowing the meaning of the words. Lakhs are piously repeating an oath recited from the rostrum.

The Red Fort was filled with two lakhs saffron men who came to hail their charismatic leader. The Indian Civil Service Act, was amended a day before removing the restriction on civil and ex-army officials joining RRS. One speaker was loudly shouting before the mike, *"Never was leader born, nor will be. God has destined him to rule the Billion people. His divine power derived from god is unshakable."*

Har Har Premnath! Jay, Jay Mawa! Premnath is our vision! Premath future of the nation!

Speeches followed, tracing the days of legend to the history of success of NPP. There was a demand to rewrite the history of the nation. Sea of superstition and bundles of classical caste ridden social system, were all sanctified with a cry to issue orders to bring back old social order. Nithyanswami inflamed the crowd. *"My loving Rashtirya Rakshna soliders, the rebellion spirit in me very strong. With our glorious past of Sathya, Dwapara, Thretha, and present Kaliyugas, four time life cycles of our earth and divine Avatars in every Yuga, we were able build a Hindu kingdom. But, we lost this punya boomi to foreign borns in the end of Kali Yuga. But we are destined to rebuild the Baratha Kanda. To-day, we are putting a long step in our political history. We are going to revive Hindu Bhoomi. In fact, I see an avatar in the human form to-day. Our Premnath Mawa has come to revive the Hinduism and build a kingdom of Hindus in India. Prophesies and the godly signs are showing that we are going to be in the golden era of great governance. Nostradamus 16th Century Astrologer from France, predicted that our great Hindu leader will rule India from 2014. Those who oppose by being a Hindu, the demons, they have to undergo a mental therapy. Those who are from other religions will have a realization of truth and automatic indoctrination of their belief. They shall know that they cannot convert this holy land by inducting unholy ideas of other religions.* P.M. was silently looking at some notes. He is sure that Swami Speech will receive a fireworks to-morrow in the front page, over shadowing his oration. He is going to face more brick bats. But, he loves the diversion of the opponents. They will again recite his name thousand times. Allegations will vanish as passing clouds overnight. His name will be resounding in the ears of people.

"We shall form a Uniform Civil code. Permitting Muslims to have four wives shall be banned."

Day Dawns reporter was whispering to his colleague, *"this man is jealous, because he is not having, even one official wife. I am always surprised by the statistical claims, my dear. Every census show that in ratio, between Hindu-Muslims are narrowing down by one percent for every ten years. Muslims as on to-day are 13% to 14 in the latest census and it was almost 11% during Independence. How this man says that Muslims are going to be more than Hindus in 2020? According to him, Muslim women in India have to deliver 62 crores children in six years. Is it possible? Secondly, man-women ratio of Muslim is almost the same with more number of male per thousand. If so, assuming that one Muslim marries four wives, then, three fourth of Muslim boys will have no wives? What they will do man? If this swami demands same provision for Hindus, bloody you will have no girl to marry all through life.* His friend was already wild as he is not able to get one coffee house in the vicinity. *"Oh shit, what a great mathematician you are! Idiot, when you come to political meeting, you shall simply hear them and clap your hand. Don't use your brain, I told you hundred times. I have recorded all your questions, either you get me a good coffee or I will ask Swami himself to answer you, when he comes down. What is your preference? "His friend's finger was pointing out the Café.*

P.M was in a terrible disturbed mood. His attempt to push through the Constitutional amendments has failed. More the time taken by parliament, the more damage the bill will suffer. Madan Vyas spoke for half an hour. "*Crores of Indians are attracted to our magnetic leader. Those who says that I am not, please go and have a blood test to find out what kind of adulteration you have. Perhaps you may be suffering with a new iron-patriotism-deficiency.*" The whole crowd cheered and laughed. Vyas told the crowd that Prime Minister will address the final rally at MEERUT HIGH WAY to-morrow.

More than twelve organizations, who worked along with RRS in different name and banner participated. At seven that night, an important secret meeting took place. Conspiracies for a nocturnal attacks were hatched.

"We will teach a lesson! Every corner of the city shall see the blood flow. In future no fellow will carry the flag of other oppositions and speak against NPP."

CRAB sensed terror action in some of the areas in Turkmen gate, Jamai nagar, Seemapur, Jame Masjid. Old Delhi slums were targeted, especially the Muslim settlements which had decisively voted against N.P. Party. The lawless ruffian gangs started moving for a genocide. Payments met to hirlings. The fury of intolerance, fanatical frenzy, emboldened by the historical success of capturing the central power, now opened them an opportune to revenge the minority.

Opium gurus were let out on road with their semi-nude morcha and trishul weapons making horror shows. CRAB sent a warning report to PMO office. They gave the list of criminals involved.

10 years before Desh Hindu Parishat held their international conference in Karnataka. Gambling on the emotional surge, the frenzy gangs went round Muslim hutments and simply stabbed and butchered. Many poor Hindu immigrants from other state were also were killed because of their common hutments. It was recorded as a clash between the communities inside the slum. 40 to 60 Muslims and 20 to 30 Hindus and other communities were murdered ruthlessly by the organized gang which came from M.P. to the conference. Police completely blacked out the information. Muslims understood, fury of the swords of enemy is not a horrid weapon to face, but silence of the saviours is not pardonable.

A gangs of local rogues moved parallelly, in the city with long swords, country made bombs, pistols and rods in hundreds of travel vans, open jeep and more in two wheelers were going round with a threat and shouting. The local mafia was also moving along with communal groups. The signal was for ethnic cleaning is yet to come. But the local gang had different agenda of slum clearing for builders lobby. For these forces, slashing humans and walking through bloody path are irresistible passion.

"The Blood purge will be worse than the invasion of Huns and barbarous Chengiskhan. Carnage. Massacre scenes of India`s Partition will be re-enacted." Shouted Rohit prajapathi, a gangster, Secretary Vadodara Labour Union. Drawing a

salary of Rs.8000-00 from a factory, owner of two bungalows and a BMW car and a vault with 12 crores of hard cash. He is a captain of the reserve army to provoke violence or to fuel fire, to silence the opponents, wherever NPP wants to create political problem. Wherever his gang passes, the routes will be in flame.

He cried, *"Will this be same mayhem of 1969, in 1981, in 1985, in 1990, in1992 or something unimaginable like 1947, we do not know. But the blood spilled in the capital will send a red signal all over India."*

"To day, there is no identity crisis nor someone to halt us on our way. We, the Rashtriya Rakshna Samiti and the state are inseparable. Many of our pogrom and decade long bitter battles will be answered at Midnight or on the dawn. Where the fire will break out, who will burn whom, when we will end the curse of this nation all will get a reply to-morrow morning. We command and they obey-this will be the final verdict of to-morrow." His journalist friend whose is connected to Central Bureau of Investigation, Ahmadabad revealed that 8 to 9 secret meetings had taken Place among the Rashtirya Rakshna Samithi groups. He informed that some of the old guards are afraid that it will result in mayhem and carnage. Human valour and massive armed saffron brigade will be damaged, if the conflicts turned to be modern war with bombs and rockets, missiles, local factory build proto-type model drones. In Delhi, arsenal procurement of several hundred crores for the past 3 months is reported. Communal clash will become a civil war. It will take another 25 years to rebuild the nation. But the twelve inner group is determined. Now the main operation has been taken over by Madan Vyas.

Especially, areas that are sensitive and vulnerable, the extremist groups, Muslims and young bloods started to build their own defense strategy months back. They know death is sure to come, but determined not to end without making equal fall of human bodies on the other side.

Stone throwing in some area took place. A Torch Light March with saffron flags took place among the slums. Four shops in the Asahapur locality was burnt. Two cars carrying DMP picture was stopped and burnt in another place. Next day dawn in Turkmen gate, the dead body carriers were ready to be deployed. The sword wielding RHP were on rampage, destroying markets, stoning, damaging moving vehicles, blocking roads, targeting minorities turned Delhi a graveyard of culture and civilization. Police force was totally frozen in fear and were afraid to intervene. RRS and their allied organizations are pouring in New Delhi to back PM's historic move of government.

Report started flowing that nationwide protest is raising against the stone throwing, violence and candle light parade led by educated sections of the society. Largest procession of workers of hundreds of industries suddenly came to the streets in Kolkata. Many progressive student movements came with a slogan- *stop communal menace, Stop Delhi violence, arrest the brutal. Is it Delhi Police-dead police? Control violence or Resign Premnath, Suddenly, University student from JNU came in thousands and police had a tough time to control as they were started moving to PM house.* "Students are aware that this violence and communal conflict will turn to into fire and it will end nowhere without burning the half the nation.

It was Friday. Muslim masses went in large number to Masque. After the prayer, meeting took place. Burning speeches reached a shocking level, some of the young men were for a holy crusade war and swore that they will shed their blood and soul as martyr will make Allah happy. Senior Imam Bukari calmly told them that repercussions will be a national conflict or even civil war.

He spoke, *"We bow before law not one inch before brute force- Let death give us the honour we long for. We never will accept a Jewish status under Nazi regime. But we shall not injure the democracy by our errors. Our Masjid committee has decided, we will not clash with RRS. Three days we will retreat and defend our localities. We are not alone, several million Hindu friends all over the nation has decided to counter this. In one hour all the RRS state office bearers and M.Ps houses at their states, will be seized as per the report received from our friends. Our community leaders in four states confirmed that twenty thousand people have surrounded the house of NPP M.P. at Rajasthan and Tamilnadu. Police is rushing to control them. Please respect our friends. Mumbai one lac people are at India Gate two hours before, for twenty four hours dharana. Promise in the name of Allah that we will not harm the peace. Give us three days of silence and peace. Delhi shall not witness dead bodies and stream of blood. Promise us."*

A wave of campaign suddenly unleashed all over the country and 200 M.P. have contacted their states. Huge anti-communal march is shaking the nation. Instructions were sent by all parties to organize massive 12 hours rally or squatting before 300 NPP M.Ps house forcing them to appeal to P.M. to stop this holocaust at Delhi. NPP MPs contacted party president and sought permission to rush back home as the families are facing tension and pressure. Home Minister received information that 10000 demonstrators are now sitting before his home at Bhopal.

Two o clock, in the afternoon, Mr. Sameer Babu called him. *"Bukari Sab, We appreciate your most sensible yet painful decision. Please keep your boys not to venture out not ventilate their reaction. Yes, the attack is confirmed. We had collected 14 videos of stone throwing, intimidations, torch light parade, shops and car burnings and hate campaigns. We have collected 300000 signatures and sent one set to PMO office and another U.N. Human right commission through mail. UN and international organizations have received the video clippings. They met half an hour before. Twenty seven social organizations worked together with flash news. Social media is activated now. Imam Sab, you are interested national harmony.*

Information we are receiving 88,000 individuals are communicating 22 million people on the danger of communal clash. A new chain campaign has started "Tell the Nation." BBC, CNN and eight international news channels have released the clippings and Government of India is actually is highly embarrassed. All the video clippings are now reaching your Mosque office. All the international human right organizations have condemned. Worldwide reactions are stunning. People are coming to street every town and cities. You please hold your boys for another 15 to 20 hours."

Imam innocently asked *"How do you know the numbers?"*

Sameer explained how social media protests are responded and how everyone will know how many have sent the protest by viewing and how many have promised further to participate physically over the programmes organized by the organizations in every city.

Imam was really moved. *"Sameer Babu, they attempted to kill you, they burnt your Time line, and still you are fighting after all your personal tragedies."*

"Imam Sab, How do expect me to be in golden castle all the time. Let me also run for my life, then only I can sense how painful life is as fugitive. Forget me, I am giving all these clippings of past 8 hours. 27 cities in India, processions have commenced and one lakh marching at Mumbai. Talk to someone at Mumbai and Kolkata, you can see the angry reactions. They burnt my Life Line but they also kindled my inner fire to fight. Please do not react in Delhi. You please take the lead and instruct all the imams and Muslim organizations"

"If blood bath takes place, if the government of India and the Prime Minister do not stop this, we will demand a Nuremburg type trail as conducted against Nazi leaders-Signed by President, World Peace Movement, London started scrolling in the TV News Channels. Internationally, seventeen organizations were actively spreading the news of attack done yester night and the next move for a massive massacre debated, dissected. RRS groups found that their plots are back firing all over the world. Surprisingly, all the Delhi Muslims are totally silent, not one leader is prepared to talk to T.V.channels. One TV anchor went to Turkman gate and tried to provoke an Imam and asked him, how they

are going to beat back the RRS. The Imam took a glass of tea and asked the T.V. anchor to drink. While drinking he moved coolly commenting, *"Boy, I have paid for your tea, enjoy and move, O.K."*.

The live telecast showed the calm and brave face, they are showing in a most horrid and threatening condition. They were casual in their day to day business including driving the vegetable Lorries to the RRS venue for their morning kitchen supply. RRS President U.P. was burning on seeing the total fearless movements of Muslims in the city. What has happened to them? He switched on the TV. Mochas, red flags, student walking out of schools and colleges, candle light mochas, banners of anti-communal slogans, city after city, state after state and massive demonstration before Indian embassies in London, Washington, Paris and Bonn and Moscow. Bloody shit, he never had seen such worldwide movements. All fellows, who were knock down in the general election have joined all over the nation and showing us black flag and burning our ass!

Sameer told "Sab, *All the mails are also documented, dispatching will be done in two minutes to you. Tell your boys to mail to their friends."*

*"What is the Purpose"*Bukari asked.

"Your boys are experts, ask them, they will tell you". Especially "New age Muslim" website group. They have wonderful network. They have already contacted all these seventy organizations, one lakh people have reached of various national integration movements have reached Ahmadabad for a procession. In

Kerala, Bangalore, Kolkata and Chennai with Black badges people marching. In Delhi, the local news channels are blacking out. Government is receiving information that they face international sanction and demand to effect oil blockade. In Britain and Washington, Indian Embassies had witnessed demonstration two to three hours back. U.N. Secretary has called Indian Representative and told them to inform their prime minister to stop this hooliganism and violence. Bukari Sab, you please wait in 10 minutes Prof. Nadir is bringing everything to show this to your committee, in your Mosque. People are with you everywhere."

"Can I tell you one thing Sameer quoting the Holy Quran, "He may reward those who believe and do good works? It is these who will have forgiveness and gain an honourable provisions. - Allah will always be with you, my boy". Sameer was really moved as though he is getting a blessing from his parents. *"Thank you, for your blessing Imam sahib, I demand nothing more than this. Can I tell you one a word? Your and your Moulvies saved the nation form a calamity by controlling your boys in spite they were burning with anger and humiliation."*

Oh, Insha Allah, Allah will always be merciful and safe guard us." He was sitting in his office. Prof. Nadir came with his laptop. The whole India is reacting. People were shouting and angrily protesting against the wild and barbaric behaviours of the hooligans. Bukhari was really shocked to see the waves and waves of people displaying protest banners. It is really an unbelievable huge democratic movements. Tear drops fell on his white kurtha. This nation loves my people. This sublime happiness and the expression of brotherhood is more than million tonnes of gold. It wiped out the pains in him.

PMO office was buzzing with large number of visitors. Many state leaders were sitting to see the Prime Minister. Strange Illusions of creating a movement against the minority is boomeranging. Whoever charted the programme with Predatory instinct are going to bleed. PMO Chief Secretary received a call from UN representative from India . *"Look, Mr.Ramsay, there seems to be continuous riot and chaos in Delhi. There is an organised plan for human genocide to night. More than 3 million emails have almost blocked the UN net traffic. Photos of stone throwing, torchlight parade by saffron organizations and videos have flooded the human right commission. Never had they received so much, so much mails from individuals and organizations. From Geneva, Human Right Commission had sent to me a mail. I have forwarded the communications. Major western press have collected the copies of communications from UN office. He had clearly warned, despite of all the warnings, if any unpalatable incidents or human right violations take place, documents will be placed in UN Council to take action against Indian Government. U. S. Press had released headings, predicting blood bath. In U.K. Guardian has consolidated the past violence and massacres and an article has appeared on line. To-day, One hour after a press meet Human Right Commission chairman is much agitated. I am told to respond. Consult with PM and please respond. Any official vagueness will be condemned internationally".* Chief Secretary went inside and PM was sitting with home minister and Madan Vyas. Madan Vyas simply waved his hands to ask PMO secretary to go out. But Ramsay placed two page note on the table of P.M. before moving out. Last line was unusually in bold letters. *"Prime Minister is advised to reply in One Hour i.e. 16.00 hrs."*

In the midnight, 3000 Savakis stealthily were moving round. To-day, their plan was to complete the program. Dangerous weapons, fuel cans, country pistols and iron bars were held by hundreds of speaks. Four different areas were targeted and they moved in Jeeps, vans and trucks to their spots. Seventy to eighty trucks suddenly appeared from nowhere, in all eight places. SCRP policemen nearly 4000 jumped and started running in all directions with their rifles. Similar SCRP troops moved to other slums too in as a wave. More than 23000 were arrested with hand bombs and inflammable oils, daggers, rods and dangerous weapons. Wherever resistance was seen, immediately they were answered by smoke bombs, and rubber bullets. Announcements were repeated that the sevaks will face bullets. Shoot at sight is issued if any group found causing violence and arson. All were rounded off. Seventeen miles away from Delhi, the whole lot of hooligans were let out in a big school ground, wherein their meals and food, tea were waiting. No names were noted, nor were cases booked. Bombs and pistols were alone seized for their own safety by SCRP men.

The mob landed from different directions. In front of them, ***Madan Vyas*** was waiting there with his Z security. Vyas was about speak to them. One Criminal Investigation officer came to him, *"Sir, nearly 2000 other local rowdy elements are also in the crowd and it is not wiser to allow them out as they* *will not bother to hear your words. Already 110 country made pistols, bombs and 300 hand grenades were seized in front of the press people."* Madan was perplexed, *"What to do, now."* Criminal Investigation officer advised, *"We will save our face together. You ask your state leaders here to segregate their cadres and form a separate special meet for 15 minutes. The remaining we will round it off and we will report that we have cornered all anti-social elements with arms and bombs who were trying to create violence and riots to loot the slums. We know these rogue elements and many faces are known to us."*

"You issue statements absolving your party cadres and also report that law and order were restored by Delhi Police."

Madan Vyas was completely taken aback by the wonderful suggestion and smiled at the officer and told, *"You all shall come to my party leader position leaving this dress, for such flash ideas"*. Out of the crowd police picked up 1700 to 1800 goondas and again loaded them in their vans.

In next one hour morning T.Vs flashed the faces of thugs and row of arms and grenades captured by the Special Central Reserve police with arrested 3300 rowdy elements. Delhi riot is an opposition game and their paid gangs to denigrate and damage the ruling government.

All the state leaders called the cadres and instructed that the Maha Samvesha, the biggest public meeting is arranged in Meerut Road, where P.M. is going to come with an historic issue. Members are advised to maintain party directions. By 8.00 a.m. all the sevaks were returned to their camps.

Home minister briefed to his ministers that four lakhs RRS members have landed and tension was mounting. *"We hold the nation in a threat and ransom. Such a massive response is seen. While opposition is diverted, if we spread fear and political coercions, the passing of the bill is not impossible. See to-morrow, we are adopting alternative strategy. All our members shall be inside the house whole day. Other things we will do"*

"Yes sir," how it can be done in Rajya Sabha? After that 50% of the states shall pass this amended bill to be approved by President of India."

"Do not bother all those things, we will finish our business in Lok Sabha to-morrow"

"Sir, we have to give notice, copies to be circulated among the members. Debate has already commenced with the paper publication. Do we circulate the amendments?

"All procedures can wait, we can amend the regulation and we can abide to all procedures later." Home Minister briskly moved out.

Minister for foreign affairs was totally puzzled, *"If the bills passed, some secretary of foreign affairs will be appointed and he will go all over the earth, what will be our fate?"*

CHAPTER XX - DEC 2014

"NECESSITY IS THE ARGUEMENT OF TYRANTS; IT IS THE CREED OF SLAVES."

Parliament was buzzing with an unusual attendance of members. The day New Age Party and left parties wanted to place an urgent motion about the breach of law and order and dangerous pogrom of communal elements. NPP members raised the issue of death of Mr. Baji Rao, the tallest leader of RRS in car accident and Mr.Purandar Vittala, their cultural wing President. Madan puri, Patna M.P. got up,

"Hon. Speaker, even police is yet to identify whether the co-passenger died in the accident is Sri. Purandarji or someone else, why the hon. Members wants to pay homage to him. Are you sure that he is also murdered?" There was a Pandemonium and shocking reaction from the ruling party became uncontrollable.

"Expunge his remarks", Home Minister got up and told the speaker. Rishi Barath got up and asked speaker to permit the member to speak.

Madhav puri, the parliament member again shouted, *"What is wrong in my statement? Who has killed Mr. Baji Rao, he may be your leader, but many of you do not know that Poojya Guruji and I were 20 years close friends before I left your party? Pundit Purandarji and my relationship is just brotherly. Your senior leaders know? Do not try to black out the details of their assassination? I am not going to be silent and I will follow the criminals here, even if the same brutality is applied to me by the assassination squad. I will be demanding a judicial enquiry against Mafia leaders who organised this assassination. We know, who had done this. If I am jail for my statement, I am ready to face the crude authoritarianism."*

Speaker rose up and told that as the matter is under investigation, he can wait to complete the process. Members started raising for a judicial enquiry and some ruling party members objected. Home Minister turned and found that sixty percent of ruling party members are silent and in fact expressing their dissent against the government`s attempt to hush up.

Speaker told that the House is adjourned for half an hour. When the house again assembled, the member got up and told *"I apologize if I had hurt the sentiment of the members. I have a great respect for both the tall leaders of this country. I still do want to pay homage to Mr. Baji Rao, who is no more with us. I demand the house to pass a resolution for an impartial enquiry on his assassination. Mr. Purandra Vittala my heart is not convinced and I pray for his long life. I walk out of the parliament to avoid paying homage to that living genius. In the world this is the only parliament which is mourning for a living great leader."* Opposition leaders simultaneously got up and told that they are mourning for the death of Poojya Baji Rao and another unknown victim of conspiracy. After two minutes walked out.

Home minister secretly confided to his colleague, *"This rascal is a very close associate of Purandar. Some mystery is in his language He knows more than what he says. Be careful with this spy. Do not put inquiry commission or some bloody things."*

While all are walking out one Member approached Madav puri and asked why he exposed Mr.Purandar's existence.

"I have to disclose to this house that one who is dead by accident is actually assassinated and the other one is still alive, whom they call dead. Hell, let NPP members know and believe me before they mourn for the death. I have courage to voice the truth. I will go beyond these walls too to-day to reveal"

His friend mocked, *"Be careful man, they will put you in the 'Missing' column first and later send you up"* His finger was showing the roof. Some six opposition members were found in the seat.

The Law minister got up. There was no agenda for him. It is a rare scene for the ministers to get up and speak in this house. All were done by honourable P.M. He found that only NPP members were in their seat. *"Hon. Speaker, powers provided under article 368 of the constitution to amend, to add, to repeal we are placing 99th and 100th amendment to the constitution of India to bring a historic change in the fundamental formation of Government for the better democratic and strong government to turn our nation healthy super power of the world."*

Six opposition members were suddenly electrocuted with 440 volt shock. Other members were yet to return to their seat. Bell in the lounge rang up and house again commenced the business. But the doors were not opened. In the Lower house the bill was introduced.

Law minister informed the house, *"I hereby place 99th and 100th constitutional amendments before the house and appeal to the members to approve the same."*

Preamble:

"99th Amendment to the constitution is placed to repeal the articles No 54 to 55 in order to amend and to retain other relevant provisions of clauses, intentions, expression appearing in any other articles of the constitution about the election of President and vice-president of India. The repeal of the provisions referred above is to enable the election of President and Vice President of India by direct voting by the people of India. The elected President will be empowered to hold both legislative and executive powers".

"ARTICLE NO.54 AND 55 THUS REPEALED"

The 100th Amendment incorporated as new article 56(A) replacing the original.

"No person except a natural born citizen or citizen of India as on this date of adoption of this constitutional amendment shall be eligible to the office of the president, subject to other regulations so written, modified, amended, be voted directly by the people of the country as per the regulations formulated

by the election commission of India. Vice-president nominated along the presidential candidate as co-runner will be declared elected along with the President and no separate election need to be conducted."

Lok Sabha, amended both the constitutional provisions with absolute majority of 288 members voted in favour and 6 opposition members did not vote. But they could not walk out as the doors were closed. They were treated as present but abstained from voting as per the regulation. Lok Sabha adjourned for that day. Constitutional provision dating back 26th Nov 1949 lost its first validity in the same chamber of Lok Sabha after 65 years in Dec 2014. Historic amendments were passed in a historic time of 11 minutes. Ruling party members seems to be perturbed and not rejoiced by the success. One senior member commented to his colleagues, *"are we losing the moral values of this sanctum? We will be publically shamed for such breaches, politically condemned and judicially humiliated."*

House is adjourned. PM was met by Speaker. *"Sir, this voting will be easily treated as void by court as we failed to adhere many procedures. Most embarrassing situation".*

"Speaker sir, to-morrow, you agree to discuss with the opposition demand after a prolonged negations. We will go for an unending debate in Parliament. Our passing of the bill in Lok Sabha is important for our massive campaign. The purpose of hurried voting is a political strategy. Let us debate. Lok sabha passed the bills. Four years'time we are having. Supreme Court cannot interfere. It can discuss only about the constitutional validity of the act later. Let post-mortem continue, till we get majority

in Rajya sabha. Let the opposition get their throat dried. We are not in a hurry. We have to build a very big campaign, you know?"

Prime Minister hurriedly left to the mammoth rally at Meerut High way. He is carrying a message to his men for a political renaissance in India.

"So amazingly brilliant or cunning this P.M.!" Speaker of the Lok Sabha was speechless!

ooo

CHAPTER XXI

"LIBERTY IN REALITY IS ONLY A MYTH. POLITICAL FREEDOM IS NOT A FACT, BUT AN IDEA PEOPLE BELIEVE MERE PROMISES ARE CHOSEN WEAPONS TO RULE NATIONS FOREVER"

Like ocean waves, a sea of humans are moving in the conclave. Crowd is frenzy and uncontrollable. Three lakhs saffron army, organizers decided to keep the whole program in Meerut Highway not at Red Fort as originally planned. Army tents were erected with 3 lakhs cots and beds. 10000 police were deputed for security. In fact, it is all furnished as hunting jaunt of the kings of Indian kingdom. Season is cold but no cadre felt the coldness. Nineteen thousand vehicles are parked.10000 Buses are standing wherever they had small lane. From the top, crowd could watch the whole meeting by sitting at a distance of 1000 meters. SCRP was afraid of the security risk. Meerut Highways is swarmed with vehicles of all types and all brands. Knowing the risk, a helipad was constructed 2000 to 3000 meters behind the giant stage and VVIPs were allowed to land in helicopters. The whole area was treated no man land.

Morning 11.00 A.M, chief of CRAB was with home minister. RAF Colonel and Major were in the team. Home Minister was appraised by the Special Central Reserve Police. SCRP are deputing 42 battalion about 42000 men. Chief Director of Central Police will personally monitor. 1500 CCTVs, seven helicopters, forty eight gun mounted tankers will be providing securities. Thirteen trucks full of special force with A.K.47 and grenades and fire arms will be kept at high security zone. His briefing continued for more than half an hour. He was explaining with a power point program what are all the security arrangements done around the ground. All towered construction in the surrounding were manned with SCRP gun man. All the three lakhs audience will go under security check. For security reason, no one will be allowed to enter with any baggage in the inner five rings. Home Minister praised even American President did not have such security arrangements.

"*Are you satisfied with the arrangement*", Home Minister turned to Director of CRAB.

"Yes, good, Rapid Action Force is deputing 400 of its men. We will be in the scene with our uniform and identity and electronic devices for communications."

"Why, we have done so much security-why another agency sir?" DG Special Central Reserve police looked at Home Minister.

Chief of CRAB responded, "*Our agency will be there to scan terrorists and dangerous individuals DG sahib: Please hand over the pen drive. We will go through your arrangements once again and to give instruction to you if necessitated. Secondly, we want a video of the whole rally ground at present- a sky view, two kilo meter radius outside the ground".*

SCRP director general understood, that CRAB once exercise its authority all other forces shall obey. "*O.K. Sir*"

Home Minister, "*O.K., thanks, meeting over*".

In the mind of colonel some kind of tension and instinctively some violent alarm. Bloody two terror elements are freely going round in India, after blasting an airport, assassinating three leaders at Hyderabad. Like predators, annihilations, planting of bombs, conducting war within the enemy fort are going on. Oh god, Director General knows how to conduct security check for a sane crowd of 10 lakhs also. But insane brilliant terror brains are not their home birds. Colonel went round the spot. Stage was 18 feet above the crowd. Every higher structure beyond 1000 meters were noted by him and he instructed his men to check and report. Buildings, houses, hotels, construction places were inspected by him and he saw the reserve police occupying those buildings. All those who wanted to have distant dharashan of their messiah by were sitting over the buses, Colonel instructed CRPC to clear them. Reserve police cleared them by 3.00 p.m.

It was 4.10 P.M. CRAB Head Quarters received a call and it was diverted to Major Rampal. Meerut Police commissioner was on the other side. "*Major Rampal, we have a badly wounded Pak terror gang man in our custody. We have admitted him Intensive Care Unit as he was shot-four bullets! He displayed colonel and your photo.*"

The whole mass rally was preceded by a powerful display march past of RRS Saffron brigade. With a military precision the whole salutation was done. Prime Minister Premnath Mawa slowly ascended the stage from the back side of the stage. The whole crowd became frenzy and whole region was reverberating with drums, claps, slogans and shouting. Leaders after leaders were praising him as new Messiah, avatar of the new era. One told that he is the Krishna of Mahabharata to drive the nation to a great power. He was scheduled to address the crowd at 4.40 P.M. Winter will shut down the day light at any time. Colonel was worried. Once visibility is lost, tracing of any ambush is difficult. Even in the morning, it was clearly told to Home Minister, that P.M. address shall commence by 4.30 P.M. maximum. Nobody can tell, when he shall conclude.

"Major.Rampal, one badly wounded Pak terrorist. Not fluent with Urdu. Name Hakkim Surathuasin Ali. He is grievously shot on his shoulder and hip. He is having Mr. Fernando and your photo copies cut out from some Delhi Magazine. He is not disclosing anything to us. But from his few Urdu words, he wants to tell you two something very important information."

"Where is he now?"

"He is in the ICU of Meerutmulti-specialtyHospital and he was shot 12 to 14 hours before, we found him in a road side shrub 2 hours before half dead, huge blood loss and he has recovered and conscious now".

"Any arms, guns"

"No sir, some purse, Indian currency and some old ID of other person called "Ameen Habbib Rasool, France. It seems to be residential permit for migrants from Algeria. But in photo he looks like a Frenchman". Hakkim wants to talk to you now. He told that he is from Musheerabad, Pakistan Occupied Kashmir."

"Rasool photo is new or old. Scan it and send it in color to us from the hospital itself. Can you arrange some Skype or video conferencing with this man immediately? Hospital will have such facilities or some doctors, personal laptops."

Immediately, one young doctor came in his skype account and connected to Major. Hakkim, the silent partner of the dreaded leader, whose visual shades are with him appeared in the screen. He recognized Major. Yes, he is the junior partner moving along with the other terror gang leader, Identified from Vijayawada CCTV. Without any inhibition, Rajpal suddenly talked to him in Kashmiri *"Tell Hakkim are you O.K now?" "Are you from Musheerabad or nearby?"*

Hakkim was really astonished to hear someone talking to him in his tongue and that too a Major in Army. According to him, all Kashmiri people are condemned and not employed by Indian state. Here a Kashmiri talking to him as a friend. He was expecting torture chamber, with crude kicking him in his ass and plucking his nails to extract the known and unknown information. He was warned about brutality, he had seen, he had faced. He had seen the Taliban's treatments in Hindukush regions. He had never heard people talking to him so kindly and friendly manner, except a few boyhood friends or his uncle. *"Shaba, 10 k.m. from Musheerabad."*

This young man is willing to talk. Rampal`s first worry is gone. Had he resisted and tried to be silent and had his chief entered the mass rally by this time, god, the whole nation would have faced an unprecedented havoc and disaster. Rampal worked in Kashmir for 11 years and he is very fluent in Kashmiri rather he loved the musical language more.

"From Musheerabad! I had a friend in Jaland Street, next to bus stand. You know that Lahore Bank and Mousam Hotel, next to that".Hakkim was more excited that Indian Major is telling streets, shops and house and local topography. How he can guess that Rampal was spying those areas once?

"Tell me, Hakkim", he called the doctor to provide some healthy food or juice. He knows that Hakkim is going to talk to him. All were more confused. By the time the police had put 20 white clothed men surrounding the hospital. His room area was sealed it for any visitor as per the advice of Major. *"Why, your friend shot you, who is he and what is his name?"*

Hakkim was really in the world of mystery, how come Major knows that he is shot by Rasool. Before answering, major took a photo print of Rasool and showed him, *"Is he your friend."*Hakkim`s body shivered.*"Sab, brute, he is caught?"*

"Yes Hakkim, he is being followed, I am talking to you from New Delhi, you know where New Delhi is? He is in our net."

"Yes sab, by this time, Rasool must be in New Delhi with that Rocket Launcher which he took in a bus along with sniper rifles and hand bombs to attack the PM. Three days before, he was

in a big wheat field. People were leveling that for a meeting. He was taking video and some big man came to him. Rasool talked to him in French and told that he is from Paris and he is going to cover the whole mass rally addressed by the P.M. That man shook hands with Rasool and moved. Sab, he wanted me to lead the attack first, then he decided to do that himself." The dialogue was being recorded. Major wrote a slip and gave to his assistant to report that sentence to Colonel. Hakkim was drinking his juice and Major told the doctor to provide sufficient glucose. He does not want to lose one minute as his confession is very much important and crucial. He is running out of time. His assistant switched on his mobiles and called colonel and land line he pulled Director CRAB without diverting the attention of Hakkim.

"You said Bus? How can it be Hakkim. How he got the bus?" They started following the conversation.

"Sahib, day before yesterday, he gave one lakh rupee to a bus owner as advance and told that he will pay entire amount once his friends come from France. He told the owner that the team require the bus for twelve days. The bus owner was busy with a tour programme of 16 busses to Delhi for some March. He told him to have a trail run along with the bus driver. Blue color bus was decorated with saffron flags and lot of vinyl boards. Driver told that he will remove them before going out. But Rasool was particular that all the decoration shall not be disturbed. It was a blue color bus with Meerut registration. Only I read the number 4-9021 others were in English."

Major passed a slip. His senior officer immediately typed SMS, *"blue color bus, No.4-9021, UP registration, decorated with vinyl hoardings and front saffron flags used as bunker by terrorist-Trace it fast."*

Second message is sent, "Rocket launcher, sniper rifles, hand bombs are with the terrorist. This is terrorist Rasool photo".

"Sab, Rasool after crossing the city limit put the pistol on the head of the Bus driver Munimbai and told him to ring up to his boss. When, boss responded he told that the vehicle axil is cracked and he will repair the same and return. After fifteen minutes Rasool stopped the vehicle in a deserted road and pumped two bullets in the head of MunimBai and pushed and dumped his body in the nearby ditch. Sab, I drove the same to Meerut High way house and mounted one A.T.4 Rocket launcher, a few hand grenades and sniper rifles. Rasool told me that this time I will have to handle the Rocket Launchers and he will use Sniper M.107." Hakkim face is becoming pale and he started sweating. Major told him to sip some juice and relax for a few seconds.

Colonel and CRAB Chief alerted. So, the terrorist has landed in the huge rally. His rocket launcher, sniper and semi-automatic pistol have traced the target, thousands of buses. CRAB chief called Shoma transport office and asked for the MD. They told the owner Shoma, is a RRS man. He had gone to Delhi with 16 buses and 4000 men. Shoma M.D.was pulled out from the crowd, when he responded his mobile. When he was asked, whether all the buses have come to Delhi. He told one bus with UP-AL-4-9021 is held up somewhere. Blue bus is fully decorated with banners and flags No.UP-AL-4-9021.

Prime Minister PremnathMawa was floating among the celestial stars. His right hand Madan Vyas came to Mawa and told him to commence his speech. He told that the crowd has been completely magnetized and it is the right moment to incite them.

He went before the Mike and said, *"Shining star of nation, the messenger of god, our beloved leader Honourable Prime Minister of India, Shri.PremnathMawa will speak. The whole world is watching to-day to hear his message to the nation. Every part of the earth, they are looking him as the prophet of the century.*

I have one important information to share with you. To-day, the Lok Sabha has passed the amendment to elect the President of India directly by the people. Lok Sabha has deleted the articles treating the President of a nation as dummy all these days. Our party has proved that there is a higher power than the constitution."

Pointing out Premnath, *"He will lead not only India, he will lead the whole world in the coming days. I invite my most worshiped leader, Future President of India, to speak now".*

The crowd rose up and roared, making the whole atmosphere blasting with noise. Drums were beaten, bells were rung, sevaks were jumping and flowers were raining from among the crowd. For 10 minutes, he was silently watching, greeting, acknowledging, responding with a broad smile, posing for TV and photos, measuring the euphoria and echo. He raised his hands, the whole crowd suddenly became silent.....

The crowd was totally silent, Ferdando turned to the podium. Prime Minister of India, dramatically raising his hands, looking at the vast sky as though praying. He had discarded the bullet proof glass, around him. Colonel was totally nervous. Next twenty to 30 minutes, a hell is going to break, if they fail.

Devil is among this half a million crowd. In what form and with what weapons? If that devil strike here, nation is going to have blood bath. To-Morrow the sun may rise but colonel may not be there to see. This hysteric and madling mob will sure to hack the uniformed men and turn them as lifeless forms in ravage. If we fail, we all perish.

To trace a terrorist in 3 lakhs crowd! Mobile rang up. "*Sir, please keep the mobile on*".

CHAPTER XXII - DEC 2014

"EITHER I WILL COME BACK AS THE GREATEST HERO OF THE EARTH OR MAIMED AND CHOPPEDAS SLAUGHTERED PIECESOFFLESH AND BONES THROWN IN SOME MARSHY LAND OF INDIA. BUT WILL NEVER BE CAUGHT AND JAILED BY THOSE DOGS."

The demon is waiting for its prey past 16 hours, undetected by 40000 security men. It is two kilo meter away from the ground wall, crossing the highway. The blue bus is equipped with explosives, sniper rifles, and rocket launcher. If all goes as per his plot and if it blasts, the history will paint the security force of a nation as the most impotent one. The beautiful bus with all party banners and flags is far of across the marshy land to blow up everything. How that had reached there, no one knows. It is beyond the danger zone, nobody cared.

Colonel commanded his men to identify but not to enter in any vehicle. He moved to the open space away from the crowd towards Meerut Road. All the other sides are completely protected with armed vehicles and past three days. Barbed wires were used as fence so that no one can come in. Security jeeps are on petrol inside. Meerut High way is the only opening for three lacs crowd to move in and come out. Still the traffic was opened to vehicles. Can any passing vehicle shoot the missiles and move forward? He advised to SCRP chief to stop heavy vehicles movement including buses from 3.30 to 6.00 p.m. His instinct did not compromise!

Brigadier Ameen Habib Rasool, now is an army, a lone solider with his most dangerous mission and weapons. He is close to the target. He does not know that the troops of SCRP men and RAF men have identified his bunker cover up, but yet to find his location. He was setting his target to hit the stage from the side. Hakkim could have been useful, if he continued. But that bastard betrayed. His body must be rotting in that jungle. His sharp shooter pumped three bullets. Rasool had to move to avert public attention. Or in his usual style he could have walked to his victim and blasted his skull with his guns. Splashing of the blood is a crude pleasure often he enjoyed. The automatic target ranger identified the exact distance and directions. It is already loaded with missile with blast grenade head. Rasool took his binocular and wanted to see, whether Prime Minister has come to the mike as speaker podium is only visible to him. It is a waste to shoot some twenty saffron men who were moving here and there on the stage.

Lookout shall be beyond 2000 meters as the rocket launcher is capable of hitting target exactly within a range of 4300 meters. CRAB chief told that it is difficult to launch missiles sitting on the top of the bus as more than100 Reserve Polices are on the roof moving here and there. Secondly there are hundreds of hurdles. Orders were passed to 300 men to move to the terminus where buses were parked. After, 11.00 minutes RAF men were showing the number to SCRP forces to identify a blue bus.

One Young SCRP responded as RAF man approached him to trace, the man in the photo and bus number.

"How can we trace sir, in this junk yard? See the parking, it is all like wild buffalos of Africa. 700 buses are parked on the road and all ministers have to cross that area. Some fellow can walk slowly and put a grenade in the pocket of the minister and safely walk. See some drunkard has gone mad and ran his vehicle even in the wheat field which is totally a swamp and tried to climb the big slop there." He showed his finger to a bus standing two kilo meters far off on the other side of high way. *"To-morrow, we will be again called to bring a crane to lift."*

RAF man looked at the direction. About 1500 to 2000 meters beyond high way: Something, his natural instinct started telling him to recheck his target. His first lesson in his department is, don't give weightage to instinct to ignore anything. He got on the top of a jeep nearby and checked through his binocular. He saw a blue bus was standing in a slanting condition. Evening sun shine was reflecting on its glass. The attempt to reach the top of the small muddy hill has failed and wheels are struck. Blue colour, well decorated with vinyl boards and banners. No, it is not any drunkard's deed. He jumped up on the top of nearby bus there, look through his binocular and search for the number plate-UP-AL-4-9021. Behind him was the SCRP man. He noted that SCRP Jawan name and number patted his shoulder. "*Excellent clue my friend. You will be rewarded.*" He switched on the powerful wireless.

"Colonel Fernando, Colonel Fernando, attention please, attention please- RAF Force 702 reporting. Are you hearing sir?

"Yes, 702, Colonel here -report"

"The bus traced 200 meters east of main entrance, horizontal 1900 meters after crossing the High way. You can see a hillock and the bus slantingly standing, facing the hill top. I have verified the number-4-9021. Roof ventilation door is just opened, sir.Due to sun rays we are not able see any movements."

Major Rampal continued his investigation. *"Who were with you Hakkim at your village? My mother and she is also sick. I talked to my uncle at Musheerabad and he told that she is requiring medical aid and money. I asked Rasool some money to help her. He said after finishing all his work, while returning he will give me the money."*

"Did he tell how long he is planning to stay before returning? Is he not having money?"

"No sahib, he is having two lakh Indian currency and 2.5 lakhs American dollar in his bag. I wanted at least Rs. 5000 for my mother`s treatment. The Peshawar leader promised me, agreed provide Rs.3000 every month to my mother. After one

payment, no money was paid –my uncle told me. They cheated me, they cheated my mother, and she is dying, dying, dying".

Major silently observed his reaction. *"Hakkim, I will ask my friend to pay some money to your mother, sure, mother is always mother, whatever brutal her son is, am I correct Hakkim?"*

Hakkim lifted his head and wiped out his tears. *"Yes Sab, Punish me and hang me for all my crimes, Save my mother. In fact, she does not know that I am in India. She will scold me as wild pig and brutal wolf as she used to tell about my dad".*

"But how Rasool got all these arms and where he kept them, how he transported that across the border?"

"No sir, these arms, he purchased in India from some Whiteman. Hakkim narrated the whole story after they left Hyderabad till they came to Meerut. Hakkim was tired and still blood is oozing from his right shoulder and hip joints. His voice was feeble and his eyes were closing.

"Hakkim, you need rest, can you answer me two important questions? Doctor, can you give him some injection or some drips, to keep him alert to answer." Doctor injected two vials of vitamins directly in his glucose bottle. After two minutes again the young man became a little better. Doctor explained that this man is surviving because of his life at mountains and rough terrains. Any other city breed would have gone dead, in two hours after being shot. *"How he delivered the Improved Explosive Devises to the Afghan at Delhi Airport?"*

It is 4.40 p.m. Suddenly 702 cried, *"No sir, some object is moving in the rear side, sir."* Colonel was shocked when his blue tooth received the information. 1000 meters away Prime Minister is on the rostrum, the Highway. Stage is set 900 meters from High way almost 3000 meters away the rocket launcher is installed. Rostrum is more exposed to targeted attack. Crowd turned silent.

He mounted on the SCRP van and with the Binocular and asked for the direction. *"Turn towards the entrance Arch and three large flags on the right side. From there to me it is 1900 metres. You can see the field and a mount beyond the marshy land, Can you see a bus?"*

"Anybody is there? Colonel asked the RAF 702. Colonel was rushing in his vehicle to the Highway from the other entrance where much less human movement is. Hundred troops have taken position and another fifty were advancing rapidly. RAF sharp shooters crossed the road. Shooters reached the firing range of 1000 meters. SCRP men were instructed not to move beyond the road as it will cause collateral damage without wireless communications.

No sir, the SCRP told me that this bus is lying down from yesterday night and nobody is able to go because of the marshy land surrounding. I am seeing some movement but not sure?" The bus is tilted exactly in 30 degree and its roof window is open in the rear side. A small metal tube is protruding. The nostle head was slowly moving. Colonel is almost 900 metres with his M.107 sharp shooter.

Hakkim raised his head slowly and told what they did with the poor garbage worker and planted ammunitions and suicide bombers coat. *"Sir, on completion, Rasool phoned and asked his contacts to send the other man from Arab airport."*

"You were using the car?"

"Yes sab, we stole it in a workshop, number plate was changed." Hakkim face was becoming pale due to strain voice is silencing.

"Hakkim, Hakkim, one last question? Don`t bother, Rasool will be arrested or shot in a few minutes. But why he shoot you?" Tears were flowing from the eyes, a few seconds of silence. He seems to have been relaxed. The sedatives also slightly induced him to speak, without any control.

Major was in a tension. Anyone now linked to Rasool is still there? What would happen if Hakkim is dead? His admission are coming voluntarily because of the breach of relation with his chief and hatredness. Hakkims evidence and information is explosive. One of his officer who is sitting on the side of the computer was recording and wherever Major wants to communicate and to gather further information, he was going on posting mails.

Hyderabad: Check, How much Indian currency Mr.Rahamad had drawn from bank or took out from home on the day of his death? How many thousands of dollars in his custody, at home? Hold all the connected local crooks in custody till we interrogate. Rahamad driver be advised not to leave the city.

HYDRABAD; Check all the mobile communication with Rahamad and others from the 20 days before.

INDORE: Check: Rain Drop hotels, front views by scanning and entry two French/foreign nationals list. Engagement of heavy vehicles to transport to Meerut road in 7 days. Driver missing.

Delhi: Check: take out the coloured scanned copies of AT 4 rocket launchers, M 3 Carl cruster, M.107 sniper

Meerut: Check: Reported car loss from the garages in 10 days

Delhi: Check: Blood sample taken at Hyderabad outside under the tree and blood sample taken in the counter attacks made during the conflict between the Airport contract labour and terrorist.

Major added: Check at Meerut, the ID of the murdered Driver and visitors records or CCTV at the Bus owner office. RAF cadre knows how to act independently once the particular task comes before them.

"Sir, while commencing from Pak border Rasool told `Either he will come back as the greatest hero of the earth or slaughtered pieces of flesh and bones, thrown in some marsh of India, but will not be caught and jailed by these dogs.' We entered India near Kutch border, moved to sea coast again. We came to Kandla Port area in a small boat. He found that carrying an explosive coat, weapons, which he brought from Karachi is more dangerous, if he is caught. So, went to a parcel service

at Kandla and sent it to Meerut address and took the bill. We were caught, but we were released by police. From Kandla, we moved to a place called Bhopal. Later on reaching Meerut he collected the dress material parcel directly from the logistic service centre. We again went to Jaipur and I found that Rasool was having lacs and lacs of rupees and dollars, drinking lot of brandy and whisky with foreigners, killing own Muslims just because they refused to agree with his ideas."

"Someone in Delhi while talking to me told that Kashmir is ruled by Muslim Chief Minister only. When I told Rasool, he slapped me. I was told that it is Hindus who are ruling and millions of Muslims are dying. When I was talking to a Kashmiri at airport taxi stand, he told that some Sheik Abdulla, his son Farooq Abdulla and now his son Omar Abdulla were ruling the state all sixty years. I was asked to fight against the brutal Hindu leaders of the state. But I found a young Muslim is the Chief Minister."

"In Hyderabad, I heard the Muslim leader telling that they are enjoying better freedom and life in that state than Pakistan. I found their life style and their huge bungalow, cars and dresses. I was mislead. I was made a fool. But I know that I am with a Vampire. It is drinking the blood of our own people. When I saw him murdering the poor driver MunimBai at Meerut, I felt that I will be shot any time. I one or two times told him that I want to go home as my mother is serious. He placed the gun at my forehead and told he will shoot. I needed money, I needed freedom and I do not want to kill Muslims. I was told to drive the vehicle from Meerut. His purse was kept in the dash board. I lifted and started driving the vehicle. Rasool closed his eyes,

the movement bus started moving 100 meters in the front side. I pocketed his purse. I drove another 300 metres and stopped. He suddenly woke up and raised his gun. After seeing the traffic junction, he closed his eyes. He was dead tired, but deadly alert. I know, if not now, I will have no opportunity to escape. I slowed down the vehicle as there was a railway crossing. I suddenly opened the door and jumped. I was running mad among the shrubs. Suddenly I was struck by one bullet on the shoulder and another pierced my hip. I lost my consciousness." *"Relax, Hakkim, I will tell the doctors to take care of you, relax'.* Hakkim closed his eyes.

What is waiting for him, he knows. A death that will relieve him of all tortures. His friends may praise him that third generation of Surathuaisin Ali has sacrifice his life fighting against the Indian Army. No one will know that he was cheated, brain washed and facing death because his own terrorist partner shot him mercilessly. His main grievance, he is going to die without seeing his bed ridden mother. He has no fear for death. Major ordered that he shall be kept under drug. He is one of the major terror cadre, which RAF searching. Rampal called the Commissioner and told him that he shall keep this capture, a secret as he has got another associate who may escape if he gets a clue. Commissioner did not say anything. He had already passed the news about the trapped man eater to Delhi IG. He will get medal for his revelation.

No more information from Hakkim is of any use now. Major contacted Colonel. Colonel simply said, *"Rush here, we have traced him"*

Madan Vyas, Secretary NPP was proudly looking at the charisma and glory of his leader standing behind. Here is a hot wave in the cold winter, it will set fire to entire nation, if decided. Prime Minister Premnath Mawa raising his hands, looking at the sky started the prayer in a thunderous voice,

"Namaste SadhaVatsaluMathrubhoomi".

The whole crowd started chanting along with him. Again the crowd sat silently. PM turned and there was a huge photo of Poojya guruji appearing in a 3D screen. Throwing flower from the basket, PM went to the screen and bent down to touch his feet. Rasool looked through his binocular, the rostrum was empty. P.M. was not seen. PM came to the mike, pointing out the sky, he said,

"My beloved friends, Time has come, time has come to fulfil the dreams of our poojya guruji. The celestial stars are now telling us, your nation is going to have golden era after long spell of misrules of a dynasty. We were liberated from the British Empire but became slave of a Kashmiri, descendent of Parsi, ultimately Italian immigrant. They were Indians, but anti-nationals."

His words carried all venom and anger. Looking around, *"Unfortunately we had few Indian prime Ministers too as fill in the blanks. But even in 5th standard question paper there was not one question about Sri.Lalbhadur, Narasimhagaru or V.P.Singh or a greatest statesman Shri Atalji or others"* The crowd was howling, roaring with laughter and rejoicing over the smileys.

"God thought something wrong. So mystically guided the People to return the nation to Indian borns." The whole crowd was laughing at the satire. *"Now we assure you hundred percent safe rules of our land by Bharath blood. The 'evil dynasty' will be removed from the future political history of India"*

"They were running the government. They said many lies and people believed. What was happening here! All these days, the terrorist were moving like tourists everywhere. Terrorist were using this land as their weapon testing ground".

"In fact, we were strong, our military might in 1965 Pak war made the enemy to surrender. We reached Lahore and our army surrounded the city. We have a mighty force. Our army is the third largest military armed forces with 23,25,000 soldiers and other personnels in the pay roll. Huge money we spend next USA and China, some where about 86 billion dollars. Yet, we hear the gun shots in borders, intrusions in Kashmir to Kanyakumari. Our Army is bold, but we were not ruled by any brave P.M. Army will be braver as your PM is bold." The whole crowd roared to the sky.

"My dear friends the terrorist will finds this land, in future, as their burial ground. We have decided to give space to them only for burial and not to live. I am going to grand one burial stone for each terrorist, shot dead in future." The whole crowd laughed.

"You saw the Delhi Airport operation a few days back. We will send a message to everyone who try to put their feet beyond the borders. India is not your play ground to throw bombs and run. We will wipe out everyone mercilessly." SCRP chief handed

over a note to Madan Vyas. After shocked expression, determined Vyas carried the chit to his master.

After reading PM raised his head and told the crowd, *"I told you, two seconds back, that this land will turn to be the burial ground of terrorists. One hour back, our police commissioner has shot one Pakistani terrorist at Meerut. Terrorist is fighting for his life in our hospital. You know where he is supposed to be in this hour? This mass rally, to be in this ground, with powerful arms and grenades. He admitted this in death bed. Even if he still survive after the bullets that have made holes in, death is assured to him by ropes."* Crowd greeted with a thunder. P.M. in front, seems to be an avatar with Trishul. How brave this man killing terrorist after terrorist?

Suddenly he raised his voice and shouted *"We will annihilate all the terrorists one by one. We will use all our forces to weed out all these anti-national elements. Premanth Mawa, will turn the pages of history and build a powerful security all over the sub-continent. Terrorising the terrorist will be the new Indian message to world."*

The madding crowd turned frenzy rejoicing over the death of the terror elements. *"But, will you be with Premnath Mawa for the future missions, for the political moves, changes we bring in parliament, tell me?"*

The whole crowd roared in one voice "*Yea, Yea we will*"

"Will you go to every corners of India to tell the people to throw the MPs out of their constituency, if they refuse to support a presidential form of government? Will you do that?"

The crowd voiced *"Yes, we will"*

"We need our legislative power more to make the country powerful. We need our executive powers with wider authority to implement all our plans. 43 countries, 43 countries in the world are having a Presidential form of government. From USA to small state Maldives. I cannot tap the opposition parties' doors every night and ask them, terror groups are landing- can I send my RAF?"

"I cannot wait for some non-entity opposition to extent permission to implement a welfare scheme to my people. I demand the liberty to rule. Our nation cannot wait last in queue as 135 or 138, telling you all, we will overcome, we will come up, and we are growing, after sixty six years. Your government has planned to change the obsolete constitution. Otherwise, we will not move forward. We are an army with a mission. We are the nation's hopes. We are your unseen glorious future.

So, we will repeal the old laws, transform judicial system that are coming in our onward march. The role of dynasty ended and ended forever. The glorious imaginations of the comrades of red flag to rule the nations have slowly drenched in rain and dried in sun and finally they now see saffron flag in their citadel." "We have brought a historic change, we are giving the eternal liberty for the people to elect their president directly". There was huge roar and clap.

"A change in the constitution is done in Lok Sabha, a victory over the parliamentary system, a walkover, over the copse of majoritism,"

Rasool got up from his rear seat and took the binocular to check the Rostrum. Prime Minister is addressing the gathering. He turned to see the crowd for a second. Suddenly, he was shocked to see the army men in five hundred meters and Colonel Fernando was aiming with his sniper rifle. Something hit the glass windows in front of him. All were shattered and the whole row of window glass split into pieces in a second. He could see that more than hundred bullets are shaking the bus and even trying to tilt the rocket launcher His hands automatically went to his holster to pick the gun. But he knows that it is no meaning to shoot one bullet as the advancing troop consists of 100 to 120 armed group. His hand was holding a hand grenade. He swung back and tried to hold the Rocket launcher.

The Algerian-Arab lady delivered the child due to her love or hate with French paramour. He learnt the art of killing amidst the Algerian terrains. Demonstrated power and fearlessness at the street of Paris, took refuge to Libyan army, and turned to be the commander the army of Islamic liberator by becoming their Brigadier at Hindukush. This most dreaded terrorist Rasool after years of 22 wars and shoot out is to-day being honoured by the spray of bullets. It was tearing him all over the body. Bus started sliding on one side. "Do *it and die, do it and die*"-he is prattling. His steel like body is drilled with hundreds of bullets. Blood is oozing out of every pore.

Brigadier. Ameen Habib Rasool, is enjoying drilling by the bullets. Never has he known what fear is. He continued his last operation, pulled the trigger and the missile was released. India will remember him ever as he is the only one terrorist who waged war against 40000 armed men and shot the Prime Minister of India over a wheat field. He is another hero in his training camp. His name will be the latest lesson along with Abu-Nodal to Bin-laden and hundreds of terrorists. Hundreds of AK-47 will be fired on the sky in the remote mountains of Hindu Kush, Karakorum and Afghan deserts. "Ameen *Habib Rasool Amar Rahe, Long Live*"-, those boys will shout. So many writers will turn his life as a fiction or movie. Seventeen years, he was expecting this, in France, in Algeria, in Libya, in Iran, in Syria, in Afghanistan, in Pakistan. But it came at last, it came in India. He was thrown out of bus by the force of bullets and he fell on the sand. Evening sky turned blank. He did not feel the rays of sun nor pain of the fall. He is hearing the 21 Gun salute and all those boys are renting the air *"To Ameer Rasool, our greatest hero"*. He did not see anyone nor able to hear anyone near. Gun salutes!

Suddenly, the attention of the leaders and three lakhs crowd was diverted, as there was non-stop firing and flow of bullets from the entrance of the convention. As firing and blasting sound renting the whole air. SCRP Chief took his walk-talky. He was informed to cover the Prime Minister as some terrorist has entered the camp. Z security of the PM literally lifted PM and ran out of the podium. They care no protocol or public image. They normally wind up the VIP as a baggage and shift him in a hurricane speed to an utmost safe location.

RAF is continuously shooting him down across the Meerut High way. Suddenly a whistling jet made a shrill sound and crossed the meeting venue on the west. Many ducked their heads as something was swishing over. Huge blast and flame sent a wave of horror and three helicopters went to pieces and their sheets were flown in the air. Again it must be SCRPs or RAF men must have fallen as victim as protection force at helipad. Colonel was slightly depressed again. How many brave men he has got to lose like this? Helipad is built up a little high and helicopter is also twenty feet high. If the missile travelled another 4 feet high, it would have crossed the helicopters and would have landed in wheat fields.

Colonel was the first to go near the bus. While coming round the bus, he found a body of tall well built fair man thrown four feet away from the bus. More than 30 bullets had hit him and made him shapeless. His left hand was still holding a hand grenade. But he could not take it to his teeth to remove the pin. Every piece of his muscle was torn by bullet. Looked inside, no one was there. The rocket launcher has slipped down amidst the seats. CRAB Chief received the message for Colonel Fernando. *"Events management-Operators terminated"* Amidst the anarchy and chaos, the SCRP director moved three armed trucks full of reserve police and two behind the convoy of the Prime Minister, who was shaken by the dangerous missile attack. None of his party leaders were allowed to go near him.

Actual designing of M Carl Gunstar rocket launcher is so precise, that it will mark exact target and distance once set automatically. But, the target slipped by the shaking of the bus and rain of bullet hits on rocket launcher. More than that, shooting the right side tires changed its direction and distance. CRAB chief was really stunned by the flash of micro second application of brain and command by his colonel by shooting the right tiers of the bus and tilting the whole to change the direction of the missile to an empty field. Two seconds delay would have sent the missiles 2000 meters away from helipad to a bare land beyond security zone. But, one second which the punctured tyre took to tilt the vehicle, blasted the helipad instead of the leaders and large decorated stage.

Ten metres from the vehicle, colonel walked and slipped down. He was thinking of the men in helipad. Captain Rampal has taken charge of that area already. He saw his men are taking photos, putting cordon around the vehicle. Four to five RAF men stood on his side to guard him. Colonel turned and watched the rally which has turned into a madding crowd. People were fleeing from the scene. Helicopters are still burning and the smoke is seen hundred feet high. No one was paying any attention to the announcements of SCRP director.

Colonel`s mobile rang. He was irritated and handed over to the lieutenant nearby. He took the phone, *"sir, this is for you."*

"Shit, reply to them, I do not want to answer any bloody crank." A giggling sound was heard from the mobile.

He laughed and mockingly said, *"Sir, some important person wants to talk only to you, Sir please."*

He raised his head and looked at the Lieutenant, why the hell this idiot is smiling. He removed the wet sand on his shirt and took the mobile.

"Hi, Hero, why you are lying down. Darling, are you O.K?" Suddenly all his nerves tickled with a spirit. He looked around.

Where is she!

CHAPTER XXIII - DEC 2014

"AND WITH A COURAGE NEVER TO SUBMIT NOR TO YIELD, THE UNCONQUERABLE ULTIMATELY ROSE FROM THE BED OF THE MARSH"

He is yet to find Mayuri`s where about. *"How do you know, I am here?"*

"I knocked one binocular of your Personal body guard, that golden pumpkin nice looking guy and he showed me your location."

"Stupid, if any charming lady is seen, he will pour out heroic tales and disgrace all my two years training given to that idiot to shut their ass in such dangerous times"

"Why you are jealous about that pumpkin guy? What training, you give to your cadets? To lead a bloody hermit life like you, even after 30s? She heard him laughing.

"Anyway *Thanks*" -she repeated

"What for?

*"You called me charming, most beautiful: Darling, are you hurt, why you are lying down?"*A sense of anxiety is traced.

"Bloody, exhausted and drained, still pulse is beating on my forehead, why, you want me to be hospitalized again?" colonel asked.

"Yes darling, I can be with you at least four or five days and have nice honeymoon. Giving lot of my energy tab like this?" She showered kisses in the mobile.

Colonel got up and looked around, searching everywhere. She is casually crossing the marshes and moving towards him. Her jeans are turning dirt with clay and soil.

His lieutenant loudly told to the other guard *"You know technology is so advanced, energy bullets are sent though mobiles by lovers?"*

"Dirty Beggar", colonel threw a handful of mud on his friend. He found his cupid is crossing the marsh and none of the RAF men stopped her.

RAF knows the rule, that beautiful angel is licensed to break their cordon.

ooo